D0880347

MISS PETTIGREW LIVES
FOR A DAY

Persephone Books N° 21
Published by Persephone Books Ltd 2000

This reprint 2011

First published in 1938
by Methuen

© 2000 The Estate of Winifred Watson
Illustrations © Mary Thomson 2000
Preface © Henrietta Twycross-Martin 2000

Endpapers taken from a 1938 furnishing fabric
by Marion Dorn reproduced by courtesy of
the Victoria & Albert Museum, London

Typeset in ITC Baskerville by Keystroke,
Wolverhampton

Printed and bound in Germany
by GGP Media GmbH, Poessneck

on Munken Premium (FSC approved)

ISBN: 978-1-903155-10-3

Persephone Books Ltd
59 Lamb's Conduit Street
London WC1N 3NB
020 7242 9292

www.persephonebooks.co.uk

MISS PETTIGREW LIVES
FOR A DAY

by

WINIFRED WATSON

✳✳✳✳✳✳✳

with a new preface by

HENRIETTA TWYCROSS-MARTIN

PERSEPHONE BOOKS
LONDON

PREFACE

****

Miss Pettigrew Lives for a Day (1938) is an enchanting version of *Cinderella*, and the story of its re-printing by Persephone Books is also a kind of fairy tale.

I suppose I first read this novel some time in my early teens, because it was my mother's favourite book, the one she went to, I now understand, not only for an escape into laughter and joyful fantasy, but because in some ways Miss Pettigrew, middle-aged, poor, and a governess, mirrored my mother herself. She was a single parent at a time when that was a difficult thing to be (I was born in 1942), and she worked at times as a governess, a cook and as headmistress of a small private school; there was very little money, little in the way of family or friends, and much uncertainty about the future.

But my mother was an incurable optimist, and her favourite book reflects the conviction that everything will be all right in the end, as indeed it was. I therefore grew up with Miss Pettigrew, who later accompanied me to Oxford, to a life in London as a university lecturer, and finally into retirement in Cambridge, where by chance one day I lent 'my mother's favourite book' to another academic, who read it enthusiastically, referred to it while teaching, and even went into the University Library one rainy day to cheer herself up by re-reading it.

Thus *Miss Pettigrew Lives for a Day* was clearly a book with more than family piety to recommend it; and when a couple of weeks later, on another grey day, the *Persephone Quarterly* dropped through my letterbox and I read its request for title-suggestions, I amused myself by e-mailing Persephone Books, and later took my treasured family copy up to Great Sutton Street in person. Again the novel was greeted enthusiastically, and I was asked to write the preface. 'What fun', I thought, and headed into the University Library full of confidence: Winifred Watson had written six novels in all during the 1930s and early '40s, and I had no doubt I would easily find all I needed on her.

Alas, not so; reviews of her books were uninformative, Methuen's records had been lost during the war, no biographical details were listed in the standard sources, in short I drew a blank. And then the library dug out the original paper slip-covers to the novels, one of which said that Miss Watson had been a Newcastle typist before she became a novelist. A phone-call to Newcastle Central Library followed, but although very helpful, the librarians could supply no details apart from a note giving a married name and an address dating from 1974. BT was consulted, the number duly rung and the enquiry put as to the whereabouts of Miss Winifred Watson. To our complete astonishment and delight a firm Newcastle voice replied, saying 'I am she'.

So an interview was arranged and I went up to Newcastle

and chatted for two hours with Winifred Watson, still at 93 living independently in Jesmond as she has done almost all her life, and as lively, charming and perceptive as her books would lead one to expect. She has, she maintains, had a perfectly ordinary and uninteresting life. But of her six novels, her favourite was always *Miss Pettigrew Lives for a Day*.

Winifred Watson was born in 1906 into comfortable circumstances, since her father owned one shop in Gateshead and three in Newcastle that catered for working people; as she explained to me, in those days working people did not feel comfortable coming into the city centre to use the 'grand shops', and hence had their own shops in separate areas. I think this helps to explain the very vivid sympathy with urban working-class poverty that is shown, for example, in *Hop, Step and Jump* (1939), the novel that follows *Miss Pettigrew Lives for a Day*. But for Winifred as a young woman in pre-war Jesmond life was secure and happy: there were two older sisters, and twin brothers. Winifred and her sisters were educated at St. Ronan's boarding school at Berwick-on-Tweed, and from there she went to Commercial College before becoming a secretary. In this first job there was so little to do that Winifred had a lot of time to read novels, and one day when one of her sisters asked what she was reading, she said it was awful nonsense and she could do better herself, at which her brother-in-law told her to get on with it . . . So she did, and wrote the whole of her first novel, *Fell Top*, (1935) in the mornings at work.

In her second job there was much less time to write, and *Fell Top* was put aside until purely by chance her sister saw an agent's notice asking for new novelists to submit work. Winifred was advised to tell the agent she had a second novel ready, and was put under contract for her next four books. The non-existent second novel had then to be written, and Winifred's wedding, which had been planned for June of 1935, was held in January instead, so that she would have the summer to concentrate on her new book, *Odd Shoes* (1936). After her marriage, Winifred continued to write under her maiden name and her husband seems to have been proud and supportive of his wife's literary career.

Fell Top, a fashionably rustic novel of the kind mocked by Stella Gibbons in *Cold Comfort Farm* (1932), made an instant name for the young novelist: the reviews were all impressed by the sombre power of a grim story of sexual jealousy and murder, written by a young, and, going by the publicity photos, very pretty unknown. Methuen's gave *Fell Top* a launch lunch at Tilley's, then the grandest restaurant in Newcastle, the first time that a London publisher had held such an event in the town. Photographs of the new author appeared in all the local papers, the local great and good attended the lunch, and the classicist E.V. Rieu, then managing director of Methuen's, even came north to speak in Winifred Watson's honour. A radio adaptation of this first novel followed, and a second lunch at Tilley's in 1936 launched *Odd Shoes*, which was set in mid nineteenth-century Newcastle and was equally well-reviewed as the work of a promising young writer.

With one rustic novel and one historical novel already published, Winifred Watson changed direction dramatically with her next novel. But when presented with the draft

✳✳✳✳✳✳✳✳✳✳

version of *Miss Pettigrew Lives for a Day*, Methuen's readers were taken aback: what they wanted was more of the same, 'women's fiction' with passionate goings-on in rural settings of yore, not a West-End fantasy featuring a governess, a night-club singer, cocaine, cocktails and comedy. Winifred apparently took them to task and told Methuen's they were making a mistake, but she obliged with *Upyonder* (1938), another steamy rustic novel that drew a disapproving comment from one local reviewer, who complained that 'some of the dialogue and incidents seem not only somewhat wanton but so salacious that they detract from the value of a very ingenious plot.' When both novels were published in 1938 the reception of *Miss Pettigrew Lives for a Day* proved its author right. There was an American edition, a translation into French, and in 1939 Winifred Watson even agreed to a request for a German translation, saying that, as she posted the letter, she knew England would be at war with Germany by the time it was received. And she was right.

What the reviewer who condemned *Upyonder* as salacious can have made of *Miss Pettigrew Lives for a Day* one dreads to think. Nothing in Winifred Watson's previous books could have prepared the Methuen readers for this change of direction, and what astonishes is the sheer fun, the light-heartedness and enchanting fantasy of an hour-by-hour plot that feels closer to a Fred Astaire film than anything else I can think of. Sophisticated and naive by turns, *Miss Pettigrew Lives for a Day* is also charmingly daring: Miss Pettigrew herself may be of unimpeachable virtue, but she learns to regret this, and to admire her two mentors, Miss La Fosse with her

ix

several lovers (and possibly not one, but *two*, illegitimate children) and Miss Dubarry, owner of the best beauty parlour in London, who explains 'If you act "marriage or nothing" they generally give you marriage. I was very lucky. I went to his head, but he couldn't stand the pace. He got a nice tombstone and I got the parlour.' And so it goes on, sparky dialogue, no dialect, and no turgid inner life: a novelist has found her style. The glamorous thirties night-clubs, the splendid evening dresses, the men tailored to swooning-point, all come to life in the book and are vividly captured in Mary Thomson's delicious line drawings. Yet Winifred Watson had never, and has never, been in a night-club in her life: 'when you write, if things feel right, people believe them' she said to me.

By the time war broke out Winifred Watson had written her fifth novel *Hop, Step and Jump* (1939), another variant on the Cinderella theme which combines an initial setting of contemporary urban squalor with the optimism and humour of *Miss Pettigrew Lives for a Day* and, like the latter book, remains a cracking good read. Her last novel, part murder-mystery and part psychological study set in a contemporary upper-class milieu in London and the home counties, was published in 1943.

This last novel, *Leave and Bequeath*, was dedicated to her mother-in-law 'in gratitude for her many kindnesses'. But behind the dedication lies the abandonment of writing: after 1943 Winifred Watson neither published nor wrote any more, except for 120 pages of an unfinished and now lost novel. The cause was circumstances, not a deliberate decision: one evening during the war she was alone in the house and baby Keith would not settle in his back room upstairs, so she brought him down to the sitting-room. She remembers looking at him laughing on the settee, and hearing the bomb: in Keith's room the fireplace was blown onto his bed, and in adjoining houses several people were killed. But being downstairs he survived, to grow up, marry, and have two children. At the time, the bombing meant homelessness, but as Winifred said 'In those days, women of my mother's generation simply *could not* live alone, they didn't know how'. So Winifred's mother-in-law moved in with a married daughter, Winifred took over part of her mother-in-law's house, and Mrs.Watson in turn moved in with her daughter. And that was the end of writing: as Winifred said to me, not sadly but very matter-of-factly, 'you can't write if you are never alone'. Six years later, when she again had a house of her own, the moment had passed and she seems to have abandoned writing without great reluctance, as something that belonged to a different era of her life.

Although the six novels form two distinct groups, three north-country novels set in the previous century and three with contemporary settings, what stands out when reading them in sequence is how different they are: rustic novels, a historical novel, a comic fantasy, a 'poor girl makes good' and a war-time murder with family complexities. Yet they all share themes and are typical of 'women's novels' of the period in that they focus upon women's lives, and on difficulties overcome and trials surmounted before the inevitable happy ending is reached.

****

When we met earlier this year Winifred Watson said firmly that women read women's novels and men read men's novels, which was perhaps truer when she was writing than now. Her novels are plot-driven: she knew exactly what was going to happen before she put pen to paper. They are primarily stories, a good read, to be borrowed from the library and returned, just as Winifred was doing when she first said she could write something better than *that*, and was told to get on with it, then. In many respects, Winifred Watson's north-country novels anticipate Catherine Cookson's, since they deal with the development and resolution of sexual and family tensions in ways that may flout convention and the law, but that allow women to survive and ultimately flourish. I have not come across any evidence suggesting that the young Cookson read Winifred Watson's novels, but given how popular and widely publicised they were in Newcastle during the 1930s, it would be surprising if she had not.

The common theme running through these novels is women having second chances, adapting to change, moving on, just as Winifred Watson herself experimented with different genres: changing direction was characteristic of her as a writer. And in the end she changed into no longer being a writer, which I regret, but which she does not seem to. She said to me 'I have had a very happy life'. And in *Miss Pettigrew Lives for a Day* she wrote a very happy novel.

Henrietta Twycross-Martin
Cambridge, 2000

MISS PETTIGREW LIVES
FOR A DAY

✸✸✸✸✸✸✸

CONTENTS

CHAPTER ONE

9.15 a.m.—11.11 a.m.

MISS PETTIGREW pushed open the door of the employment agency and went in as the clock struck a quarter past nine. She had, as usual, very little hope, but to-day the Principal greeted her with a more cheerful smile.

'Ah! Miss Pettigrew. I think we have something for you to-day. Two came in when I had left last night. Now let me see. Ah yes! Mrs. Hilary, maid. Miss LaFosse, nursery governess. Hmn! You'd have thought it was the other way round. But there! I expect she's an aunt with an adopted orphan niece, or something.'

She gave Miss Pettigrew particulars.

'There you are then. Miss LaFosse, 5, Onslow Mansions. The appointment is for ten sharp this morning. You'll make it nicely.'

'Oh thank you,' Miss Pettigrew said weakly, nearly fainting with relief. She clutched the card of particulars firmly in her hand. 'I'd nearly given up hope. Not many of my kind of post these days.'

'Not many,' agreed Miss Holt, and, as the door closed behind Miss Pettigrew, 'I hope that's the last I see of her,' thought Miss Holt.

Outside on the pavement Miss Pettigrew shivered

slightly. It was a cold, grey, foggy November day with a drizzle of rain in the air. Her coat, of a nondescript, ugly brown, was not very thick. It was five years old. London traffic roared about her. Pedestrians hastened to reach their destinations and get out of the depressing atmosphere as quickly as possible. Miss Pettigrew joined the throng, a middle-aged, rather angular lady, of medium height, thin through lack of good food, with a timid, defeated expression and terror quite discernible in her eyes, if any one cared to look. But there was no personal friend or relation in the whole world who knew or cared whether Miss Pettigrew was alive or dead.

Miss Pettigrew went to the bus-stop to await a bus. She could not afford the fare, but she could still less afford to lose a possible situation by being late. The bus deposited her about five minutes' walk from Onslow Mansions, and at seven minutes to ten precisely she was outside her destination.

It was a very exclusive, very opulent, very intimidating block of flats. Miss Pettigrew was conscious of her shabby clothes, her faded gentility, her courage lost through weeks of facing the workhouse. She stood a moment. She prayed silently. 'Oh Lord! If I've ever doubted your benevolence in the past, forgive me and help me now.' She added a rider to her prayer, with the first candid confession she had ever made to her conscious mind. 'It's my last chance. You know it. I know it.'

She went in. A porter in the hall eyed her questioningly. Her courage failed at ringing for the lift so she mounted the main stairway and looked around until she discovered No. 5. A little plate on the door said Miss LaFosse. She looked at her watch, inherited from her mother, waited until it said precisely ten, then rang.

There was no answer. She rang again. She waited and rang again. She was not normally so assertive, but fear gave her the courage of desperation. She rang, off and on, for five minutes. Suddenly the door flew open and a young woman stood in the entry.

Miss Pettigrew gasped. The creature was so lovely she called to mind immediately beauties of the screen. Her golden, curly hair, tumbled untidily about her face. Sleep was still heavy in her eyes, blue as gentians. The lovely rose of youth flushed her cheeks. She wore that kind of foamy robe, no mere dressing-gown, worn by the most famous of stars in seduction scenes in the films. Miss Pettigrew was well versed in the etiquette of dress and behaviour of young women on the screen.

In a dull, miserable existence her one wild extravagance was her weekly orgy at the cinema, where for over two hours she lived in an enchanted world peopled by beautiful women, handsome heroes, fascinating villains, charming employers, and there were no bullying parents, no appalling offspring, to tease, torment, terrify, harry her every waking hour. In real life she had never seen any woman arrive to breakfast in a silk, satin and lace *négligé*. *Every one* did on the films. To see one of these lovely visions in the flesh was almost more than she could believe.

But Miss Pettigrew knew fright when she saw it. The young woman's face, when she opened the door, had been rigid with apprehension. At sight of Miss Pettigrew it grew radiant with relief.

' I have come . . .' began Miss Pettigrew nervously.

' What time is it ? '

' It was prompt ten when I first rang. The hour you named, Miss . . . Miss LaFosse ? I have been ringing for about five minutes. It is now five-past ten.'

' My God ! '

3

Miss Pettigrew's surprising interrogator swung round and disappeared back into the room. She did not say come in, but for a gentlewoman to face destitution was a very serious crisis: Miss Pettigrew found courage, walked in and shut the door behind her.

' At least I shall ask for an interview,' thought Miss Pettigrew.

' It was prompt ten when I first rang '

She saw the whisk of draperies disappear through another door and heard a voice saying urgently,

' Phil. Phil. You lazy hound. Get up. It's half-past ten.'

' Prone to exaggerate,' thought Miss Pettigrew. ' Not a good influence for children at all.'

She now had time to take in her surroundings. Brilliant cushions ornamented more brilliant chairs and chesterfield. A deep, velvety carpet of strange, futuristic design, decorated the floor. Gorgeous, breathtaking curtains draped the windows. On the walls hung pictures not . . . not quite decent, decided Miss Pettigrew. Ornaments of every colour and shape adorned mantelpiece, table and stands. Nothing matched anything else. Everything was of an exotic brilliance that took away the breath.

' Not the room of a lady,' thought Miss Pettigrew. ' *Not* the kind of room my dear mother would have chosen.'

4

'And yet . . . why, yes ! Quite definitely yes, the kind of room that perfectly suited the lovely creature who had so abruptly disappeared.'

Miss Pettigrew cast a sternly disapproving eye about her, but behind her disapproval stirred a strange sensation of excitement. This was the kind of room in which one did things and strange events occurred and amazing creatures, like her momentary inquisitor, lived vivid, exciting, hazardous lives.

Shocked by such flighty thoughts Miss Pettigrew took her imagination severely in hand and forced it back to the practical.

'Children,' pondered Miss Pettigrew. 'Where could one possibly teach or play with children in an impossible room like this ? Ink or dirty marks on those cushions would be desecration.'

From behind the door of what was, presumably, the bedroom, Miss Pettigrew could make out a heated altercation in progress. The low, pleasantly grumbling tones of a man's voice,

'Come on back to bed.'

And Miss LaFosse's high, exhorting voice,

'No I won't. I can't help it if you're still sleepy. I'm awake and I've got a lot of things to do this morning. I can't have you lying snoring here all morning, 'cos I want to get this room tidied.'

Soon the door opened and Miss LaFosse appeared again, almost immediately followed by a man, clad in a dressing-gown of such brilliantly coloured silk Miss Pettigrew blinked.

She stood apprehensive, clutching her handbag in quivering fingers, awaiting the chilling inquiry of what her presence meant. Hot waves of nervous dread made her perspire just a little. She was always at her worst at interviews. Suddenly she felt terrified, defeated, forlorn, before ever the battle commenced. People like these . . . *any* kind of employer . . . would never again pay her for her services. She stood as dignified as possible, stoical, terrified, awaiting her dismissal.

The young man glanced at her amiably, without a trace of surprise.

' 'Morning.'

' Good morning,' said Miss Pettigrew.

She felt so weak she simply sat down bang on a chair.

' Did she rout you out of bed as well ? '

' No,' said Miss Pettigrew.

' A wonder. Early to be abroad and fully clad, isn't it ? '

' It is thirteen minutes past ten,' said Miss Pettigrew severely.

' Ah ! Up all night. Don't believe in these all-night binges myself. I like my sleep. Dead all day if I don't get it.'

' I have not been up all night,' said Miss Pettigrew, beginning to feel bewildered.

' I always did admire women.'

Miss Pettigrew gave it up. These conversational pyrotechnics were beyond her. She stared at him. He was dapper, neat, brisk, with brilliant, liquid brown eyes and dark hair. He had a jutting nose, a full-lipped mouth and a look about him that said he was not a man to play tricks with, yet a hint he could be pleasant enough if folks were pleasant with him.

' And yes,' thought Miss Pettigrew ; ' somewhere in his ancestry there has been a *Jew.*'

He said in a conversational tone to no one in particular,

' Well, you may be in a hurry and satisfied with orange juice, but I'm not. I'm hungry. I want my breakfast.'

6

'Breakfast?' gasped Miss LaFosse. 'Breakfast! You know my maid's left. I can't cook. I can't cook *anything* but a boiled egg.'

'I hate boiled eggs.'

Miss LaFosse's eyes swivelled round to Miss Pettigrew. Her expression became imploring, beseeching.

'Can you cook?'

Miss Pettigrew stood up.

'When I was a girl,' said Miss Pettigrew, 'my father said that after my dear mother I was the best plain cook he knew.'

Miss LaFosse's face became illumined with joy.

'I knew it. The minute I laid eyes on you I knew you were the kind of person to be relied on. I'm not. I'm no use at all. The kitchen's through that door. You'll find everything there. But hurry. Please hurry.'

Flattered, bewildered, excited, Miss Pettigrew made for the door. She knew she was *not* a person to be relied upon. But perhaps that was because hitherto every one had perpetually taken her inadequacy for granted. How do we know what latent possibilities of achievement we possess? Chin up, eyes shining, pulse beating, Miss Pettigrew went into the kitchen. Behind her Miss LaFosse's voice carried on,

'Now you go and get shaved and dressed, Phil, and by the time you are ready breakfast will be ready. I can set the table.'

In the kitchen Miss Pettigrew looked about her. Everything was up to date. Tiled walls, refrigerator, electric oven, pantry stocked to overflowing, but, 'oh dear, how untidy,' thought Miss Pettigrew! 'And yes, not clean. Whoever had charge here was a . . . a slut.'

She took off her coat and hat and set to work. Soon the blissful aroma of fried ham and eggs and coffee

7

filled the air. She discovered an electric toaster. Toast took its correct place. She went back into the room.

'Everything is ready, Miss LaFosse.'

Miss LaFosse's face took on a brilliant smile of thanks. Her hair was now brushed and her lips carmined and a faint film of powder gave bloom to her face. She still wore the gorgeous, silk *négligé* that made her look so breath-takingly lovely that Miss Pettigrew thought, 'No wonder Phil wanted her to go back to bed.' Then blushed a painful, agonizing red of aghast shame that such a thought could even touch the fringe of her virgin mind. And then . . . and then she thought, '*Miss* LaFosse. It couldn't be.'

'There,' said Miss LaFosse solicitously. 'You've gone all red. It's cooking over a hot stove. That's why I've never cultivated the art. It simply *ruins* the complexion. I'm terribly sorry.'

'It's all right,' said Miss Pettigrew with resignation. 'I've reached the age when . . . when complexions don't matter.'

'Not matter!' said Miss LaFosse, shocked. 'Complexions *always* matter.'

Phil came back into the room. He was now fully dressed and wore a lot of rings with very shining stones. Miss Pettigrew privately shook her head.

'Not in good taste,' she thought. 'Gentlemen never wear all those rings.'

'Ha!' ejaculated Phil. 'My nose smells breakfast and my stomach says its waiting for it. Stout woman.'

Miss Pettigrew smiled happily.

'I do hope it's cooked to your satisfaction.'

'Sure to be. My hostess is a useless hussy. I'm glad she has useful friends.'

He beamed amiably. Then abruptly, boldly, frankly,

8

Miss Pettigrew acknowledged to herself that she liked him.

'I do,' she apostrophized her shocked other self determinedly. 'I don't care. I do. He's not quite . . . quite delicate. But he's nice. He doesn't care whether I'm shabby and poor. I'm a lady, so he's polite in his way to me.'

Perhaps it was because he was different from any other man she had ever met. He was not a gentleman, yet there was something in his cheerful pleasantries that suddenly made her feel more comfortably happy and confident than all the polite, excluding courtesies that had been her measure from men all her life. Miss LaFosse was speaking to her.

'I've set a place for you. Even if you've had your breakfast a cup of nice coffee *never* comes amiss at this time.'

'Oh !' said Miss Pettigrew, touched. 'How . . . how exceptionally kind of you.'

She suddenly wanted to cry, but she didn't. Surprisingly she lifted her head firmly and said authoritatively,

'Now you two sit down and I'll serve breakfast. Everything's ready.'

Phil enjoyed his breakfast. He ate leisurely through a grapefruit, ham and eggs, toast and marmalade, fruit. Then he leaned back comfortably in his chair and dug out of his pocket a packet of villainous-looking cheroots.

'Dash it all, I'm sorry,' he apologized to Miss Pettigrew. 'Haven't got a cigarette on me to offer you. Always mean to carry 'em and always forget.'

Miss Pettigrew fluttered in her chair and looked a little pink with pleasure. She couldn't look quite as antiquated as she had always imagined if a man thought she smoked.

'I do wish you wouldn't smoke those nasty things,' grumbled Miss LaFosse. 'I don't like the smell.'

'Force of habit,' said Phil apologetically. 'Bought 'em when I couldn't afford cigars, and now I don't want cigars.'

'Oh, well. Every one to his taste,' said Miss LaFosse philosophically.

All this time Miss Pettigrew's delicate female perceptions had been aware that their hostess was in a high state of agitation behind her smiling front. Suddenly Miss LaFosse jumped to her feet and made for the kitchen.

'I must have some more coffee.'

Miss Pettigrew followed her with her eyes. She saw her stop in the doorway and make frantic signs of appeal. Miss Pettigrew had never been an actress in her life, but now she gave a brilliant performance. She rose to her feet with just the right touch of tolerant amusement in her voice.

'I'd better go my-self. She's quite capable of pouring it over herself.'

In the kitchen Miss LaFosse clutched her arm frantically.

'You must get him out. My God! What shall I do! You must get him out at once. You can do it without his guessing. I'm sure you can do anything. Please, please get him out for me.'

10

She wrung her hands in distress, her lovely face quite white with agitation. The kitchen pulsed with drama. No one could have resisted Miss LaFosse's appeal, let alone Miss Pettigrew with her susceptible heart. She felt strong with compassion and sympathy, though for what she hadn't the faintest idea. Yet behind her solicitude, rather guiltily, Miss Pettigrew felt the most glorious, exhilarating sensation of excitement she had ever experienced. 'This,'

'You must get him out'

thought Miss Pettigrew, 'is *Life*. I have never lived before.'

But feeling pity wasn't enough. This lovely child looked to her to act. Miss Pettigrew had never in her life before dealt with a situation that needed such finesse. What should she do? Her mind ranged in panic over her past life. From what experience could she draw? She thought of Mrs. Mortleman in that Golder's Green post and her terrible husband she had managed so well. If only . . . Miss Pettigrew, from nowhere, felt an amazing, powerful assurance pouring into her veins. This beautiful creature believed in her. She would not fail her. Could a Miss Pettigrew not be a Mrs. Mortleman?

'I have never,' said Miss Pettigrew, 'told a black

lie in my life, and very few white ones, but there is always a time to begin.'

'He mustn't guess I want him away. You're sure you won't let him guess.'

'He won't guess.'

Miss LaFosse flung her arms round Miss Pettigrew and kissed her.

'Oh, you darling! How can I thank you? Oh, thank you, thank you . . . you're sure you can manage?'

'Leave it to me,' said Miss Pettigrew.

Miss LaFosse made for the door. Calmly, collectedly, full powers in control, Miss Pettigrew chided her gently.

'You've forgotten the coffee.'

Miss Pettigrew filled the coffee-pot, turned around and went back into the room. Her heart was thumping, her cheeks were flushed, she felt weak with nervousness, but she had never felt so exhilarated in her life. Things were happening. Miss LaFosse followed meekly behind.

Miss Pettigrew sat down, poured out another cup of coffee for herself and Miss LaFosse and waited, with devilish tact, for a few minutes. That marvellous sense of assurance still upheld her. Phil looked set for the morning. At last Miss Pettigrew spoke. She leaned forward with her gentle, engaging smile.

'Young man, I am a busy woman and I have a lot of things to discuss with Miss LaFosse. Would you mind very much if I were so rude as to ask you to leave us alone together?'

'What things?'

Miss Pettigrew was not beaten.

'Oh!' said Miss Pettigrew with delicate reserve. 'Certain articles . . . of a lady's clothing . . .'

'That's all right. I know all about 'em.'

'In theory, perhaps,' said Miss Pettigrew with dignity. 'In

'. . . such ardent kisses. Not at all proper'

practice . . . I hope not. We are fitting.'

'I don't mind learning.'

'You choose to joke,' said Miss Pettigrew sternly.

'O.K.' said Phil resignedly. 'I'll wait in the bedroom.'

Miss Pettigrew shook her head with gentle amusement.

'If that suits you . . . but I don't think you'll like sitting for over an hour in a cold bedroom.'

'You can't be discussing underclothes all the time.'

'There are other feminine interests.'

'Can't I listen in?'

'You can *not*,' said Miss Pettigrew firmly.

'Why not? Ain't it pure enough for my ears?'

13

Miss Pettigrew stood up and drew herself to her full height.

'I am,' said Miss Pettigrew, ' the daughter of a curate.' He was quelled.

'O.K., sister. You win. I'll scram.'

'The contaminating effect,' thought Miss Pettigrew severely, ' of too many cheap American films.'

Miss Pettigrew herself helped him on with his coat. All this time Miss LaFosse wore an air of vague detachment, as though she didn't really care whether he went or stayed, but one must humour these middle-aged females. And once she winked at him at Miss Pettigrew's expense. Miss Pettigrew noted, and her new, indecorous self gave full marks of approval for the delicate touch it gave to the whole conspiracy.

'Well, good-bye, baby,' said Phil. 'See you anon.'

He took Miss LaFosse in his arms and kissed her, just as though he didn't care whether Miss Pettigrew saw or not. And, of course, he couldn't care. Miss Pettigrew sat down weakly.

'Oh dear!' Miss Pettigrew's virgin mind strove wildly for adjustment. 'Kisses . . . in front of me. I mean such . . . such ardent kisses. Not at all proper.'

But her traitorous, female heart turned right over in her body and thoroughly sympathized with the look of whole-hearted enjoyment registered by Miss LaFosse's face. And even though he was obviously left a little drunk with the reciprocatory fervour of Miss LaFosse's kisses, Phil still, very politely, remembered to say good-bye to herself.

A last kiss for Miss LaFosse, a last word for Miss Pettigrew, Phil opened the door and was gone.

CHAPTER TWO

11.11 a.m.—11.35 a.m.

WITH the banging of the door behind Phil, the door also banged on Miss Pettigrew's exhilarating feeling of adventure, romance and joy. She felt suddenly tired, inefficient and nervous again. She had only been allowed the privilege of seeing romance for a short time, but it was not really her portion in life. Now all the practical, terrifying worries of her daily life poured back into her mind. She was now the applicant for a post and Miss LaFosse her possible employer. She would never learn who Phil was, or what his last name was, or why Miss LaFosse so urgently wanted him away when she so obviously enjoyed his kisses.

She pushed back a wisp of straying hair with shaking fingers and gathered herself together for the always terrifying ordeal of stating her negligible qualifications.

'About . . .' began Miss Pettigrew with an attempt at firmness.

Miss LaFosse swooped down on her and caught her hands.

'You've saved my life. How can I thank you! You've saved more than my life. You've saved a situation. I was utterly lost without you. I never could have got him away myself. I can never repay you.'

15

The remembrance of stern dictums, 'To succeed, seize opportunity when it knocks,' came into Miss Pettigrew's mind. With the last remnants of her courage she began feebly,

'But you can . . .'

Miss LaFosse didn't hear her. She began to speak urgently and dramatically, but Miss Pettigrew could see that laughter lit the backs of Miss LaFosse's eyes as much as to say she quite realized she was hopeless but hoped Miss Pettigrew would humour her.

'Is your pulse fluttering?' asked Miss LaFosse. 'Is your eyesight excellent?'

Miss Pettigrew's pulse *was* fluttering, but she thought, 'One lie to-day, why not two?'

'My pulse is not fluttering,' said Miss Pettigrew, 'And my eyesight is excellent.'

'Oh!' said Miss LaFosse in great relief. 'I knew you were the calm kind. Mine is, so I *know* I'm too agitated to see. You know the way it is in detective books. You've cleared everything away, or think you have, then the detectives go around snooping and they discover a pipe or analyse some ash and find it's cigar ash and then they say, "Ha! So you smoke a cigar now, do you, miss?" And you're done for.'

'I see,' said Miss Pettigrew, not seeing at all, completely bewildered, and with visions of policemen, sergeants, detectives, descending on Miss LaFosse's flat.

'No you don't. I must explain everything. Nick's coming this morning. At least I'm perfectly certain he'll come, just to try and catch me out. He's wickedly jealous.'

She explained this with the kind of tone that said, 'There, I've told all, confessed all. Now I'm completely at your mercy, but I know you won't fail me.'

Miss Pettigrew, completely submerged in unknown waters, did her best to surmount the waves.

'You mean *another* young man is coming this morning ?' she questioned faintly.

'That's it,' said Miss LaFosse in relief. 'I knew you'd understand. Will you clear everything away, every single thing down to hair castings, that might faintly *hint* another man has been present.'

The waters nearly went over Miss Pettigrew's head, but she managed a weak, faltering voice.

'The safest course would be not to let him in.'

'Oh. I couldn't do that.'

'Why not ?' questioned Miss Pettigrew in surprise.

'I'm sort of afraid of him,' said Miss LaFosse simply.

'If,' said Miss Pettigrew with brilliant courage, 'if you are afraid of this young man, I . . . I will go to the door for you and say very firmly you are " not at home ".'

'Oh dear !' Miss LaFosse wrung her hands. 'But I don't think he'll knock. You see he's got a key. He'll just walk in. And I couldn't in any case. He pays the rent, you know. You see how it is.'

'I see,' said Miss Pettigrew in a small voice. She did see. It was nearly too much for her. She knew she should now gather her hat and coat, elevate her nose and walk out with outraged dignity. But she couldn't. She heard her voice saying very weakly,

'Then couldn't you . . . couldn't you have put off the other young man last night ?'

'Oh dear !' said Miss LaFosse, again hopelessly. 'It's so involved. I didn't know Nick was coming. I only got to know quite by chance late last night. He told me he was coming home to-morrow. He's been away, you know. I think he . . . he doubts me a little. So when Phil said could he come, I said all

17

right.   And then when I heard about Nick I couldn't put Phil off without a perfectly cast-iron excuse, and I'm not good at them.   And I couldn't make him suspicious.   He doesn't know about Nick.   He's going to back me in a new show.   You see how it is?'

'I see,' said Miss Pettigrew, shocked, excited, and, yes, thrilled.   Thrilled right down to the very marrow of her bones.   Why pretend?   This was life.   This was drama.   This was action.   This was the way the other half lived.

'So you see what you've got to do?' Miss LaFosse pleaded.   'You see how vital it is.   You're sure you can manage?'

Miss Pettigrew stood still and fought her fight. 'Stand for virtue' ran her father's teachings.   'Cast out the sinner.   Spurn him.'   All her maidenly up-bringing, her spinster's life of virtue, her moral beliefs, raised shocked hands of indignation.   Then she re-membered her place set at table, the cups of coffee, the thickly buttered toast piled on her plate, which, had Miss LaFosse only known, were the first food and drink she had had that day.

'As I said before,' remarked Miss Pettigrew, 'I have excellent eyesight.'

She went into the bedroom.   When she had rapidly erased all possible male signs from the bedroom and adjoining bathroom, even down to nail parings, she came back into the sitting-room.   Miss LaFosse was reclining on the chesterfield in front of the electric fire. She had been busy herself and cleared away all the tell-tale breakfast dishes, but she still wore her lovely *négligé* that made her look like Circe without her wickedness.

'Now,' thought Miss Pettigrew miserably, 'it is really business.   Nothing can put it off now.'   She felt

18

a sudden, unaccustomed sting at the back of her eyes. She had long ago learned that tears were never any use. 'Oh dear!' thought Miss Pettigrew suddenly. 'I'm so tired, so terribly tired of business and living in other people's houses and being dependent on their moods.'

She walked across the room slowly with the hopeless dignity of the petitioner and sat down on a comfortable chair opposite Miss LaFosse. She folded her hands on her lap and held them very firmly together. She now believed it was quite possible Miss LaFosse *might* have a few stray children tucked away somewhere, but was beginning to be doubtful whether her past obliging willingness to help in the way of deceit would now recommend her to their mother. Mothers were queer creatures where their children were concerned. Sauce for the goose was *not* sauce for the gander.

'About . . .' began Miss Pettigrew desperately.

Miss LaFosse leaned forward eagerly.

'Is everything all right?'

'Absolutely,' said Miss Pettigrew. 'You can set your mind at rest.'

'Oh, you darling!' Miss LaFosse leaned forward impulsively and kissed her again, and there, right on Miss Pettigrew's clasped hands, fell two drops of water and two more were trickling down her cheeks. Miss Pettigrew flushed a delicate pink.

'I have not,' said Miss Pettigrew in humble excuse, 'had much affection in my life.'

'Oh, you poor thing,' said Miss LaFosse gently. 'I've always had such a lot.'

'I'm glad,' said Miss Pettigrew simply.

After that they were friends and Miss LaFosse, tactfully, ignored the tears.

'About . . .' began Miss Pettigrew again.

'It's because you're so understanding,' broke in Miss

LaFosse eagerly. ' I felt it at once. I'm very good at first impressions. Here's a woman, I thought, who wouldn't let another woman down.'

' No. I wouldn't do that,' said Miss Pettigrew.

' I knew it. I've trespassed on your kindness a lot, I know, but don't you think you could stay a bit ? I mean, Nick might be here any minute. I'd appreciate it a lot.'

' Stay,' said Miss Pettigrew.

' Yes,' said Miss LaFosse pleadingly.

' If . . . if I could be of any assistance,' said Miss Pettigrew.

' You see, Nick's a very dangerous person. That's why he hadn't to learn of Phil. He's more money than Phil. He's more influence than Phil. He might quite easily do something that might hurt Phil. I couldn't have that happen. I mean, it wouldn't be fair. After all, I led Phil on. Phil's willing to back me in a show. Nick won't. He's too jealous. He won't help me an inch with my career, and however much you like a man you still want your career. So you see I couldn't have Nick trying to hurt Phil.'

' No,' agreed Miss Pettigrew firmly. ' It wouldn't be fair.'

' I know all the bad things there are to know about Nick, but it's no use. When he's there I can't resist him. I've been trying to for a long time. He's been away for three weeks and I've survived quite beautifully, so I thought now or never is the time to break. That's why I want you to stay. Meet him alone and I know I'm lost. Already I can feel quivers of expectation. So you see, when I waver, and I know I'll waver, I want you to be strong for me.'

Miss Pettigrew now forgot all about her original errand. For the first time for twenty years some one really wanted her for herself alone, not for her meagre scholarly qualifications. For the first time for twenty years she was herself, a woman, not a paid automaton. She was so intoxicated with pride she would have condoned far worse sins than Miss LaFosse having two young men in love with her. She put it like that. She became at once judicial, admonitory and questioning.

'I wouldn't think of advising normally,' said Miss Pettigrew, 'but I'm a great deal older than you and shall act in the place of a mother. If you are afraid of this new young man, wouldn't it be easy to sever all connexion with him? I mean, he can't do anything *to* you. Just fix your mind on that.'

'I know,' said Miss LaFosse sadly, 'but you don't quite understand yet.'

'I always considered I had a very receptive intelligence,' hinted Miss Pettigrew falsely.

'I know you have,' agreed Miss LaFosse. 'I see you will understand.'

She leaned forward.

'Have you ever,' said Miss LaFosse earnestly, 'had strange feelings in your stomach when a man kissed you?'

'Where,' thought Miss Pettigrew wildly, 'have I read that there is something in the stomach that responds to osculation. Or was it the stomach? It doesn't matter. I must reassure her.'

'Don't be alarmed,' said Miss Pettigrew weakly. 'I understand that it is a scientific fact that the stomach . . .'

'I'm not alarmed,' said Miss LaFosse. 'That's just it. I love it. It's no use. I can't escape him. He just looks at me and I'm wax in his hands.'

'A firm will . . .' began Miss Pettigrew hesitatingly.

'I'm a rabbit,' said Miss LaFosse, 'and he's a snake. When a snake fixes a rabbit with its eyes, the rabbit has no will. It stays there. It wants to stay there, even if it does mean its death.'

'Oh, not death,' said Miss Pettigrew, shocked.

'Worse than that,' said Miss LaFosse.

She got to her feet abruptly, went into the bedroom

'That's cocaine'

and returned with a small packet, which she opened and placed on Miss Pettigrew's knees.

'Do you know what that is?'

'It looks,' said Miss Pettigrew cautiously, 'very like a Beecham's Powder. Very good, I understand, for nerves, stomach and rheumatism.'

'That's cocaine,' said Miss LaFosse.

'Oh no! No!'

Terrified, aghast, thrilled, Miss Pettigrew stared at the innocent-looking powder. Drugs, the White Slave Traffic, wicked dives of iniquity, typified in Miss Pettigrew's mind by red plush and gilt and men with sinister black moustaches, roamed in wild array through her mind. What dangerous den of vice had she discovered? She must fly before she lost her virtue. Then her common sense unhappily reminded her that no one, now, would care to deprive her of that possession. It was Miss LaFosse who was in danger. She must save her. She jumped to her feet, tore into the kitchen, scattered the powder down the sink and returned triumphant.

'There!' she said breathlessly. 'That bit of temptation is beyond your reach now.'

She sat down weakly.

'Tell me,' she said in imploring accents. 'You have not Contracted The Habit?'

'No,' said Miss LaFosse. 'I haven't taken any yet. If I did, Michael might see. There's no flies on Michael. If he got to know he'd want to beat the daylight out of me. He's liable *to* beat the daylight out of me. Then he'd be off to murder the man that gave it me.'

'Michael!' said Miss Pettigrew faintly. 'Not *another* young man?'

'Oh, no!' denied Miss LaFosse hastily. 'Not a bit like that.'

She stared at the fire.

'Michael,' explained Miss LaFosse gloomily, 'wants to marry me.'

'Oh!' said Miss Pettigrew weakly.

'A woman's got to look out for these men,' said Miss LaFosse darkly. 'If you don't you'll find yourself

23

before the altar before you know where you are, and then where are you ? '

Bang went all Miss Pettigrew's cherished beliefs: scattered her naïve imaginings that only the men dreaded the altar: gone for ever her former unsophisticated outlook. ' I've lived too secluded a life,' thought Miss Pettigrew. ' I've not appreciated how my own sex has advanced. It's time I realized it.'

She ought to have said, ' My dear, a good man's love is not to be scorned.' But she didn't. She shut her mouth with a snap. None of that weak woman stuff here. She saw how ridiculous had been her wild thoughts of protecting Miss LaFosse. Miss Pettigrew sat up.

' You've said it, baby,' said Miss Pettigrew calmly, happily, blissfully.

' Eh ! ' said Miss LaFosse.

' American slang,' explained Miss Pettigrew. ' I heard it at the pictures.'

' Oh ! ' said Miss LaFosse.

' I have always longed,' explained Miss Pettigrew, ' sometimes to use slang. To let myself *go*, you understand. But I could never permit myself. Because of the children, you know. They might have heard.'

' Oh, quite,' said Miss LaFosse bewildered.

' I'm glad you understand,' said Miss Pettigrew simply.

' I'm glad *you* understand about Nick.'

' Of course,' said Miss Pettigrew.

She raised her head.

' He's wicked and handsome and fascinating,' said Miss Pettigrew in a clear voice, ' but he's life and excitement and thrills.'

' Yes,' said Miss LaFosse.

' And this good young man, this Michael, who wants

to marry you, has all the virtues, but he's dull. He has no fire . . . no imagination. He would stifle your spirit. You want colour, life, music. He would offer you a . . . a house in surburbia,' ended Miss Pettigrew brilliantly.

Miss LaFosse gave her a quick look under her lashes.

'Well . . .' began Miss LaFosse guiltily, 'I don't know that . . .'

'Neither do I,' said Miss Pettigrew simply. 'I cannot advise you. It would be impertinent. My own life has been a failure. How could I advise others ?'

'Oh,' said Miss LaFosse. She said nothing more.

'You look,' said Miss Pettigrew shyly, 'so lovely in that . . . that article of clothing. I can quite understand *all* the young men falling in love with you. I don't think, my dear, you need decide about your future yet.'

Miss LaFosse leaned forward, a smile parting her delightful mouth.

'Do you think so ?' she asked eagerly. 'I kept it on deliberately. You know, I think there's something sort of, well, *especially* fetching about a *négligé*, don't you think ? And men are so difficult in the morning.'

From her one tremendous experience of living in a house where the eldest daughter was about to be married, Miss Pettigrew agreed sagely.

'A . . . a sort of wanton attraction.' Miss Pettigrew blushed for her adjective. 'Very hard for the men to resist.'

'You understand perfectly,' said Miss LaFosse.

Miss Pettigrew suddenly remembered. She gasped in distress.

'But, Miss LaFosse,' said Miss Pettigrew in agitation, 'you're slipping already. You mustn't do it. You shouldn't want to be attractive. You should dress your plainest. You should try and repel him.'

'I know,' confessed Miss LaFosse guiltily, 'but I just can't help . . .'

They heard the faint sound of a key being gently inserted in the lock. They each gave a wild glance at the other. Then Miss Pettigrew was treated to a brilliant piece of acting. Miss LaFosse lay back quickly.

'I always consider,' said Miss LaFosse in a lazy, languid voice, 'that blue suits me best. It brings out the colour of my eyes.'

The door opened and shut. Miss Pettigrew sat in dumb admiration while surprise, unbelief, joy in turns took deceitful possession of Miss LaFosse's face. She jumped to her feet. There was a flutter of draperies, a rush across the room with outstretched arms.

'Nick,' cried Miss LaFosse.

Miss Pettigrew averted her eyes hastily.

'Oh dear!' thought Miss Pettigrew. 'Not . . . not again . . . so publicly. And I *always* thought they exaggerated kisses on the films.'

CHAPTER THREE

MISS LAFOSSE disengaged herself from the new-comer's arms and Miss Pettigrew saw him clearly for the first time. Graceful, lithe, beautifully poised body. Dark, vivid looks: a perfection of feature and colouring rare in a man. Brilliant, piercing eyes of a dark bluish-purple colour: a beautiful, cruel mouth, above which a small black moustache gave him a look of sophistication and a subtle air of degeneracy that had its own appeal. Something predatory in his expression: something fascinating and inescapable in his personality.

Miss Pettigrew rose slowly from her chair with a queer feeling of helplessness. She understood immediately Miss LaFosse's subjection. It only needed one look. She had seen his counterpart a dozen times on the films, young, fascinating, irresistible to women, supremely assured of his power, utterly callous when the moment's fancy passed. She had seen the heroine a dozen times nearly lose happiness because of his attentions. But there was no hero to save Miss LaFosse.

' Queer,' thought Miss Pettigrew helplessly, ' one reads about these men. One sees them on the films. One never thinks to meet them in daily life, but they do exist after all.'

Miss LaFosse stood away from her visitor. Her cat's look of contentment after cream became tinged with a nervous tension. Nick now noticed Miss Pettigrew. His face immediately darkened. He flung Miss LaFosse an angry, questioning glance.

'Oh!' said Miss LaFosse. 'This is my friend . . . my friend . . . Alice.'

She gathered herself together and made a more polite introduction.

'Alice, meet Nick. Nick, this is my friend Alice.'

'How-do-you-do?' asked Miss Pettigrew politely.

'How do?' said Nick curtly.

His glance flicked over her and Miss Pettigrew became aware at once of her age, her dowdy clothes, her clumsy figure, her wispy hair, her sallow complexion. She flushed a painful red. Her mind disliked him at once: her emotions were enslaved.

It wasn't only good looks. His looks were merely an extra, naturally helpful but not necessary. It was something in the man himself. The room was in an instant filled with his presence. All the women of any company would at once be rivals for his notice. Perhaps it was an aura that sent out waves of challenge to the female in every woman. Miss Pettigrew felt it. Miss Pettigrew responded to it. She couldn't help it. Her feminine susceptibilities simply turned traitor on her and she would have given ten years of her life for him to kiss her as he had kissed Miss LaFosse. She almost did hate Miss LaFosse for her youth, her beauty, her charm. Not for long, though. She was not as stupid as all that.

He was not good. Miss Pettigrew knew that: from what Miss LaFosse had told her and from something about the man himself. That was why he was so fascinating. Miss Pettigrew's intelligence was quite up

28

to the subtle attraction of a spice of wickedness against the dullness of too much virtue.

'Oh dear!' she thought. 'These men. They're wicked, but it doesn't matter. They simply leave the good men standing still. If only Michael had been a little less good and proper he might have had a chance, but as it is, against a man like this, what ordinary man has a look in? It's no use, we women just can't help ourselves. When it comes to love we're born adventurers.'

She sighed. The problem was going to be a difficult one. She quite forgot in her excitement that any minute she might be ejected summarily. She had now completely identified herself with Miss LaFosse and felt she had known her all her life.

Miss LaFosse was standing eyeing them both a little nervously. Her smile had lost its lovely assurance and had that faintly placating nervousness about it of a woman who longs for, yet doubts, her complete power over a man.

'Come and sit down,' said Miss LaFosse to Nick propitiatingly.

'Oh, my dear,' thought Miss Pettigrew, 'that other manner is much the best. A . . . a sort of regal indifference. This kind of creature respects that. The minute he thinks you're all his, you'll lose him.'

Her worldly wisdom almost dumbfounded her. She had to call him in her mind creature, upstart, mountebank, to save herself falling in love with him. If he had only once looked at her, kissed her, the way he had Miss LaFosse, she knew she would have been his slave.

'Who would ever have thought it,' worried Miss Pettigrew, 'at my age? I am a very stupid woman. As if I didn't know he thinks I'm an old back number and wants me away.'

29

In truth the very air round Nick was thick with anger at her presence. He had come jealously prepared to find Miss LaFosse not alone, but he had not expected a Miss Pettigrew. This old fool seemed set for the day. Miss Pettigrew felt these waves of thought. Suddenly all her old deprecating nervousness crowded back on her.

'Should I go?' she thought in terror. 'After all, I am an intruder. I expect even Miss LaFosse is thinking I'm an interfering busybody and wishes I would have the sense to go and didn't really mean she wanted me to stay.'

Hot with discomfort she began to tremble a little. All her lovely, new sense of assurance vanished. She was Miss Pettigrew, the inefficient nursery governess again, nervous, futile, helpless. She fumbled at the back of a chair. Then she looked at Miss LaFosse.

Miss LaFosse gave her a brilliant, friendly, reassuring smile.

And quite suddenly Miss Pettigrew was immune: safe from his dislike: safe from his charm. He could turn on his fascination act as much as he liked. She wouldn't fall for it. He could be as rude as he liked, and she thought, if goaded, he could be very rude; she was impervious to insult. Here she was and here she would stay. Only Miss LaFosse could turn her out.

Miss Pettigrew sat down on her chair again, serene, composed, set for the day.

Nick glared at her, met the solid wall of her indifference, and turned slowly to Miss LaFosse.

'I thought you would be alone.'

Miss LaFosse jumped at his deadly tone.

'But you said to-morrow,' she pleaded nervously. 'You distinctly said to-morrow.'

'I know, but I pushed the business through a day

30

earlier and came straight back. I thought you would be glad to have me back sooner.'

'Oh, darling, I am glad.' Miss LaFosse came to him with outstretched arms. 'I've missed you like hell. I thought you'd never come back.'

'Very bad beginning,' worried Miss Pettigrew. 'Not at all the kind of greeting to lead up to a parting.'

Nick looked placated. He gave her a quick kiss, merely as a taste of what was to come, finishing with an understanding glance. Obviously she didn't like to be rude to the old fool, but he didn't mind in the slightest. He put her to one side and came to rest in front of Miss Pettigrew.

'I didn't catch the name,' said Nick in his most insulting voice.

Miss Pettigrew sat secure beneath the mantle of Mrs. Jackaman, four situations previous. How superbly she had countered the insults of an abominable husband by a bland unawareness, until blaspheming he had torn from the house and left her to a little peace.

'Pettigrew,' said Miss Pettigrew helpfully; 'so uncommon, isn't it? My dear father used to say . . .'

'Too uncommon not to let it travel around,' said Nick ominously.

'Ah!' said Miss Pettigrew sadly. 'I've never been a good traveller. I remember once . . .'

'I've been away three weeks,' said Nick, beginning to get warm.

'Well now, I do hope you had a nice holiday,' said Miss Pettigrew kindly. 'Do you intend to travel much further? The weather has been so unsettled.'

'I have something to say to Miss LaFosse,' said Nick, getting still more furious.

'Something you forgot to write? But there, the post these days is disgraceful. But the telephone is such a convenience I simply cannot think what we would do . . .'

'I thought she would be alone,' said Nick, holding back an explosion with difficulty.

'Great minds . . .' said Miss Pettigrew brightly. 'Just what I hoped myself. I was so glad to find Miss LaFosse alone to-day. I've been looking forward to such a long chat, but it was nice of you to pop in as you passed.'

Nick was red in the face. Miss LaFosse painfully awaited the explosion.

'Most of her friends have tact,' said Nick pointedly, in a last raging effort towards peaceable ejection.

'There now,' said Miss Pettigrew cheerfully. 'I knew you had. It makes it so much easier. So nice of you to understand. As soon as I saw you I thought . . .'

'To hell with what you thought. Will You Go ?' exploded Nick.

'No,' said Miss Pettigrew.

'!!!. . .? ? ?. . .!!!. . .? ? ?. . .!!!'

'Oh !' gasped Miss Pettigrew.

Miss LaFosse started forward. She threw a wild look at Miss Pettigrew's shocked countenance, and a distracted look at Nick's raging one.

'Nick, darling, do sit down and let me have a look at you.'

Nick was too dumbfounded to resist. She helped him off with his coat. She pulled him on to the chesterfield and sat down beside him. Nick gave Miss Pettigrew one more glare, shrugged his shoulders and proceeded to forget her. As Miss LaFosse had thought, the *négligé* was very seductive.

By this time Miss Pettigrew was getting almost hardened.

'Well,' she thought weakly, 'they don't seem to mind.

Why should I ? I think before, perhaps, I've held too narrow views. This . . . this lovemaking seems a very pleasant business.'

She sat up and began to take quite an interest in the technique.

' Ah ! ' thought Miss Pettigrew sagely, ' with Phil it was only a business, a pleasant business, but only part of the day's routine. But with Nick, every gesture, every caress conveys the impression you are the one woman in the world. Who could resist him ? '

After a while Miss LaFosse and Nick relaxed for air. He now took Miss Pettigrew quite philosophically. If the old lady—every one to Nick was old over thirty-three —didn't mind a bit of petting, he wasn't the one to deprive her of her enjoyment. She rather cramped his style, but it was still early. Night was, after all, the best time. Worth-while pleasures never lost their flavour for a little postponement.

He sat up.

' I could do with a drink.'

' So could I,' agreed Miss LaFosse. ' You know where the stuff is.'

' O.K. What'll it be ? '

' Well,' pondered Miss LaFosse, ' mix me one of your Specials, Nick. There's a wallop in them that sets you up for the day.'

' Anything you say. What's yours ? '

' Me ? ' said Miss Pettigrew.

' You.'

' A drink ? '

' It's been mentioned.'

Miss Pettigrew nearly said, ' Oh, no thank you,' in a flutter of genteel denial. But she didn't. Not her. Not now. She stopped herself in time : just in time. She was going to accept now everything that came along.

33

From this one day, dropped out of the blue into her lap, she was going to savour everything it offered her.

'I will take,' said Miss Pettigrew, with calmness, with ease, with assurance, 'a little dry sherry, if you please.'

She considered the 'dry' the perfect touch. Not Sherry. Any one could say that. 'Dry sherry.' That showed poise, sophistication, the experienced palate. It raised her prestige. She had no idea what the dry meant, but she remembered distinctly the husband of her last situation but one, who had always terrified her by his booming irritation, cursing this 'damned dry sherry' and she was quite sure what he didn't like, she would.

Nick looked unimpressed.

'Sure you won't have a Horse's Fillip, too?'

Miss Pettigrew's resolution to experience everything wavered a little.

'Oh, I think not,' she said hurriedly, 'not in a morning. Just a little dry sherry, please.'

Nick went into the kitchen. Miss LaFosse leaned forward. She felt responsible for Nick's behaviour and his language was not suitable for ladies like her new friend.

'You mustn't mind Nick's language,' she whispered. 'I mean, he doesn't *mean* anything. It's just like you or me saying "Oh bother" or "drat it".'

Miss Pettigrew raised her head. Her expression became very firm.

'My dear, I don't like to be unpleasant, but I'm afraid *I don't believe* that excuse. I am a lot older than you and during my lifetime I have heard a great many people say they don't mean a thing, when they know perfectly well they do. It's just a weak excuse for a bad habit. If I were you I would use your influence on that young man to, well, moderate his language. You know, my dear, in the end a young man thinks a lot more of a young lady who insists on decorum in her presence. I . . . I hope

34

you don't mind my telling you this, but I am, as I say, almost old enough to be your mother.'

There was the loveliest twinkle in Miss LaFosse's eyes, kindly, affectionate, but she veiled it discreetly. She wouldn't have hurt Miss Pettigrew for worlds.

' I'll try,' said Miss LaFosse meekly. ' I'll do my best. I'm quite sure you're quite right about it.'

They could hear the clink of glasses in the kitchen and Nick moving about. He was humming with a low, cheerful sound a popular tune. Suddenly the humming stopped, to be succeeded by a terrifying silence. Miss Pettigrew looked at Miss LaFosse. Miss LaFosse looked at Miss Pettigrew. Her face was suddenly strained with the expression of rigid apprehension worn on Miss Pettigrew's first view of her.

The kitchen door opened and Nick stood on the threshold. Miss Pettigrew felt a sudden shiver run down her spine. All his pleasant amiability was gone. His face was menacing, frightening. Miss Pettigrew understood at once that it was no mere joke that some men were to be feared. Her vague, developing belief that all these amazing interludes were some kind of charming joke she had been privileged to share vanished abruptly and she realized she was now in the middle of a new situation that no longer held humour.

She saw Miss LaFosse's lovely face go almost green with fright under Nick's terrible stare.

' Since when,' asked Nick in a low, deadly voice, ' have you started smoking cheroots ? '

Miss Pettigrew's first impulse was to explode into giggles and she saw that the same unbalanced mirth threatened Miss LaFosse behind her terror. She could hear, quite plainly, Miss LaFosse saying, ' Then the detective snoops around and says, " Ha ! So you smoke a cigar now, do you, miss ?" '

Miss LaFosse was quite incapable of speaking. Miss Pettigrew saw that everything now depended on her.

Her mind whirled dizzily, then burst like a rocket into dazzling light. She remembered Mrs. Brummegan, her last employer: chest like a hill, nose like a horse, mouth like a clamp, chin like a hatchet, voice like a rasp, manner calculated to awe a brigadier. Her life with Mrs. Brummegan had been two years of sheer, un-

diluted hell. But she was thankful for it now. It all lay in the manner. Manner can put over anything, and who, better than she, knew just how Mrs. Brummegan did it? No one ever dared doubt Mrs. Brummegan. This was her moment.

Miss Pettigrew stood up. She stalked across the room, arrogance and contempt in her stride. She picked up her handbag lying on a chair. She turned: she glanced at Nick, chin up, eyes blazing, voice rasping.

' Young man,' said Miss Pettigrew, ' if there's one thing I completely abominate it's the effeminate type of man that snoops round a house like an old, peeking busybody. I am Miss LaFosse's guest. If she doesn't mind, it's no business of yours. If I want to smoke cheroots, I'll smoke cheroots, instead of those damned, silly cigarettes. I've reached the age when I can please myself and I mean to please myself and to hell with your opinion. Have one. I can recommend them.'

Miss Pettigrew opened her bag. She took out a worn packet of cheroots. She held it out. It was a crisis. She snorted, she glared.

Nick was vanquished. He reached out, took the packet, compared the cheroots. He dropped the half-burned end on the rug and ground it with his heel. He walked over to Miss LaFosse and stood over her. He said in a soft voice that made Miss Pettigrew shiver,

' You wouldn't fool me, would you ? '

Miss LaFosse made a

' Since when,' asked Nick in a low, deadly voice, ' have you started smoking cheroots ? '

lightning recovery. She was not an actress for nothing. She jumped to her feet with a petulant gesture.

' Oh, for God's sake, Nick ! When will you stop having heroics ? I said I wouldn't have any men in the place. Now are you satisfied ? Where's that drink, or have I got to get it myself ? '

' Sorry.'

He flung an abrupt arm round Miss LaFosse and kissed her. Miss Pettigrew did a hasty disappearing act into the bedroom.

'Oh dear!' she gasped to herself. 'There's times when two *are* company. I didn't know there *were* kisses like that.'

She was in such a trembling state of reaction after Mrs. Brummegan that she felt like collapsing, but she didn't dare. She had to sustain Mrs. Brummegan to the end. She quite forgot in the heat of the moment that it would be the best thing possible if Nick did fly off the handle and depart in a rage. Nick had frightened her. He had frightened Miss LaFosse. He must not be allowed to do it again. After a hasty terrified glance at herself in the glass, she returned to the sitting-room.

Nick was bringing in the drinks on a tray. Miss LaFosse was sitting quietly with the radiant, shining look on her face of the woman who has just been thoroughly and satisfactorily kissed. It caught at Miss Pettigrew's heart. It made her look so defenceless. Then Miss Pettigrew remembered again.

'He's got her again,' thought Miss Pettigrew, ' but I won't let him. I'll save her yet.'

Nick brought up her drink. Miss Pettigrew took her glass without a word and downed it like a toper, without a single thought of its possible effect on her wits.

'That,' remarked Miss Pettigrew, 'was very good. I'll have another.'

Miss LaFosse and Nick were still sipping their first. Nick gave her an admiring glance. She had gone up in his estimation. The old dame had guts: smoking cheroots and bending her elbow with the best.

'Sure you won't have a whisky?' he offered solicitously. 'There's sure to be some in the cupboard.'

The old dame had guts . . . bending her elbow with the best

' No, thank you,' said Miss Pettigrew blandly. ' I prefer them light in the morning.'

Her voice hinted at dark hours of intemperance in the evening.

' Oh dear ! ' she thought wildly, ' it can't possibly be me speaking like that. What's come to me ? What's happening to me ? '

But she didn't care. Not really. The thought was only a guilty, placating concession towards her former values. The excitement of adventure had entered fully into her, and also, perhaps, a little of the wine to her head. She was ready for anything.

Nick brought her drink.

' Young man,' said Miss Pettigrew, ' when you are not being a fussy old woman, I quite like you.'

' Thanks,' said Nick with a grin. ' You're a lady.'

They drank to each other.

This friendly little interlude had not at all lessened Miss Pettigrew's determination to tear Miss LaFosse from his grasp. It was merely the polite exchange of amenities during an armistice.

They finished their drinks. Nick stood up.

' I've got to see Dalton. Business. Or I'd take you to lunch. He's putting up half the money and we're opening a new place. Can't afford to offend him. See you to-night.'

' Oh ! ' exclaimed Miss LaFosse. She weakened. ' When ? '

' I'll collect you when your turns are over and we'll come straight back.'

Miss LaFosse's hand was lying along the arm of her chair. He leaned forward, closed his hand on her wrist and stood looking at her. Miss LaFosse raised her eyes to his and they remained silent.

Miss Pettigrew felt a fainting sensation inside and a queer feeling, that was almost pain, right in the pit of her stomach, precisely as Miss LaFosse had once said. The look was not for her. No one had ever looked at her like that, but she knew exactly what Miss LaFosse was feeling : breathlessness, terror, ecstasy ; a slow melting of all her senses towards trembling surrender. And the look on Nick's face made one want to give him anything he asked. Even Miss Pettigrew felt the effect, knowing what she knew. To an outsider it was two lovers for the first time catching a glimpse of innocent, earthly paradise : to an insider, like Miss Pettigrew, it was a very wicked man seducing a darling lady to her damnation.

Yet only by an effort of common sense could Miss Pettigrew keep in mind that Nick was really an evil, selfish man, who a year to-day might be looking at another woman with the same compelling urge, while poor Miss LaFosse might be ruined and broken-hearted. Miss Pettigrew could never forget the cocaine and she was not an ignorant fool.

By the rapt look on Miss LaFosse's face and air of defenceless submission, Miss Pettigrew knew she was wavering : knew she had wavered, but before she could speak the fatal words of surrender, Miss Pettigrew came into action like a howitzer.

She thudded across the room with the Brummegan stalk. The sherry bottle and glasses were standing on the tray. She splashed out another drink and lifted the glass negligently in her hand. Through years of endurance she knew to a calculated nicety the demolishing effect of a negligent gesture.

' Young man,' said Miss Pettigrew in the most strident voice her throat could compass, ' you can come back for a drink if you like, but no late hours, I warn you. I'm not as young as I was and I will not have my short stay here ruined by disturbed nights leaving me half-dead next day. I sleep with Miss LaFosse and while I'm here she comes to bed early, and I'm not having you hanging around to all hours. I'm too old a friend of Miss

LaFosse and too old myself to pretend to be polite, and that's that.'

Nick's hand sprang from Miss LaFosse's as from a hot poker and he spun round.

' What ? '

' What what ? '

' Are *you* staying here ? '

' You know I'm staying here.   I said so.   Until to-morrow the invitation was and until to-morrow I stay, and what's it got to do with you, pray ? '

' ? ? ?...! ! !...? ? ?...! ! !' exploded Nick again.

Miss LaFosse turned a startled gaze on Miss Pettigrew, denial, indignation, resentment, eloquent in her glance. Miss Pettigrew returned the look, steadily, sternly, remorselessly.   Miss LaFosse remembered.   She blushed. She rallied her drooping forces about her.

' You said to-morrow, Nick darling,' quavered Miss LaFosse.

' Telegrams are cheap,' stated Miss Pettigrew.

' How the hell should I know my . . .'

' I was lonely,' faltered Miss LaFosse, ' with you away.'

' I'm coming round to-night.'

' There's only one bed.'

' What the . . .'

' Come if you like,' broke in Miss Pettigrew amiably. ' You can sleep on the chesterfield.   They say it's healthy to sleep with your knees bent.   But nothing,' she eyed the couch, ' will make *me* sleep on it.   At my age I insist on my proper bed.'

Nick was beaten.   The old dame was his match and seemed to have a claim on hospitality.   He must curb his temper and mind his step.   The girl friend had a temper of her own which could crop up at the most inconvenient of occasions.

Nor had he any intention of sleeping on a lonely sofa.

He preferred a comfortable bed for his nightly rest. The couch, plus Miss LaFosse, might have held some inducement, but the couch as a place of rest, with Miss LaFosse sleeping in tantalizing innocence in the next room, held none.

He went to his hat and coat and picked them up. Miss LaFosse hovered about him nervously. He put on his hat and coat in silence and moved to the door. Miss Pettigrew saw firmness, indecision, surrender, battle on Miss LaFosse's face.

'If she succumbs now,' thought Miss Pettigrew, 'she is lost. I can do no more. If he goes away without speaking she will probably run after him.'

Then Nick spoke.

'Maybe I should have wired.'

Miss Pettigrew drew a deep breath. Miss LaFosse twined her hands nervously. She gave a timid, pleading smile.

'I'm . . . I'm terribly sorry.'

'See you to-morrow then.'

'To-morrow,' promised Miss LaFosse hastily.

'Maybe,' thought Miss Pettigrew grimly.

'Take you to lunch.'

'Lunch,' agreed Miss LaFosse.

He moved and took hold of her arms above the elbows and pulled her to him.

'After all, you'll keep.'

Miss Pettigrew thought his young face with its old look of experience a little frightening. He took hold of Miss LaFosse's chin and tipped up her face.

'No good thing was spoiled by a little waiting.'

He kissed her. The door closed behind him.

CHAPTER FOUR

12.52 p.m.—1.17 p.m.

IMMEDIATELY the door closed behind Nick tension relaxed. It was like coming out of a fog into clear, bright air. Miss Pettigrew drew a long breath. Her legs felt wobbly. Reaction had set in. She felt weak, unstrung, thoroughly upset. She found a chair and sat down. Suddenly she burst out crying.

Miss LaFosse was standing staring at the closed door. Nick had gone. She had let him go. She didn't know why. She was a fool. She had never so much wanted him as now, when he was gone. She was on the verge of running after him. Miss Pettigrew's tears made her swing round. She forgot everything in concern.

'Don't do that. Please don't do that.'

All the terrible things she had done crowded into Miss Pettigrew's mind: the lies she had told, the drink she had taken, the swear words she had used.

'I've never sworn in my life before,' wailed Miss Pettigrew.

'No?' marvelled Miss LaFosse.

'Never. Not even in my mind. Our Vicar once said that to swear in your mind was just as bad and even more cowardly than to swear out loud. He did neither.'

'What a man!' said Miss LaFosse in awe.

'He was,' agreed Miss Pettigrew.

44

'But I didn't hear you swear,' consoled Miss LaFosse.

'You must have been too upset. I said "damned" and "hell" and meant them . . . that way.'

'Oh!' said Miss LaFosse with a reassuring beam. '*They're* not swear words. They're only expressions. I assure you, fashions change in words, same as everything else. I think they've quite come out of the sinful category now. There now, what you need is another drink.'

She went over to the tray and further depleted the sherry bottle. She came back with a brimming glass.

'Come along now. It's only sherry. I know you like your drinks light in a morning.'

Miss Pettigrew looked up. Her tears began to dry. Her face took on a look of dawning wonder and remembrance.

'Oh!' gasped Miss Pettigrew. 'Oh, I did. I dealt with a situation.'

'Oh boy!' said Miss LaFosse with reverence. 'You sure did.'

Miss Pettigrew's eyes began to shine through her tears. She was tremulous, bewildered, unbelieving.

'I did. I saved it.'

'Oh, quick,' hurried Miss LaFosse. 'Drink your sherry, and tell me how you did it.'

Miss Pettigrew refused it.

'No, thank you, my dear. I have had two already and a little I pretended to drink. It's a wise woman who knows her limit. I have never been rendered ridiculous by alcohol yet and I have no intention of starting now.'

'You're sure you're all right then?'

'Quite.'

Miss LaFosse swallowed the sherry herself and sat down.

'Oh, quick,' she implored. 'Quick. I can't wait to

45

hear any longer. How . . . Did . . . You . . . Do
. . . It ? I forgot the kitchen. I never thought about
the kitchen. I never looked for any signs there. Rank
carelessness. I was born careless. You were marvellous.'

Miss Pettigrew made a hasty disclaimer of any
brilliance.

' It was very simple,' she said earnestly, ' very simple
indeed. Nothing really to it. Please don't think I'm
clever or you'll be disappointed. When I was tidying
the bedroom I discovered the packet and I thought my
bag was the safest place for it. When Nick came in so
angry I remembered and the rest all followed. There
was nothing to it, really.'

' Nothing to it ! ' said Miss LaFosse. ' Nothing to it !
It was brilliant, marvellous. The best bit of acting I've
seen in years.'

' Oh no ! It wasn't acting. It was copying.'

' Copying ? '

' It was Mrs. Brummegan.'

' Mrs. Brummegan ? '

' My late employer. If you'll forgive me speaking ill
of the absent, a dreadful woman.'

' But I don't quite follow,' said Miss LaFosse,
bewildered.

' I endured her two years,' said Miss Pettigrew simply.
' I had to. I was in a very good position to know the
effect of her personality. I did my best to emulate it.'

There was no wool in Miss LaFosse's brain. Her eyes
shone.

' Oh ! ' she breathed. ' A Mimic. A born mimic.
God ! What a performance ! I wouldn't have said
you had it in you. You were wonderful.'

' Oh no,' denied Miss Pettigrew, deprecating, thrilled,
delighted as a child.

46

'You've never thought about entering the Profession, have you?'

'The Profession?'

'The stage, you know.'

'The stage!' gasped Miss Pettigrew. 'Me?'

'There's a great dearth of really good character actresses,' said Miss LaFosse earnestly. 'You know how it is. The ones that started young, when they're getting on and have the experience, they don't like to be relegated to minor rôles. They don't like the old boys to say, "By Jove, I remember her when we were both young. You should have seen her then, my boy, when she played lead in 'Kiss me, Daddy'." No. They don't. They like to stay young and play young leads, and when they can't they quit. I don't blame them. I'll do it myself.'

'You're on the stage yourself?' queried Miss Pettigrew, tactfully leading the subject from her own histrionic powers.

'Yes,' agreed Miss LaFosse, 'but I'm resting just now, only I'm working while I'm resting. I didn't want to sign a poorer contract while Phil was getting ready to back me in " Pile on the Pepper ", so I refused to sign a small contract and I'm singing just now at the Scarlet Peacock.'

'A very odd name,' murmured Miss Pettigrew, 'Scarlet Peacock?'

'Very,' agreed Miss LaFosse, 'but it's very fetching, don't you think? Nick is partner in it with Teddy Scholtz. Nick's a bit conventional and wanted to call it " The Scarlet Woman ", and Teddy's a bit unimaginative and wanted to call it " The Green Peacock." So they cut for it, only they didn't know they'd got hold of Charlie Hardbright's fake pack and they both cut the Ace of Spades. Neither would give in and cut again, so they split the difference and called it " The Scarlet Peacock ".'

' How terribly interesting,' breathed Miss Pettigrew. ' I mean, you know, knowing the *inside* histories of things. I've always been on the outside before.'

' Yes,' agreed Miss LaFosse. ' You're certainly on the inside when Nick's around.'

Talking about Nick brought him close again. She got up and began fiddling with an ornament on the mantelpiece with her head half-turned from Miss Pettigrew. Her merry, laughing face was clouded and a little unhappy.

' You see how it is,' said Miss LaFosse in a muffled voice; ' he just . . . gets you.'

' Yes,' agreed Miss Pettigrew.

' There's some men like that.'

'Assuredly.'

'You can't explain it.'

'Not to other men.'

'There's no words for it.'

'Being a woman,' said Miss Pettigrew, 'I don't need any.'

Miss LaFosse leaned her elbow on the mantelpiece and rested her brow on the palm of her hand. Her voice sounded a little hopeless.

'He's bad and I know it and I want to break with him. While he's been away these three weeks I determined when he came back I would finish everything. I even asked you to help me to be firm. But you saw how it was. The minute he returned I was soft again. If you hadn't been there I'd have agreed about to-night and everything he asked, but you mayn't be there next time.'

Miss Pettigrew saw things needed firm handling. She was getting to know her new rôle and was beginning to find a certain zest in attacking problems boldly.

'Sit down,' said Miss Pettigrew. 'Looking back I don't know why I acted as I did. It was purely automatic. I never thought. He has a very . . . very *intimidating* personality. You were afraid. I was afraid. But something had to be done about it, so I did something. I was very foolish. I should really have let him discover about Phil, even if it meant sacrificing Phil to his anger, then all would have been safely over between you. I cannot think why I destroyed the opportunity.'

'But I'm so glad you did,' breathed Miss LaFosse.

'Sit down.'

Miss LaFosse sat down.

'You need a talking-to,' said Miss Pettigrew.

'I wouldn't be surprised.'

'If you don't mind,' said Miss Pettigrew, 'I'll talk.'

49

'Not at all,' said Miss LaFosse. 'Please do.'

'You're pitying yourself,' accused Miss Pettigrew. 'You think it's very hard you should be picked out to love a person you think you shouldn't love. You don't think it's fair and you're a little aggrieved at so much worry and so you're pitying yourself.'

'I suppose I am,' agreed Miss LaFosse honestly.

'In my life,' said Miss Pettigrew, 'a great many unpleasant things have happened. I hope they never happen to you. I don't think they will because you're not afraid like me. But there's one thing I found fatal: pitying myself. It made things worse.'

'I expect you're right.'

'I am right. You've got to face up to facts. I did. My way,' said Miss Pettigrew simply, 'was dumb endurance. It was the only way I could. I hadn't the courage for fighting. I've always been terrified of people.'

Miss LaFosse turned unbelieving eyes on her.

'It's true,' pursued Miss Pettigrew, 'you must not judge by to-day's events. I've never acted like that in my life before.'

'I couldn't dumbly endure.'

'No,' agreed Miss Pettigrew. 'I'm glad. You'd probably kick back and end safely somewhere. But you've got courage and I haven't.'

'I'm glad you think so.'

'Agreed to the courage,' said Miss Pettigrew firmly. 'Now you've got to use it.'

'Oh.'

'He's gone,' said Miss Pettigrew.

'Yes.'

'And when he went through the door you thought the world went with him.'

'You do understand things.'

'Do you feel exactly the same now?' demanded Miss Pettigrew.

'Well. No. Not now. Not so badly. Come to think of it. No.'

'I mean he's away, but you can bear him away.'

'Well. Yes.'

'And to-morrow isn't ten years away?'

'Why, no. I suppose it isn't. I'll survive.'

'Well, you see how it is,' said Miss Pettigrew earnestly. 'It's only when he's there. When he's gone you know you can live without him. Will you always remember that, so that however hard it is at the moment, will you promise me that every time in future he asks you to do anything you'll only agree to give him an answer later and wait until he's been gone fifteen minutes before deciding, when the glamour has ceased to function?'

'It's a difficult promise,' said Miss LaFosse, 'but I give it. I know it's for my own good. I can never thank you for what you've done for me to-day. You've saved me twice. You know, I've never turned Nick away before. I didn't think I ever really could, however much I hoped. Now I've done it, and do you know? I feel quite all right now. I feel kind of fine. I feel, I've done it once, why can't I do it again? I feel, why, I *can* do it again. . . . I feel,' said Miss LaFosse, warming up, 'just grand. Free. Maybe I can resist him.'

'That,' said Miss Pettigrew, 'is the spirit.'

She leaned back in her chair. Miss LaFosse leaned back in hers and sank into a contemplative dream. The clock on the mantelpiece ticked. Slowly its ticking penetrated Miss Pettigrew's brain. She turned her head and looked at the clock. The pointers were racing round and Miss Pettigrew remembered where she was. There was nothing to keep her there now. Good manners demanded her departure. She must state her errand and go. She must give up her position of equality as Miss LaFosse's ally and take her correct one of humble applicant for a job, which she felt in her bones she would never get.

She knew too much about the private affairs of Miss LaFosse. Miss Pettigrew had endured many hard knocks from human nature and understood how intolerable to a mistress such a situation would be. She felt a hopeless, bitter unhappiness invade her. But there was nothing she could do. She must at last get her presence explained and end this wonderful adventure.

She couldn't bear to do it. She had never in her life before wanted more to stay in any place. She felt she couldn't endure to leave this happy, careless atmosphere, despite momentary upheavals, where some one was kind to her and thought her wonderful. How could she possibly live out her life never knowing what happened to Phil, whether Nick's charms bore down Miss LaFosse's susceptible defences, who Michael was and what he was like? She felt the tears of loneliness and exclusion sting her eyes.

'I'll wait,' thought Miss Pettigrew dully, 'three more minutes. I'll wait 'til the pointers move three minutes before speaking. Surely I can have three more minutes of being happy.'

She prayed desperately for a knock on the door. A knock on Miss LaFosse's door heralded adventure. It was not like an ordinary house, when the knocker would be the butcher, or baker or candlestick-maker. A knock on Miss LaFosse's door would mean excitement, drama, a new crisis to be dealt with. Oh, if only for once the Lord would be good and cause some miracle to happen to keep her here, to see for one day how life could be lived, so that for all the rest of her dull, uneventful days, when things grew bad, she could look back in her mind and dwell on the time when for one perfect day she, Miss Pettigrew, lived.

But miracles don't happen. No knock came. The clock ticked on. Three minutes were over. Miss Pettigrew, always honest, even with herself, sat up. She clasped her hands very tightly. Her face shadowed with a determined, pathetic, hopeless look.

' There's a little matter,' began Miss Pettigrew bravely, ' I think we ought to get settled. About my . . .'

Miss LaFosse came out of her dream with a sigh and smiled at Miss Pettigrew.

' I was thinking of Michael,' she confessed.

' Michael ! ' exclaimed Miss Pettigrew.

Miss LaFosse nodded with a half-shamefaced look.

' I don't care who it is,' she said earnestly, ' a woman always has a kind of sentimental feeling for the man who wants to marry her, even if she has no intention of marrying him and thinks he's terrible. It doesn't matter who he is or what he's like, he at once becomes a man apart. I suppose,' Miss LaFosse looked profound, ' it *is* the greatest compliment there is and it flatters your vanity.'

Miss Pettigrew didn't like Michael. She wanted Miss LaFosse to get married. Marriage was her best safe-guard. But somehow or other it hadn't to be an ordinary marriage. She didn't want an ordinary marriage for Miss LaFosse. She wanted something happy and romantic and brilliant. It somehow hurt her to think of Miss LaFosse settling into obscurity with a dull, pro-vincial nonentity, even if he did offer her security. And she had the impression that Michael was all these things.

' I suppose,' questioned Miss Pettigrew hopefully, ' he isn't in the line for a baronetcy, or a title, or anything like that ? '

' Oh no,' said Miss LaFosse ; ' not Michael.   Nothing like that.'

' I thought not,' said Miss Pettigrew sadly.

' His father owned a fish shop in Birmingham,' explained Miss LaFosse, ' and his mother was a dressmaker.   But he came south when he was sixteen.   He's what you might call a self-made man.'

' I see,' said Miss Pettigrew in complete disappointment.

She detested Michael.   She knew just how conventional and narrow-minded these self-made men could be.   There was that Mr. Sapfish in her Fulbury post.   A contemptible man.   No ancestry.   No background behind them.   Clinging to their new status with nervous respectability.   Fearful of straying from the strait path because of their insecurity.   Frightened to experience life themselves so fascinated beyond control by some one who had.   Miss Pettigrew had read her psychology and knew of inhibitions.   The prize in their hands, what then ?   Terror of whispers and people talking.   ' His wife, you know. . . .   Watchful, nervous eyes for ever following a wife's movements.   Poor Mrs. Sapfish !   It would break Miss LaFosse's spirit. He would clip her wings.'

' Oh, not Michael ! ' prayed Miss Pettigrew.   ' There must be some one else.'

' Isn't there any one else who wants to marry you ? ' asked Miss Pettigrew hopefully.

Miss LaFosse brightened.   The conversation was getting interesting.

' Well, there's Dick,' she said helpfully, ' but he's got no money and squints.   He's a reporter, and reporters never do have any money.'

' No use,' said Miss Pettigrew firmly.

' And there's Wilfred, but he's had two children

54

already by Daisy LaRue, and I think he ought to marry her.'

'Undoubtedly,' agreed Miss Pettigrew, shocked, but with a wicked interest.

'I think he will, once he's got over me. He's very fond of Joan and George.'

'The poor darlings!' said Miss Pettigrew, all agog.

'So we'll wash out Wilfred,' said Miss LaFosse with superb magnanimity.

'And there's no one else?' asked Miss Pettigrew, disappointed.

'Well, no, I don't think so. Not at the moment. I mean, well, I haven't been working on anything very seriously just lately.'

'Well,' said Miss Pettigrew with grudging fairness, 'I haven't seen Michael yet. . . .'

The clock caught Miss LaFosse's eye.

'Good heavens!' she gasped. 'Look at the time. Quarter-past one. You must be starved.'

She turned impetuously to Miss Pettigrew.

'Oh, please! Do say you can stay. You haven't got another appointment, have you? I don't feel a bit like lunching alone.'

Miss Pettigrew leaned back. Bliss made her quite dizzy.

'Oh no,' said Miss Pettigrew in a voice which, if visible, would have shone, 'I haven't got another appointment. I'd love to have lunch with you. I'm free all day.'

CHAPTER FIVE

1.17 p.m.—3.13 p.m.

THEY lunched at home, and Miss Pettigrew prepared it. She discovered the remains of a cold chicken in the pantry. Cold chicken, to her, was the height of luxury. Miss LaFosse opened a bottle of Liebfraumilch and made her drink some. Miss Pettigrew sipped it slowly with stern caution, and beyond making her feel, if possible, a little more reckless, it had no ill effects.

They were sipping their coffee in comfortable intimacy when the bell rang. Miss Pettigrew looked up with alert expectancy. Things were starting again. Her body jerked in response, but Miss LaFosse was before her. She answered the door and brought in a box containing a huge sheaf of scarlet roses.

' Oh, how lovely ! ' gasped Miss Pettigrew.

Miss LaFosse hunted for the card.

' Until to-morrow,' read Miss LaFosse, ' Nick.'

' Nick ! ' said Miss Pettigrew in a flat voice.

' Nick ! ' repeated Miss LaFosse in a thrilled voice. ' Oh ! The darling ! '

She picked up the roses and buried her nose in their fragrance. Over her face, very slowly, dawned a look of sentimental tenderness.

' Oh ! ' she breathed again, ' how sweet of him ! '

She looked apologetically at Miss Pettigrew.

'He doesn't often send them. I mean, he's not like that. I mean, it means more from him than some one else.'

Miss Pettigrew saw Miss LaFosse was slipping. She sat up for action.

'Humph!'

'What?'

'A very nice gesture.'

'What do you mean?' asked Miss LaFosse in a hurt voice.

Miss Pettigrew gave a negligent glance at the flowers.

'Any one can send flowers,' said Miss Pettigrew. 'It's the easiest thing in the world for a man with money to walk into a shop and say send a bunch of flowers to Miss So-and-so. No trouble to him: no worry: no care, and he knows that every silly, sentimental woman is touched by the act. Odd!' said Miss Pettigrew conversationally, 'the undermining effect of flowers on a woman's common sense.'

'Well! It was very nice of him,' said Miss LaFosse defensively.

'Oh . . . very,' said Miss Pettigrew sarcastically.

'Well. What else should he do?' asked Miss LaFosse, getting a little heated.

'Are they your favourite flowers?' demanded Miss Pettigrew.

Miss LaFosse looked at the roses.

'Well, no,' she confessed. 'To tell you the truth, I've never been too partial to scarlet roses. One gets such a lot. Like orchids. All the men send you orchids because they're expensive and they know that you know they are. But I always kind of think they're cheap, don't you, just because they're expensive. Like telling some one how much you paid for something to show off. I've always loved those great bronze chrysanthemum blooms.'

57

Miss Pettigrew made a careless gesture with her hand.

'There you are. He's never even taken the trouble to find out your favourite flowers. Now, if he'd done that . . . ! Well ! There's something to it. But just to walk in a shop and order some flowers sent round like a pound of butter . . . no !' said Miss Pettigrew. 'I'm sorry. But I can't get excited over that.'

'You're quite right,' said Miss LaFosse. 'I never thought of that before. It's just as you say. It's the little things that show a man's true feelings.'

She dropped the roses on the couch.

'Oh !' said Miss Pettigrew hastily, 'I don't think it's the flowers' fault. A little water, don't you think . . . ?'

'Of course. I'll get some.'

Miss LaFosse found an empty vase and went into the kitchen for water. Miss Pettigrew stood up. She in turn picked up the roses and let their lovely fragrance envelop her senses.

'Oh !' thought Miss Pettigrew. 'If a man had ever sent me a bunch of scarlet roses, I'd have lain on the ground and let him walk all over me.'

Miss LaFosse came back and Miss Pettigrew carelessly pushed the roses in the vase. Their vivid hue added one more touch of brilliance to the room.

'Quarter-to three,' meditated Miss LaFosse. 'It's early, but we're due at the Ogilveys' at five and it's surprising how long it takes to change and get your face made up. We'd better start now. You must come and decide my frock for me.'

Miss Pettigrew followed her into the bedroom. That 'we' rang in her head. But she couldn't believe it meant herself. Some one else must be calling for Miss LaFosse. Until he came though (it would certainly be a 'he') she would savour every precious minute left with her hostess.

'A bath first,' said Miss LaFosse. 'I haven't had one yet. There's one blessing about this place. The water's always hot. In my last flat you could never depend on the hot water and I do like a nice hot bath whenever I want. I'll go first, then you can have one and we can choose a frock for you. Now will you turn on the water while I find some clothes.'

Dazed, Miss Pettigrew went into the bathroom. Dazed, she turned on the water. Dazed, she laid out soap and towels. She hadn't heard aright. Her ears were playing her tricks. Even if she had heard aright she was putting the wrong construction on it. She stood gazing at the water pouring in. She was quite drunk now. She was drunk with excitement and expectancy and joy. She was drunk with an exhilaration she had never known in her life before. Miss LaFosse was a wicked woman. She didn't care. To her own knowledge Miss LaFosse possessed two lovers, and who knew how many more she had had? She didn't care. Somewhere Miss LaFosse had a child tucked away and needed a governess. She didn't care.

'I don't care,' thought Miss Pettigrew wildly, 'if it's *two* children.'

She went back into the bedroom.

'Your bath's ready.'

Miss LaFosse disappeared into the bathroom. Miss Pettigrew surveyed the room. It was in great disorder. Cobwebby stockings of various shades strewed the floor. Underwear, masses of silk and lace, hung out of drawers and draped chair-backs. Frocks were tossed on the bed.

Miss Pettigrew shook her head.

'Tut . . . tut,' thought yesterday's Miss Pettigrew. 'A very untidy child. Very slovenly. No order. No care. Bad upbringing. A lady's bedroom should never be in this state.'

Yesterday's Miss Pettigrew subsided.

'Oh charming disorder!' thought Miss Pettigrew luxuriantly. 'Oh lovely sense of ease! Oh glorious relaxation! No example to set. No standard to keep up. No ladylike neatness.'

Even if one did work as governess for Miss LaFosse, Miss Pettigrew was quite sure Miss LaFosse would never come round with prying eyes to invade the privacy of your bedroom and judge how you kept it. She felt a soaring sense of joy just to know there were people in the world as kind as Miss LaFosse. She stood in the centre of the room and beamed round happily until Miss LaFosse returned from the bathroom.

Miss LaFosse wore nothing but a peach-coloured silk dressing-gown. As she moved carelessly her gown swished apart and Miss Pettigrew had a glimpse of beautifully modelled limbs, of flawless, pale-coloured flesh. Her face was flushed a delicate pink by the heat. The steam had fluffed her hair into tiny, curling tendrils round her face. Miss Pettigrew regarded her with shy admiration.

'You are very lovely.'

'Well, now,' smiled Miss LaFosse, 'that is very nice of you to say so.'

She slipped off her dressing-gown unconcernedly and began hunting round for another garment. Miss Pettigrew gasped, blinked, shut her eyes, opened them again. Miss LaFosse wandered round with unselfconscious ease, unaware of offending any delicate sensibilities.

Miss Pettigrew, feeling hot and flustered, chided herself.

'It is I,' thought Miss Pettigrew sternly, 'who have an evil mind. What's wrong with the human body? Nothing. Didn't the Lord make it, the same as our faces? Certainly. Would He create anything He thought wrong ? No. Isn't it only the exigencies of our climate which have demanded clothes ? Of course. It's all in the way of thinking. I've a silly, narrow mind. I've never seen anything lovelier than Miss LaFosse standing there.'

Miss LaFosse was now regarding herself in the mirror with detached appreciation.

' Though I says it as shouldn't,' said Miss LaFosse, ' I do think I've got a nice figure. I mean, do you ? You see, it's so very important in my profession. Lose your figure : lose your following. One's got to keep fit.'

' You've got the loveliest figure I've ever seen,' said Miss Pettigrew.

Miss LaFosse beamed.

' You say the nicest things. You'd make any one feel good with themselves.'

She slipped into a bit of silk and lace. Miss Pettigrew gave a gentle sigh of relief. She was quite willing to have her outlook widened, but she was a bit old to move too precipitately.

' What a mess ! ' exclaimed Miss LaFosse. ' I've lost my maid, you know, and I never can keep things tidy when I hunt clothes myself. Now. Which frock shall it be ?'

She held up two frocks. Miss Pettigrew drew a deep breath. Each was ravishing. Each the kind of frock fit to feature a film star. One had a background of midnight blue, patterned in a wild design of colours. The other was black, with a silver dog-collar and wide, transparent sleeves, fastened tight around the wrist with silver bands, and a silver girdle round the waist. Miss Pettigrew liked them both. She didn't mind which Miss LaFosse wore, but she looked solemn, wise and knowing and pointed decisively to the black. Black was always safe.

'The black,' said Miss Pettigrew. 'With your fair hair and complexion and blue eyes . . . perfect.'

Miss LaFosse struggled into the black. Miss Pettigrew fastened her up.

'They're both new,' said Miss LaFosse. 'I was going to give the bill to Nick, but if I'm going to try

Struggled into the black

and break with him, I think it's only decent to send the bill to Phil, don't you agree?'

'Oh, undoubtedly,' said Miss Pettigrew faintly.

Miss LaFosse sat in front of the mirror in preparation for the greatest rite of all, the face decoration. The dressing-table bore so many bottles and jars Miss Pettigrew lost count of them.

'Now, Alice,' said Miss LaFosse, ' sit down. You'll tire yourself out standing round like that.'

With the happy sense of being looked after, never experienced since she was eighteen and took her first post, Miss Pettigrew found a chair and pulled it close to the dressing-table.

'Excuse me,' said Miss Pettigrew. She flushed slightly. ' My real name is Guinevere. It's a very silly name, I know, given me by my mother, and not at all suitable. She had been reading Sir Lancelot and Guinevere. Alice, as you say, is much more suitable. I look,' said Miss Pettigrew sadly, 'much more like Alice.'

Miss LaFosse swung round.

'Nonsense,' she said ecstatically. 'It's a lovely name: a perfectly marvellous name. And actually your own. It gives you importance at once. It . . . it makes you somebody.' She lowered her voice. ' My own name,' she confided, 'is Sarah Grubb. There ! I've told you and I wouldn't confess it to another living soul, but I think a lot of you. You've saved my reputation to-day. When I went on the stage I took another name. I called myself Delysia LaFosse. I made up the LaFosse myself. I thought it was very good.'

' You look,' said Miss Pettigrew, ' much more like a Delysia.'

' Thank you,' said Miss LaFosse ; ' I kind of thought I did.'

' What's in a name,' quoted Miss Pettigrew dreamily.

' The hell of a lot,' said Miss LaFosse simply ; ' a damned, snooping little newspaper man with a spite against me dug up my real name once and I daren't tell you what I had to do to make him keep it out of his wretched little gossip column.'

Miss Pettigrew didn't dare think.

'Ruined I'd have been,' continued Miss LaFosse.
'Can't you see it? Sarah Grubb. Enough to damn
any one. Who could get enthusiastic over a Sarah
Grubb! But the fates were kind. He got drunk as
usual one night and got run over by a lorry so that was
one worry the less for me.'

'Very kind,' agreed Miss Pettigrew feebly.

'What's the full label?' asked Miss LaFosse, interested.

Miss Pettigrew's wits were becoming remarkably
sharpened in one day. She understood at once.

'Pettigrew,' said Miss Pettigrew. 'Guinevere Pettigrew. Very ridiculous, I'm afraid you'll think.'

'Perfect,' breathed Miss LaFosse; 'absolutely perfect.
A marvellous combination. And all your own. No
chance of some wretched little tyke making a fool of you
by dishing up an Ethel Blogg. You're sure,' pressed
Miss LaFosse earnestly, 'you've never thought of going
on the boards? I mean, with your powers of mimicry
and all that. I have a bit of influence, you know.'

'No,' said Miss Pettigrew firmly, but with a new sense
of importance, of prestige, or consequence, 'never.'

'A pity.' Miss LaFosse shook her head. 'A great
pity. A perfect name lost from the lights.'

She drew the comb through her hair.

'You have beautiful hair,' said Miss Pettigrew wistfully. She looked at her own straight, lustreless locks a
little sadly in the mirror. 'It makes such a difference.'

'All the difference in the world,' agreed Miss LaFosse.
'I'm lucky. My hair has a natural wave, but if it
hadn't, it's a perm. you want. There's nothing like a
good perm. for working a transformation. I mean, even
if you do go out in the rain, it stays in curl. Not like a
marcel, that goes straight at once and looks worse than
it did before.' She looked critically at Miss Pettigrew.

' I really think we'll have to. I don't mean to offend, but don't you think an outsider sometimes knows better what suits you than you do yourself? Alphonse is the very man. He'll know just what to do. We'll go to him.'

Miss Pettigrew sat, face pink, eyes shining, mouth trembling.

' Oh, my dear,' said Miss Pettigrew. ' You couldn't offend me, but aren't you forgetting that . . .'

There was a loud ring at the bell.

' There ! ' said Miss LaFosse. ' Do you mind . . . ? '

Mind ! Miss Pettigrew was on her feet in a flash. She closed the bedroom door firmly behind her. One never knew. Her feet nearly tripped over themselves hurrying over the floor. She stood in front of the door for one perfect, breathless second of expectancy ; then she flung it open.

CHAPTER SIX

3.13 p.m.—3.44 p.m.

'OH!' gasped Miss Pettigrew.

A lady of startling
attractions

She was nearly knocked over by the flying passage of a female body belonging to a lady of startling attractions. Miss Pettigrew gaped, blinked and devoured them avidly. The lady was young, slim, arresting. Her face was of a deep, creamy pallor, devoid of any colour except the wicked red bow of her mouth. Hair, like black lacquer, parted in the middle, was coiled in an elaborate roll at the nape of her neck. A tiny hat was perched at an acute angle at the side of her head. Black brows curved with an unnatural slant above eyes of a surprisingly vivid blue for a brunette. Long, black lashes, as thick and curled as the most famous of film star's, held Miss Pettigrew's fascinated attention. Vivid green ear-rings dangled from tiny, shell-like ears snug

66

against her head. As she moved, a delicate perfume, subtly alluring, beguiled Miss Pettigrew's senses. Her clothes . . . Miss Pettigrew gave it up. Her experience had not fitted her to describe Parisian confections. The lady had flung open her fur coat and tossed her gloves on the couch. Obviously here to stay. Miss Pettigrew turned and shut the door.

The visitor glanced distractedly round the room.

'I don't know you.'

'No,' said Miss Pettigrew.

'Is Delysia in ?'

'Yes.'

'I must see her. I simply must see her. I *can* see her ?'

'Certainly,' agreed Miss Pettigrew.

'I mean,' she threw a wild glance at the closed bedroom door, 'I'm not butting in. I hear Nick's back.'

'Miss LaFosse is alone.'

'Thank God !'

'If you will tell me your name,' said Miss Pettigrew helpfully, 'I will acquaint Miss LaFosse of your presence.'

The visitor was already on her way to the door. She threw a surprised glance over her shoulder.

'That's all right. She knows me.'

She hurried to the door and flung it open.

'Delysia.'

'Go away,' said Miss LaFosse.

'I've got something to tell you.'

'I know. When haven't you. That's why I'm saying go away. I'm busy just now. If you distract me while I'm making up my face I'll make a mistake and look a fright. I'll not be long.'

'I've simply got to talk to you.'

'Guinevere,' called Miss LaFosse.

'Yes,' said Miss Pettigrew, immediate attention.

'Edythe, meet Guinevere. She'll look after you. Guinevere, meet Edythe. For the love of God take her away and do something with her. She's a terrible woman, but I'll not be long.'

'Delighted,' said Miss Pettigrew happily.

She shut the bedroom door firmly. Miss LaFosse wanted to be alone. Miss LaFosse should be alone. She turned a little diffidently to her new visitor. She was not quite sure how one talked to young women like this. They could not all be as simple and kindly as Miss LaFosse.

'Pettigrew is the surname,' she said a little apologetically, in case the visitor should not like the familiarity of Christian names.

'Ah ! Mine's Dubarry.'

'How-do-you-do ?' said Miss Pettigrew politely.

'Lousy,' said Miss Dubarry. 'How are you ?'

'Oh . . . oh, fine,' said Miss Pettigrew, gasping, but hastily seeking sophisticated ease. 'Just fine.'

'Then you're safely married,' said Miss Dubarry gloomily, 'or you're not in love. I'm neither.'

'Neither what ?' queried Miss Pettigrew, surprised into rudeness.

'I'm not safely married and I am in love.'

'Oh !' said Miss Pettigrew, thrilled, interested, frankly curious. 'How lovely.'

'Lovely ?' exploded Miss Dubarry. 'Lovely ? When the dirty dog's walked out on me !'

'Oh, how tragic !' gasped Miss Pettigrew.

'Tragic's the word,' groaned Miss Dubarry. 'That's why I've come to Delysia. She's got brains, that woman, even if she is a natural beauty as well. Don't you be deceived.'

'I'm not,' said Miss Pettigrew.

'No, you wouldn't be. It's the men who make the mistake. They see she's got the looks and think she can't have the grey matter as well, and they try to take her for a ride. Their mistake, of course.'

'They deserve all they get,' said Miss Pettigrew belligerently, but without the faintest idea of what they were talking about.

'That's what I say. But she's got brains. She gets away with it. I haven't, so I always land in a mess.'

She glanced so unhappily round the room that Miss Pettigrew's kind heart melted.

'Have a seat,' said Miss Pettigrew kindly.

'Thanks, I will.'

Miss Dubarry sat down.

'Men are awful,' said Miss Dubarry miserably.

'I quite agree,' said Miss Pettigrew.

The subject of the conversation still eluded her, but she didn't care. She was thoroughly enjoying herself. She was in a state of spiritual intoxication. No one had ever talked to her like that before. The very oddness of their conversation sent thrills of delight down her spine. Come to think of it, hardly any one had ever troubled to talk to her about anything at all: not in a personal sense. But these people! They opened their hearts. They admitted her. She was one of themselves. It was the amazing way they took her for granted that thrilled every nerve in her body. No surprise: they simply said 'Hallo', and you were one of themselves. No worrying what your position and your family and your bank balance were. In all her lonely life Miss Pettigrew had never realized how lonely she had been until now, when for one day she was lonely no longer. She couldn't analyse the difference. For years she had lived in other people's houses and had never been an inmate in the sense of belonging,

69

and now, in a few short hours, she was serenely and blissfully at home. She was accepted. They talked to her.

And how they talked! She had never heard the like before. Their ridiculous inconsequence. Every sentence was like a heady cocktail. The whole flavour of the remarks gave her a wicked feeling of sophistication. And the way she kept her end up! No one would ever dream she was new to it.

'I never believed,' thought Miss Pettigrew with pride, 'that I had it in me.'

She stood beaming down at Miss Dubarry. Miss Dubarry sat staring gloomily at the electric fire, quite unaware of the elation she was causing her friend Delysia's friend. Miss Pettigrew thought she must do something to lighten Miss Dubarry's distress. She soared to the heights. With carelessness, with ease, with negligent poise, as featured in countless Talkies.

'Have a spot,' said Miss Pettigrew.

Miss Dubarry brightened.

'That's an idea. Blessings on the woman.'

Miss Pettigrew resorted once more to the cupboard in the kitchen. She came back with a laden tray. She had put on a bottle of most things she could discover.

'Perhaps you'll mix your own,' she said with careless airiness. 'Every one to their own poison, I always say.'

Miss Dubarry rose with alacrity.

'Just a little gin I think, and . . . where's the lime juice? Ah! Here. I think a gin and lime will do me grand.'

Miss Pettigrew watched her with veiled concentration.

'What'll yours be?' offered Miss Dubarry helpfully.

Miss Pettigrew started.

A hasty refusal came to her lips, then she changed her mind. This was no time for squeamishness. A hostess must drink with her guest.

'I'll mix my own,' said Miss Pettigrew recklessly.

'O.K.'

Miss Dubarry retired with her drink. Hastily Miss Pettigrew filled a glass with soda and just coloured it with sherry to give it a look of authenticity. She returned to her seat.

'Mud in your eyes,' said Miss Dubarry.

Miss Pettigrew knew no happy rejoinders, so made one up.

'Wash and brush up,' said Miss Pettigrew.

They drank.

'Another?' offered Miss Pettigrew.

'I don't think I'd better,' said Miss Dubarry reluctantly. 'I mean, if we're going to the Ogilveys', we'd better *arrive* sober. I mean, we nearly always *leave* drunk.'

'Exactly,' agreed Miss Pettigrew.

'And then, if Tony's there, I'll need all my wits about me.'

'Precisely,' said Miss Pettigrew.

'So I'd better not have another.'

'The bar has closed,' said Miss Pettigrew.

'Well, perhaps just a *splash*,' said Miss Dubarry.

She splashed. Already she looked a great deal more cheerful. Her air of funereal gloom had almost departed. She regarded Miss Pettigrew with interested curiosity and made no bones about satisfying her inquisitiveness.

'Friend of Delysia's?'

Miss Pettigrew stared at her toes, glanced at the closed bedroom door, looked back at Miss Dubarry.

'Yes,' said Miss Pettigrew.

'Close friends.'

'Very,' lied Miss Pettigrew.

'Well,' said Miss Dubarry, 'I always say "a friend of Delysia's is a friend of mine".'

'Thank you,' said Miss Pettigrew.

'She sees things in people I don't and she's always right, so I follow her lead.'

This sounded a little doubtful to Miss Pettigrew, so she only smiled.

'New to London,' diagnosed Miss Dubarry brilliantly.

Miss Pettigrew forbore to tell her that for the last ten years all her posts had been in and near London. Suddenly she was ashamed to acknowledge it. Obviously she had gained nothing by this advantage.

'I was born in a village in Northumberland,' she prevaricated.

'Ah!' said Miss Dubarry brightly. 'Scotland.'

'Well. Not quite,' said Miss Pettigrew.

'It's a long way from London,' said Miss Dubarry darkly.

'Yes. It is.'

'Here for good now?'

'I hope so.'

'Ah. You'll soon learn things here. There's no place like London. Takes time, you know. But you'll soon leave the provinces behind.'

'Do you think so?'

'No doubt at all, with a little expert advice.'

Miss Dubarry stood up abruptly. She circled Miss Pettigrew, eyes intent, expression concentrated. Miss Pettigrew sat petrified. Miss Dubarry frowned. She held her chin between thumb and forefinger. She shook her head. Suddenly she barked,

'You shouldn't wear those muddy browns. They're not your colour.'

' Oh ! ' Miss Pettigrew jumped.

' Certainly not. Where's your taste ? Where's your artistic discrimination ? '

' I haven't any,' said Miss Pettigrew meekly.

' And your make-up's wrong.'

' Make-up ! ' gasped Miss Pettigrew.

' Make-up.'

' Me ? ' said Miss Pettigrew faintly.

' You.'

' I haven't any.'

' No make-up,' said Miss Dubarry shocked. ' Why ? It's indecent, walking around naked.'

Miss Pettigrew stared at her blankly. Her mind was whirling: her thoughts chaotic. A mental up-heaval rendered her dizzy. Yes, why ? All these years and she had never had the wicked thrill of powdering her nose. Others had experienced that joy. Never she. And all because she lacked courage. All because she had never thought for herself. Powder, thundered her father the curate, the road to damnation. Lipstick, whispered her mother, the first step on the downward path. Rouge, fulminated her father, the harlot's enticement. Eyebrow pencil, breathed her mother, no lady . . . !

Miss Pettigrew's thoughts ran wildly, chaotically, riotously. A sin to make the best of the worst ? She sat up. Her eyes began to shine. All her feminine faculties intent on the important, earnest, serious, mighty task of improving on God's handiwork. Then she remembered. She sat back. Her face clouded.

' Oh ! ' said Miss Pettigrew in a flat voice. ' My dear . . . at my age. With my complexion.'

' It's a beautiful complexion.'

' Beautiful ? ' said Miss Pettigrew incredulously.

' Not a mark, not a spot, not a blemish. Colour !

73

Who wants natural colour? It's always wrong. A perfect background. No base to prepare. No handicaps to overcome. Blonde, brunette, pink and white, tanned, creamy pallor. Anything you like.'

Miss Dubarry leaned forward intent. She tipped Miss Pettigrew's face this way: she tipped it that way. She patted the skin. She felt the texture of her hair.

'Hmn! A good cleansing cream. A strong astringent to tone up the muscles. Eyebrows definitely darkened. Can't make up my mind about the hair yet. Nutbrown, I think. Complexion needs colour. Definitely colour. Brings out the blue of the eyes. Whole face needs a course of treatment. Shockingly neglected.'

She stopped abruptly and looked apologetic.

'Oh dear! You must excuse me. Here I am, forgetting myself again. I'm in the trade, you see, and I can't help taking a professional interest.'

'Don't mind me,' breathed Miss Pettigrew. 'Please don't mind me. I love it. No one's ever taken an interest in my face before.'

'Obviously not,' said Miss Dubarry sternly. 'Not even yourself.'

'I've never had any time,' apologized Miss Pettigrew.

'Nonsense. You've had time to wash, haven't you? You've time to get a bath. You've time to cut your nails. A woman's first duty is to her face. I'm surprised at you.'

'Ah well!' sighed Miss Pettigrew hopelessly. 'I'm long past the age now. . . .'

'No woman,' said Miss Dubarry grimly, 'is ever past the age. The more years that pass the more reason for care. You should be old enough to know better.'

'I've never had any money.'

'Ah!' said Miss Dubarry with understanding. 'That's different. You wouldn't believe the amount

74

it costs even me to keep my face fixed, and I'm in the trade and that means nearly ninety-nine per cent off.'

She found her handbag and opened it.

'Here's my card. You bring that any time you like and you shall have the best of everything. Any friend of Delysia's is a friend of mine. If I'm at liberty I'll do you myself. If not, I'll get you the best left.'

'How wonderful,' gasped Miss Pettigrew. She took the card with trembling fingers.

'Edythe Dubarry,' she read, thrilled.

'It's well seen you're no Londoner,' said Miss Dubarry. 'That name stands for something. It's the best beauty parlour in London, though it is my own.'

Miss Pettigrew's face began to shine.

'Tell me,' she begged, 'is it true? Is it really true? I mean, *can* these places improve your looks?'

Miss Dubarry sat down. She hesitated. She hitched her chair closer.

'Look at me.'

Miss Pettigrew looked. Miss Dubarry gave a friendly chuckle.

'I like you. There's something about you . . . well! What do you think of me?'

'Oh dear!' said Miss Pettigrew, much embarrassed. 'What have I to say to that?'

'Just what you like. I don't mind. But the truth.'

'Well,' said Miss Pettigrew, taking the plunge, 'I think you have very . . . very *startling* looks.'

Miss Dubarry looked immensely pleased.

'There you are then.'

Miss Pettigrew warmed to her task. If Miss Dubarry could be frank, so could she.

'You're not exactly beautiful, like Miss LaFosse, but you catch the eye. When you come into a room, every one will notice you.'

'There,' said Miss Dubarry proudly. 'What did I tell you?'

'What?' asked Miss Pettigrew.

'What I've been telling you.'

'What's that?'

'You and I,' said Miss Dubarry, 'are exactly alike.'

'Oh . . . how can you say it!' said Miss Pettigrew unbelievingly.

'You don't look like the kind of a woman to give away secrets,' said Miss Dubarry recklessly.

'I'm not,' said Miss Pettigrew.

'And when I see such a perfect lay figure as you, I can't help spreading the glad tidings.'

'No?' said Miss Pettigrew, bewildered.

Miss Dubarry leaned closer.

'My hair,' stated Miss Dubarry, 'is mouse coloured . . . like yours.'

'No!' gasped Miss Pettigrew. 'Not really.'

'A fact. I thought black suited me better.'

'Undoubtedly.'

'My eyebrows,' continued Miss Dubarry, 'and eyelashes are sandy-coloured. I have plucked my eyebrows and pencilled in new ones. My eyelashes, as well as being such a damnable shade, are short. I have had new ones fixed. Black, long and curly.'

'Marvellous,' whispered Miss Pettigrew, at last realizing the reason for Miss Dubarry's surprising eyes.

'I have the insipid, indeterminate complexion that goes with that stupid colouring. I thought a creamy pallor a great deal more interesting.'

'Absolutely,' breathed Miss Pettigrew.

'My nose was a difficulty. You score over me there. But McCormick is a marvellous surgeon. He gave me a new one.'

'No,' gasped Miss Pettigrew.

'My teeth were the greatest trouble,' confessed Miss Dubarry. 'They weren't spaced evenly. Fifty pounds that cost me. But it was worth it.'

Miss Pettigrew leaned back.

'It's unbelievable,' she said faintly, 'quite unbelievable.'

'My hair is mouse coloured, like yours'

'I forgot the ears,' said Miss Dubarry. 'They stood out too much, but, as I say, McCormick's a marvellous surgeon. He soon put that right.'

'It can't be possible.' Miss Pettigrew was almost beyond words. 'I mean, you're not you.'

'Just a little care,' said Miss Dubarry. 'It does wonders.'

'Miracles,' articulated Miss Pettigrew, 'miracles; I'll never believe a woman again when I see her.'

'Why!' said Miss Dubarry. 'Would you have us all go naked and unashamed? Must we take off the powder with the petticoat, and discard the eyeblack with the brassiere? Must we renounce beauty and revert to the crudities of nature?'

'All but Miss LaFosse,' continued Miss Pettigrew faintly but loyally. 'I saw her straight . . . out . . . of . . . the . . . bath.'

'Oh, Delysia!' said Miss Dubarry. 'She's different. She was blessed at birth.'

She glanced at the bedroom door. Her face clouded over again.

'I wish she'd hurry. I'm in an awful jam and she generally sees a way out.'

Miss Pettigrew's eyes became misted.

'How lovely!' she thought sentimentally. 'Is there anything more beautiful? Woman to woman. And they say we don't trust each other!'

'There's nothing like another woman when you're in trouble,' sighed Miss Pettigrew.

Miss Dubarry shuddered.

'Good God! Don't you believe that,' she said earnestly. 'There's not another woman I'd come to but Delysia.'

'No?' asked Miss Pettigrew in surprise.

'Well, Delysia, she's different. I mean, with her looks she hasn't got to worry about men. You can trust her.'

'Yes,' said Miss Pettigrew. 'I know you can.'

'She doesn't try to pinch your men. I mean, I don't mind flirting. A woman wouldn't be human if she didn't, but there's ways of doing it. She doesn't try to turn them off you behind your back. She says the best when you're not there.'

78

'Just like her,' said Miss Pettigrew proudly.

'Oh yes. I forgot. You're an old friend of hers. Oh dear! I wish she'd hurry. There'll be no time for her to think of anything.'

'How did you come to own a beauty parlour?' asked Miss Pettigrew tactfully, trying to turn Miss Dubarry's mind from her troubles. 'You look very young. If you don't think I'm rude, I'm very interested.'

'Oh, that,' said Miss Dubarry. 'That was very simple. I vamped the boss.'

'Vamped the boss!' echoed Miss Pettigrew weakly. 'Oh dear! However could you think of such a thing?'

'Very simple. I was eighteen . . . an apprentice. He was getting on. They always fall for the young ones . . . if you're clever, that is. I was always clever that way,' said Miss Dubarry simply. 'If you act "marriage or nothing" they generally give you marriage. I was very lucky. I went to his head, but he couldn't stand the pace. He got a nice tombstone and I got the parlour.'

'We must be fair,' said Miss Pettigrew vaguely, not knowing what to say.

'I earned it,' said Miss Dubarry simply. 'But there! You can't expect to get things without a little work. And he wasn't a bad sort. I've known worse. I was no fool either. I learned that business, even though I did get married. It's paid me. Do you know, it's worth three times as much now as when he passed out.'

'I bet it is,' admired Miss Pettigrew simply and slangily.

'I put up the prices. That's business. And I changed the name of course. I picked Dubarry. I mean, you've only got to *think* of Du Barry and you expect things. It stands for something. I think it was a very clever choice. At least,' said Miss Dubarry honestly, ' Delysia thought of it, but I was quick to be on to it.'

' A perfect name,' praised Miss Pettigrew. ' A marvellous name,' she added recklessly.

She did her best to discipline her judgment. But it was no use. She was carried away. Who was she to judge ? Wouldn't she have married *any* man who had asked her in the last ten years to escape the Mrs. Brummegans of this world ? Of course she would ! Why pretend ? Why pretend with all the other silly old women that they were better than their sisters because they had had no chance of being otherwise ? Away with cant. Miss Pettigrew leaned forward with shining eyes and patted Miss Dubarry's knee.

' I think,' said Miss Pettigrew, ' you're wonderful. I only wish I'd had *half* your brains when I was young. I might be a merry widow to-day.'

' A lot's in the chances you get,' consoled Miss Dubarry. ' Always remember that. And grabbing them when they come, of course.'

' Even if they had come,' said Miss Pettigrew with sad conviction, ' I could never have grabbed. I wasn't the kind.'

' Never say die,' said Miss Dubarry. ' You'll get your kick out of life yet.'

She patted Miss Pettigrew's knee in return, and the delicate seductiveness of her perfume again assailed Miss Pettigrew's senses.

' What a lovely scent,' admired Miss Pettigrew.

' Isn't it ? ' said Miss Dubarry complacently.

' I've never smelt anything like it before.'

' You're hardly likely to. I'm the only person in England knows the secret.'

'How wonderful!' marvelled Miss Pettigrew. 'Is it expensive?'

'Nine pounds an ounce.'

'What?' gasped Miss Pettigrew.

'Oh well! It costs me ten-and-six.'

'And people *buy* it?' quavered Miss Pettigrew.

'As much as I'll sell them. But I've found in the long run you keep a steadier market by pretending there's a shortage. You might sell more in the beginning, but let them once think there's plenty and the demand will soon fall off. My clients like to be select.'

'Ten-and-six,' said Miss Pettigrew faintly. 'Nine pounds.'

'Oh, that's just business. I mean, no one else can make it, so of course I charge. If the secret leaked out, the price would come down with a bang. It's the exclusiveness you're paying for.'

Miss Pettigrew's interest overcame her shock.

'But how, if you don't mind my asking, did you learn to make it?'

'Well, it's a long story,' said Miss Dubarry, 'told in full. I was over in France buying stock. I met Gaston Leblanc . . . he's the greatest expert on perfumes there is. Well, I mean, it was too good a chance to miss, so I put in a bit of overtime. His idea, of course, was to combine the two businesses. I'm no fool. It wasn't exactly my charms alone. Well, I didn't exactly cold-shoulder him and he gave me the secret as an engagement present. You know! Cost him nothing and the secret was safe in the family. Then I came back to England.'

'To England?' said Miss Pettigrew, bewildered.

'Of course,' said Miss Dubarry indignantly. 'Well, I mean to say! He wasn't wanting to marry *me*. He was wanting to marry Dubarry's. It wasn't as if I didn't know. I don't approve of these continental ways. He'd never have considered me for marriage without my business. Well, that's more than *I* can stomach. I do like a man to put a bit of passion into a proposal. Englishmen don't want to get into a business, they want to get into bed. We're brought up to expect it and you can't get over early training.'

'No,' said Miss Pettigrew indignantly. 'Of course not. The very idea! A business indeed!'

Miss Dubarry dug into her handbag and brought out her compact. She proceeded to paint on a new mouth again. Miss Pettigrew stood up. She stared at herself in the mirror over the mantelpiece, at the tokens of middle age that lay not so much in lines and wrinkles but in much more subtle suggestions, in something old in the expression: in the tiredness of the eyes, in the lack of brilliance about the face. Straight, lank, mouse-coloured hair: faded, tired blue eyes: pale mouth, thin face, dull, yellowish complexion.

'It's no use,' thought Miss Pettigrew, 'you can do what you like with paint and powder, but you can't get away from the unhealthy complexion brought by lack of good food. And I don't see where good food's coming to me.'

Suddenly she felt flat, lifeless and terrified again. Immediately the nervous worry sprang into the face in front of her. It was ageing, destructive. It demolished all signs of youth.

Miss Pettigrew hastily turned her eyes from her own image. She stared at Miss Dubarry, sitting in her expensive clothes, with her sleek, black head, her crimson lips, the beautiful arresting pallor of her face.

'No,' thought Miss Pettigrew hopelessly, 'you could never at any time turn me into her. Even when I was young. It isn't only the paint. It's something inside you.'

She moved to sit down again. The bedroom door opened and Miss LaFosse emerged.

CHAPTER SEVEN

3.44 p.m.—5.2 p.m.

MISS LAFOSSE came into the room, black draperies floating, silver collar, silver girdle, gleaming, fair hair, like a pale gold crown, shining. At once, in Miss Pettigrew's estimation, Miss Dubarry sank into the shade.

'Ah!' thought Miss Pettigrew with a feeling of possessive pride, 'art can never beat nature.'

'Delysia!' cried Miss Dubarry, springing to her feet. 'I thought you would never come.'

'Now be calm, Edythe,' begged Miss LaFosse. 'You always get too excited.'

'So would you if you were in my place.'

'Yes. I suppose I would,' agreed Miss LaFosse soothingly. 'It's easy talking when it isn't yourself. But how have you and Guinevere been getting along? Sorry to keep you waiting.'

'Oh, fine. We've had a grand talk. I've been showing off. It's a soothing feeling.'

'Oh no, she wasn't,' denied Miss Pettigrew hastily. 'She was only telling me things because I asked.'

Miss LaFosse chuckled.

'I believe both of you.'

'Oh, Delysia!' Miss Dubarry's voice broke.

All her unhappiness came back into her face again.

84

She nearly wept. Her face puckered, but she could not imperil her make-up. She sat down on the couch and tried to gain control of herself.

'I know,' said Miss LaFosse with comforting sympathy. 'I'm ready. Where's the cigarettes . . . here? Have one.' She lit one for herself and Miss Dubarry and sat down beside her. 'Now. Tell me.'

Miss Dubarry gulped in the smoke.

'Tony's left me.'

'No!' said Miss LaFosse incredulously.

Miss Pettigrew sat a little away. She felt she was intruding. These two were real friends. They had forgotten her. She felt she ought to go but didn't like just to walk out of the room without a word. Miss Dubarry knew she was there, so it wasn't her fault if she eavesdropped. She didn't want to go. She wanted instead to know who Tony was and why he had left Miss Dubarry, but she was also beginning to have a lost, forlorn feeling that all these exciting people, with their experiences and adventures, should only touch her life for one short period.

Miss Dubarry nodded her head.

'It's true,' she said dully.

'But you've quarrelled before.'

'Yes. But not real quarrels. There's a difference.'

'I know,' agreed Miss LaFosse. 'What's happened?'

'Well. You know how Tony is? He's so jealous if you just speak politely to the liftman he thinks you have designs on him.'

'I know. But you must confess you've a very intimate way of being nice to men.'

'Yes, I know all that. But it's just habit. You know that. Until you've made your way, you've got to be like that, and the habit's just stuck.'

'Yes,' agreed Miss LaFosse again.

85

'There isn't any one but Tony. You know that. There never has been. I mean, you might marry for business first time, the way I did, but you don't fall in love for business once you're settled in life. I'd even marry him, if he asked me. But he's never asked.'

'Perhaps he doesn't like to. I mean, it's a lot to give up, your freedom, with your own business and plenty of money. There's no need to get married. He probably thinks it would be cheek to ask. The way it is . . . well, it's just in the way of affection. Break off when either of you likes. But marriage is serious. He's probably thinking of you.'

'I think that's what he does think. I'm almost sure it is. I earn more with my business than he does, you know. I wouldn't care if he'd only say so, then I'd know where I was. I mean, if he'd only say he was serious. I'd soon make him agree to marriage.'

'Men are funny,' agreed Miss LaFosse.

'Well. He expects it both ways. Me to be faithful, like married, yet not married and nothing even said.'

'It's the funny way they have. Expect you to read their minds.'

'Well. I was willing. I'd rather have Tony that way than no way, but I didn't see why I shouldn't have a bit of innocent fun. You know he had to go abroad for six weeks and I got running around with Frank Desmond. Nothing to it, you know. Just amusement. Well, a party of us motored out to his week-end place one night. The others left ahead of us. I just stayed for one more drink, and when we got to Frank's car the lights wouldn't work. He's no mechanic and we hadn't even a torch to give us light. It was pouring like the devil and black as pitch and a mile to the village, so what could I do but stay the night ?'

'Well, obviously nothing,' concurred Miss LaFosse.

' I'd have done the same myself. But I suppose Tony's got to know.'

The tears nearly came through. Miss Dubarry's mouth trembled.

' Yes.'

' I suppose,' queried Miss LaFosse tentatively, ' it was all innocent.'

' That's what hurts,' mourned Miss Dubarry pathetically. ' You know what a fascinating devil Frank is. It isn't as though you wouldn't have liked a bit of fun with him. But because of Tony, well, I didn't. And now I might just as well for all he'll believe me.'

' Oh well ! They say virtue is its own reward.'

' I'd rather have the fun, if the reward is to be the same in any case.'

' I suppose Tony won't believe you.'

' No. I can't do anything. You know what a reputation Frank has. Tony simply won't believe either of us . . . I even lowered myself to drag in Frank. He says of course he'd lie for me.'

' Of course he would,' said Miss LaFosse drearily. ' That's the worst of it. I mean, Tony knows he'd lie, so how does he know when he's not lying ? Oh dear ! It's terribly difficult.'

' I know. That's the way it was.'

Miss Dubarry's voice choked. A few of the prudently withheld tears spilled over. She caught Miss LaFosse's arm.

' Oh, Delysia ! You've got to think of something. I can't live without him.'

Miss LaFosse made comforting noises. Miss Dubarry dabbed her eyes, then she looked up with a show of indignation.

' Crying over a man ! Can you beat it ? You must think I'm mad. I am mad. The idea ! He's

87

a horrid, suspicious beast. I never want to have anything more to do with him in my life again.'

' Very heroic,' sighed Miss LaFosse, ' but unfortunately untrue.'

Miss Dubarry collapsed again.

' I thought immediately of you. I thought you might
think of something.'

' I'll try,' said Miss LaFosse hopelessly. ' But . . .
Tony ! And you can't even say you didn't stay the
night.'

' I know.'

' It's a problem.'

' I came straight to you. I heard Nick was back.
I didn't know whether you'd be available, but I risked
it.'

' Oh yes. Nick's back.'

' I thought you said he said to-morrow.'

' He did.'

' Are you still coming to the Ogilveys' then ? '

' Oh yes.'

' When did he come ? '

' This morning.'

' Where's he now then ? '

' I don't know. He didn't stay.'

' What ? '

' Only an hour.'

' He's not . . . he's not . . . wavering ? ' said Miss
Dubarry, aghast.

' Oh no ! Guinevere wouldn't let him. That was
the real reason.'

' What ? Wouldn't let him ? '

' She didn't like him.'

' You're joking.'

' Ask her.'

' He'll be back any minute though ? '

' No.   To-morrow.'

' He's not coming back to-night ? '

' No.'

' What ? '

' Guinevere wouldn't have him.'

' Good God ! ' said Miss Dubarry faintly.

' It's the truth.'

' He stood for it ? '

' He had no choice.'

' You're kidding.'

' He was no match for Guinevere.'

' God save us ! '

Miss Dubarry moved round.   She stared at Miss
Pettigrew.   Awe, amazement, incredulous disbelief
showed in her face.   Dawning reverence ousted all other
emotions.

' *You* turned *Nick* out of his own flat ? '

' Oh dear ! ' fluttered Miss Pettigrew, ' not as bad as
all that.'

' I was in a jam,' said Miss LaFosse.

' You too ? ' said Miss Dubarry faintly.

' Nick said he was coming to-morrow.'

' I know.'

' So Phil stayed here last night.'

' Good heavens ! '

' I learned too late about Nick.'

' Obviously.'

' Phil's backing my new show. I couldn't offend
him.   A girl never knows in this life.'

' Of course you couldn't.'

' He doesn't know about Nick.'

' Not good tactics.   I agree.'

' So there he was.'

' What happened ? '

' Guinevere put him out.'

89

' No.'

' Yes.'

' Did he guess ? '

' Not an idea.'

' And then Nick came ? '

' Yes,' said Miss LaFosse. ' He found one of Phil's cheroots.'

' No ! ' gasped Miss Dubarry.

' Guinevere handled that too. She offered him another. She had him eating out of her hand.'

' Holy Moses ! ' breathed Miss Dubarry. ' And he fell for it ? '

' The way *she* did it,' said Miss LaFosse simply, ' you'd have fallen yourself.'

' Explain,' said Miss Dubarry in a weak voice. ' Full details. Nothing missed out.'

Miss LaFosse explained. Miss Pettigrew twittered, fluttered, blushed, made little disclaiming noises. Her face shone. She had never felt so proud of herself in her life before. She had thought nothing of it at the time, but the way Miss LaFosse explained it, well, perhaps, after all, she *had* worked a miracle. Miss LaFosse's obvious delight in her achievement sent her into the seventh heaven of bliss. Nick, it appeared, was a much more formidable character than she had imagined, and that had been bad enough.

' What a woman ! ' said Miss Dubarry.

She came over and took Miss Pettigrew's hand.

' Guinevere,' she said simply, ' the disguise hid you well.' She touched Miss Pettigrew's clothes. ' I made a mistake. You're the goods.'

' That's what I think,' said Miss LaFosse.

They looked at each other.

' If she can deal with Nick . . .' said Miss Dubarry weakly.

90

'That's what I thought,' said Miss LaFosse.

They both turned and looked at Miss Pettigrew.

'It's a chance,' said Miss Dubarry.

'No instructions,' said Miss LaFosse hastily. 'She works better alone. She'll think up something when she gets the right cue. That's her way. We mustn't muddle her.'

'Of course not.'

'He'll be there?'

'He said he was going.'

'What's the time?' asked Miss LaFosse.

'Ten-past four.'

'Oh Lord! And Guinevere's still to dress. You're the very person to advise. Something that'll do for this afternoon and to-night as well. She needn't take off her coat this afternoon. We want to look as though we're leaving when we arrive. You know what the Ogilveys are like.'

'Stand up,' said Miss Dubarry earnestly to Miss Pettigrew. Miss Pettigrew stood up. Miss Dubarry regarded her with a frown.

'She's about your build.'

'That's what I thought.'

'Your things might fit.'

'We'll make them.'

'Oh please!' said Miss Pettigrew in a nervous voice. 'If you want to go, please go. Don't worry about me. I couldn't intrude on your friends.'

'Intrude on the Ogilveys,' said Miss Dubarry in a surprised voice.

'Intrude on Terence,' said Miss LaFosse.

'Intrude on Moira,' said Miss Dubarry.

'They don't know there is such a word,' said Miss LaFosse.

'As long as I'm not putting you out,' said Miss Pettigrew weakly, too excited at the prospect of further excitement to stress her excuses. 'But please don't let me be a nuisance.'

'A nuisance,' exclaimed Miss Dubarry, 'when it's you doing us a favour. You've got to save me. Please, please, don't forget that.'

'Oh, Guinevere!' implored Miss LaFosse. 'You won't let me down. You've simply got to do something about Tony.'

Miss Pettigrew said no more. Why plead against your own happiness? She let her spirits soar. She simply stood and let elation pour through her like a shot of Nick's cocaine. She didn't care what happened. She was ready for it. She was intoxicated with joy again. Past questioning anything that happened on this amazing day. She was bewildered as to what she had to do with Tony, but then, so many of their remarks were obscure, she simply let it pass.

'Where are we going?' asked Miss Pettigrew.

'To a cocktail party at the Ogilveys'.'

'A cocktail party!' said Miss Pettigrew blissfully. 'A cocktail party! Me?'

'Why not?' demanded Miss Dubarry.

'Why not?' echoed Miss Pettigrew. Her face became one shining light. 'Oh women!' said Miss Pettigrew. 'Lead me to it.'

They led her into the bedroom. She had a quick bath while Miss Dubarry and Miss LaFosse concentrated on Miss LaFosse's wardrobe. She put on silk underclothes laid out for her by Miss LaFosse. She had never worn real silk underclothes in her life. At once they made her feel different. She felt wicked, daring, ready for anything. She left her hesitations behind with her home-made woollens.

'The psychology of silk underclothes has not yet been fully considered,' mused Miss Pettigrew happily.

She came back into the bedroom like a debutante. Even her legs, quite uncovered below the last short frill of lace, caused her no blushes.

Miss Dubarry sat her in front of the mirror.

'No,' said Miss Pettigrew firmly. 'I think not. I'd rather see the final result: nothing spoiled by watching the intermediate stages, thank you.'

They moved her from the mirror. The most important moment of the day had arrived.

'The face,' said Miss Dubarry.

'Can you do anything with it?' asked Miss LaFosse nervously.

'With that to start on,' said Miss Dubarry, 'I'll do a job.'

She stood away and regarded Miss Pettigrew. She walked round her. She cocked her head on one side. Her brow grew corrugated. Miss Dubarry, in her professional guise, was a different woman. No nervousness, worry, or indecision. All gravity, firmness, competence: the expert at work.

'Look at that jawline,' said Miss Dubarry. 'Clean as a whistle. No mass of fat to be massaged away. Look at that nose. Perfect. You can do a lot with a face . . . but a nose! That takes a surgeon, and there's not many will risk that.'

'Beautiful,' agreed Miss LaFosse.

'When you're over thirty-five,' lectured Miss Dubarry, 'make-up must be sparing. There's nothing worse than a middle-aged woman with too much make-up. It accentuates her age, not lessens it. Only a very young, unlined face can stand the lavish emphasis of too many cosmetics. The effect must be delicate, artistic, the possibility never strained that it can, after all, be natural, so that the beholder is left wondering which it is, art or nature.'

Miss Dubarry set to work. Miss Pettigrew had her face pommelled, patted, dabbed, massaged; cream rubbed in, cream smoothed off; lotion dabbed on, lotion wiped off. Her skin tingled; felt glowing, healthy, rejuvenated.

'Well!' said Miss Dubarry at last, 'it's the best I can do here. It's not like my own place. But you can't have everything.'

She looked consideringly at Miss Pettigrew. Miss Pettigrew glanced back nervously. She felt a little guilty, as though, somehow or other, she should have wafted herself into Miss Dubarry's shop, though it was beyond her comprehension that any more bottles or jars could be needed.

Miss Dubarry tipped Miss Pettigrew's face to the light.

'You see. I haven't *blackened* the eyebrows and lashes. I've merely delicately darkened them. Would you say they weren't natural? No. You wouldn't.'

'Can't be bettered,' agreed Miss LaFosse. 'You're a genius, Edythe.'

'Well, I'm pretty good in my own line,' acknowledged Miss Dubarry modestly.

She admired Miss Pettigrew a moment.

'Now!' she said briskly. 'The frock.'

'Are you sure you won't have the green and gold brocade?' asked Miss LaFosse wistfully.

'No. I will not,' said Miss Dubarry firmly. 'Much too elaborate for Guinevere. She hasn't the right atmosphere for it. Not vulgar enough, if you want the exact truth. If you weren't the kind of woman who can wear anything and look right, Delysia, you'd have no taste in clothes at all. Guinevere *can't* just wear anything. She's got to *be* right.'

94

'Anything you say,' said Miss LaFosse meekly.

'The black velvet,' said Miss Dubarry.

They put it on. For a breathless second they hardly dared look. But it fitted. Not perfectly, but enough not to notice.

'I thought she was about my figure,' said Miss LaFosse with a sigh of relief.

'Thank heavens,' thought Miss Pettigrew wildly and extravagantly, 'for short rations and no middle-aged spread.'

'A necklace,' said Miss Dubarry. 'Something chaste and ladylike.'

'There're my pearls,' said Miss LaFosse. 'They're not very good ones, but who knows ?'

'The very thing.'

'No,' broke in Miss Pettigrew very firmly. 'I will *not* wear any one's pearls. I should not enjoy a single minute thinking I might lose them. Thank you very much, but no.'

Miss Dubarry and Miss LaFosse looked at each other.

'She means it,' said Miss LaFosse. 'When Guinevere says no she means no.'

'The jade ear-rings,' said Miss Dubarry. 'The necklace to match. Glittering stones are not Guinevere's medium of expression.'

Miss Pettigrew trembled towards further speech, but Miss LaFosse said hastily,

'They're only imitation. You needn't worry. A relic of my less palmy days, but Edythe always liked them.'

They went on.

'And to-night,' said Miss Dubarry, 'she must have a spray. Something delicate, mainly green and cream, to carry out the colour touch, but one single flower may

have a brilliant colour. And real flowers. Not artificial. Real flowers express her personality . . . something fresh and natural about her.'

' Unspoiled,' said Miss LaFosse.

' And with her brains.' Miss Dubarry shook her
head.

' Almost unbelievable,' agreed Miss LaFosse.

' You'd have thought the dictatorial air.'

' Not a sign of it.'

' Thank God ! ' said Miss Dubarry.

' I'll choose it myself,' promised Miss LaFosse.

' You'd better. Funny, how these brainy people so
seldom know how to look after themselves. Minds
must be above it. No insult meant.'

' None taken,' said Miss Pettigrew.

' And now,' said Miss Dubarry, ' the hair.'

She let down Miss Pettigrew's locks.

' Absolutely straight, but the kind that takes a perfect
Marcel. Sometimes if there's a trace of natural wave
it doesn't do so well . . . oh ! ' Miss Dubarry looked
blankly at Miss LaFosse. ' You don't need curling
tongs. Your hair's natural. You won't have any.
We're sunk.'

' We are not. I have,' said Miss LaFosse with pride.
' You remember the night Molly Leroy lost her curls
in the rain coming here and had draggly ends all even-
ing, and it spoiled her night . . . well, ever since then
I've kept a pair for my guests in case of need. And
I got a gadget as well to heat them with.'

Miss LaFosse produced the whole outfit like a con-
jurer producing a rabbit from a hat. Miss Dubarry
set to work.

' No time for a shampoo. Pity, but it can't be
helped. Fortunately her hair isn't greasy. Just a few
loose waves. We haven't time for an artistic dressing.'

Her clever fingers flew. Miss Pettigrew sat almost unconscious with excitement. She had never, in all her life before, interfered with the simple gifts presented by nature. 'Why,' asked her mother, 'attempt to improve on God's handiwork? Will He be pleased? No. He gave you that face and that hair.' He meant you to have them.' Miss Pettigrew sat savouring to the full a blissful sense of adventure, of wrongdoing: a dashing feeling of being a little fast: a worldly sense of being in the fashion: a wicked feeling of guilty ecstasy. She enjoyed it. She enjoyed it very much.

'Finished,' said Miss Dubarry. 'A side parting. A few, loose, negligent waves back from the brow— the impression of being natural and just a little carelessly dressed. A sophisticated coil at the nape of the neck the idea of worldly poise for all the carelessness.'

'There.' She stood away from her handiwork.

'My Holy Aunt!' breathed Miss LaFosse. 'Would you believe that hair can make such a difference to a person?'

'Am I ready?' quavered Miss Pettigrew.

'Ready,' said Miss Dubarry.

'Fixed,' exclaimed Miss LaFosse.

'A satisfactory job,' agreed Miss Dubarry modestly.

'I don't believe my eyes yet,' marvelled Miss LaFosse.

'It's a good subject,' said Miss Dubarry. She allowed enthusiasm to overcome modesty. 'Though I says it as shouldn't, I'm proud of my work.'

'Can I look?' implored Miss Pettigrew.

'The mirror's waiting,' said Miss Dubarry.

Miss Pettigrew stood up. She turned round. She stared.

'*No*,' whispered Miss Pettigrew.

'*Yes*,' chorused the Misses Dubarry and LaFosse joyously.

'It isn't me,' gasped Miss Pettigrew.
'You in the flesh,' said Miss Dubarry.
'You as man intended,' encouraged Miss LaFosse.

Then they were both silent. This was a sacred moment. This was Miss Pettigrew's moment. They gave it the honour of silent admiration.

Miss Pettigrew stared

Miss Pettigrew stared. She caught the back of a chair for support. She felt faint. Another woman stood there. A woman of fashion: poised, sophisticated, finished, fastidiously elegant. A woman of no age. Obviously not young. Obviously not old. Who would care about age ? No one. Not in a woman of that charming exterior. The rich, black velvet of the gown was of so deep and lustrous a sheen it glowed like colour. An artist had created it. It had the wicked, brilliant cut that made its wearer look both daring and chaste. It intrigued the beholder. He had to discover which. Its severe lines made her look taller. The ear-rings made her look just a little, well, experienced. No other word. The necklace gave her elegance. She, Miss Pettigrew, elegant.

That delicate flush ! Was it natural ? Who could tell ? That loosely curling hair ! No ends, no wisps, no lank drooping. Was it her own ? She didn't recognize it. Those eyes, so much more blue than memory recalled ! Those artfully shaded brows and lashes ! That mouth, with its faint, provocative redness ! Was it coloured ? Only by kissing it would a man find a satisfactory answer.

She smiled. The woman smiled back, assured, composed. Where was the meek carriage, the deprecating smile, the timid shyness, the dowdy figure, the ugly hair, the sallow complexion ? Gone. Gone under the magic of ' Du Barry's ' expert owner and manager.

Miss Pettigrew, rapt, thrilled, transported, gazed at herself as her dreams had painted her. A lump came into her throat. Her eyes became misty.

' Guinevere,' screamed Miss Dubarry in a panic. ' For God's sake, control yourself.'

' Guinevere,' gasped Miss LaFosse. ' Control, I implore you. Your make-up. Remember your duty to your make-up.'

Miss Pettigrew made a valiant effort.

' Most certainly,' said Miss Pettigrew with dignity. ' " England expects ! " I am quite aware that due care is essential.'

' Shoes,' said Miss Dubarry.

Miss Pettigrew tried on a pair.

' Why ! ' marvelled Miss Pettigrew. ' They are a trifle too large.'

'Well, that's a blessing,' said Miss LaFosse thankfully. 'It's better than too small. We'll stop and buy a pair of soles.'

'Now her coat,' said Miss Dubarry.

Miss Pettigrew had a terrified vision of all her splendour being eclipsed by her shabby brown tweed. But no! She suddenly found herself encased in a fur coat so soft, so silky, so blissfully warm, she knew she had never known luxury before.

'Oh!' gasped Miss Pettigrew. 'Oh! I can't believe it. All my life I've *longed* to wear a fur coat, just once.'

'No hat?' asked Miss Dubarry.

'None of mine are suitable,' decided Miss LaFosse. 'She'll have to go without. No one will notice.'

Gloves, handkerchief, a new handbag.

'Ready?' asked Miss Dubarry, after a last touch to herself.

'All set,' agreed Miss LaFosse. 'Let's get going.'

A last look round: a final inventory. They all made for the door.

CHAPTER EIGHT

5.2 p.m.—6.21 p.m.

MISS PETTIGREW found herself wafted into the passage. She was past remonstrance now, past bewilderment, surprise, expostulation. Her eyes shone. Her face glowed. Her spirits soared. Everything was happening too quickly. She couldn't keep up with things, but, by golly, she could enjoy them.

'I don't care,' thought Miss Pettigrew rapturously. 'My dear mother would have been shocked. I can't help it. I've never been so thrilled in my life before. She always said be careful of strangers, you never know. They may be leading me to destruction, but who can possibly want to destroy a middle-aged spinster like me? I refuse to credit it. I don't know why these things are happening. I don't care. They're happening. That's enough.'

'Feeling O.K.?' asked Miss LaFosse solicitously.

'Lead on,' said Miss Pettigrew joyfully, radiantly.

'Taxi, miss?' asked the porter downstairs.

Miss Pettigrew had never been in a taxi for pure frivolity before. It was the final touch: the gesture perfect. She sat back and watched the London streets fly past her with the sense of being in a dream, but a perfectly sensible dream. No nightmare round the corner. She didn't know where they went. She had always been terrified of the London maze and had never yet learned to get her bearings. They stopped and bought a pair of soles. They went on. They stopped in front of a house. All the windows were lit. They got out. Miss LaFosse paid off the taxi. They knocked and were admitted. No one challenged Miss Pettigrew.

'We're very late,' remarked Miss Dubarry.

Had never been in a taxi for pure frivolity before

The maid led them to a dressing-room. There were no other occupants.

'That's all right, Maisie,' said Miss LaFosse. 'We know the way.'

The maid left them.

Miss LaFosse and Miss Dubarry powdered their noses.

'Come along now, Guinevere,' said Miss LaFosse. 'You must powder your nose again. It isn't done not to. Last gesture before entering a room—powder your nose. It gives a sense of confidence.'

With trembling fingers, nervous, clumsy, contented, for the first time in life Miss Pettigrew powdered her own nose.

'Do you know,' she said happily, 'I think you're right. It does add a certain assurance to one's demeanour. I feel it already.'

'Attaboy,' praised Miss Dubarry.

They walked downstairs. From behind a closed door came high sounds of revelry. Suddenly Miss Pettigrew felt qualms. She stood rooted to the spot. Stage-fright engulfed her. She forgot absolutely what she now looked like. Her glimpses had been too short. She would need solid hours of close concentration to get her new image soaked in. She simply felt as she had always felt: Miss Pettigrew permanently seeking a new job, nervous, incompetent, dowdy and shy. She began to shake. They would laugh at her, stare at her, make remarks. She couldn't bear it. She couldn't face any more ridicule. She had had so much in her life.

Miss LaFosse and Miss Dubarry had also stopped.

'We're here,' said Miss Dubarry in a weak voice.

Miss Pettigrew stared at her. All Miss Dubarry's gay insouciance had gone. She looked limp as a rag: drooping, nervous, more terrified than herself. She was so surprised she forgot her own nervousness again.

'Buck up, Edythe,' Miss LaFosse implored. 'You can't let him see. Everything will be all right. She's bound to think of something.'

They both turned to Miss Pettigrew.

'You won't forget Tony,' said Miss LaFosse urgently.

'I'll point him out when we get in, if he's there,' said Miss Dubarry with equal urgency.

'How kind,' thought Miss Pettigrew, touched.

She's so friendly she wants me to see her former young man, even if they have quarrelled.'

' I should love to meet your young man.   Thank you very much,' said Miss Pettigrew earnestly.

' There,' said Miss LaFosse proudly.   ' What did I tell you ?   She's thinking of something already.'

' Please . . .' began Miss Dubarry.

' No instructions,' begged Miss LaFosse again. ' They only *muddle* people.   You must let her do her own act.   It's far the best way.'

' You won't forget,' said Miss Dubarry with a last despairing reminder.

Miss Pettigrew hadn't the faintest idea what they were talking about, but so many of their speeches were odd and beyond her comprehension she didn't trouble herself and there was certainly no time to question.   Miss LaFosse opened the door, and she was swept in.

She blinked, dazzled.   The room was full of people, men and women.   Their jumbled voices assaulted her ears.   It was a large room.   At the far end was what looked like a counter and behind it a lot of bottles. She had very little time to gather clear impressions because at their entry there were loud cries and they were immediately surrounded by people.   Miss LaFosse and Miss Dubarry were obviously popular.

' Delysia.'

' Edythe.'

Miss LaFosse beamed.   A surprising transformation took place in Miss Dubarry.   She laughed, talked, joked.   No sign of depression or unhappiness.   Miss LaFosse had firm hold of Miss Pettigrew's arm.   She piloted her round.   Miss Pettigrew said ' How-do-you-do ?' politely to, she was sure, about a hundred people. No one stared at her.   No one laughed at her.   No hostess gave her a freezing welcome.   She did not

She blinked, dazzled. The room was full of people

know for sure who her hostess was. She had a vague idea that a dreamy woman, in a brilliant scarlet frock, who said, ' Delysia darling, how good of you to come,' *might* be she. But then another woman in diaphanous green said, ' Delysia, my pet, how sweet to see you.' So doubt could enter.

She found a drink in her hands, placed there by a charming young man with dark, wavy hair, a cajoling voice, and a wicked twinkle in his eyes, but Miss LaFosse gave an urgent shake of her head.

' I wouldn't,' she whispered. ' I mean, not that drink. That's Terence's own. I'll get you one myself. I mean, I wouldn't like to hurt your feelings, Guinevere, but I don't think you're *very* used to strong liquor, and, well, there's Tony, you know, and that's *very* strong.'

' Just as you advise, my dear,' said Miss Pettigrew, flustered. ' I wouldn't dream of doing anything you didn't advise.'

Miss LaFosse brought her another.

' Now,' said Miss LaFosse in a moment's breathing space, ' would you like a seat, and, if so, where ? You mustn't tire yourself before to-night.'

' I think,' said Miss Pettigrew simply, ' I will stand just over there, so that if I look up I can see myself in the mirror across the room. Please don't think that pure vanity dictates this wish, though I admit a little is present. I am not accustomed to myself yet, and if I can glance up every now and then merely to re-assure myself of what I don't look like, it will give me tremendous strength and encouragement.'

' An excellent idea,' agreed Miss LaFosse.

She led Miss Pettigrew to the desired vantage-point. Miss Pettigrew at once took a surreptitious peep at herself in the mirror. She gave a tremendous sigh of relief. She still retained her new personality. There was little to distinguish her from any other woman present. Very carelessly she loosened her fur coat to show off more of the velvet gown. She felt so elated she didn't care whether she was left alone or not. She was here to watch and enjoy and remember. That was sufficient. But she wasn't left alone. Miss LaFosse disappeared after a time, but to Miss Pettigrew's surprise others immediately took her place. In fact a considerable number of people in turn took her place. They spoke to her pleasantly and offered her drinks, which, of course, she refused, and seemed to regard her with deference. Miss Pettigrew grew more elated and more excited every minute. She couldn't understand it. She seemed to be holding quite a little court of her own. She didn't find conversation at all difficult, as she had dreaded. She merely agreed with what any one said to her and smiled, and they at once looked gratified. If she did venture a remark of her own they took it with such a look of wondering admiration she began to think she had never before had a chance to test her conversational powers to the full.

She laughed so much and shook her head so much, every now and then she was sure she was becoming untidy and dishevelled and a little disordered. Then, all she had to do was take a peep at herself in the mirror at once to be reassured. No Miss Pettigrew, governess, stared back at her, but a strange lady, whose disarray had a distinctive and becoming charm.

And still people came for a little friendly intercourse. She was happily innocent of Miss LaFosse's chattering. Miss LaFosse couldn't keep a good thing to herself. Details could not be given, but a brief sketch, of an imaginary incident, couldn't be resisted.

'Yes,' said Miss LaFosse. 'The most brilliant mimic I've ever seen in my life.'

'Good party,' said Reggie Carteret, variety star, to Florence Somers, vaudeville beauty.

'Moira certainly draws the crowds,' agreed Miss Somers.

'Who's the lady ?' asked Reggie.

'Miss Pettigrew.'

'Don't think we've met.'

'What ?' With assumed condescension, 'Never seen her take off Mrs. Brummegan ?'

'Mrs. Brummegan ?'

'Mrs. Brummegan.'

'Never heard of her.'

'Never heard of Mrs. Brummegan ?'

'No.' Anxiously, 'Should I ?'

'You certainly should.'

'Then I'd better.'

'Can't afford not to be in the know these days,' agreed Miss Somers.

'You're right. Doesn't pay.'

'Well, bye-bye,' said Miss Somers. 'There's Charlie. See you anon.'

'Good party,' said Reggie Carteret to Maurice Dinsmore, superior juvenile lead.

'Pretty fair,' said Maurice carelessly.

'They certainly always manage to get the new celebrities.'

'Celebrity ! Who ?'

'Miss Pettigrew.'

'Miss Pettigrew ?'

'Never seen her take off Mrs. Brummegan ?' incredulously.

'Mrs. Brummegan ?'

'Surely you know Mrs. Brummegan ?'

'Oh . . . ah ! Yes. Come to think of it, I believe we've met. At the Desmonds, wasn't it ?'

' Probably.'

' Miss Pettigrew do her well ? '

' Brilliant mimic. Knock spots off Dora Delaney.'

' You don't say so.'

' Umm . . . don't breathe a word, but I believe Phil Goldberg's going to back her. She's a friend of Delysia's and Delysia's got Goldberg . . . like that.'

' Good Lord ! ' said Maurice.

' Fact. Friend of Goldberg's, well, who wouldn't want to know her ? '

' Who wouldn't ? ' agreed Maurice.

He hastened away.

' Ah ! Hello, Eveline,' said Maurice to his more superior lady juvenile lead.

' Howdy, Maurice.'

' Met the lady ? '

' What lady ? '

' My dear girl, surely you know her.'

' Don't breathe a word, I believe Goldberg's going to back her '

' Know who ? '

' Miss Pettigrew.'

' Oh . . . ah . . . Miss Pettigrew.'

' Future star.'

' Oh . . . er. Come to think of it, I believe I have read notices.'

' Never seen her do Mrs. Brummegan ? '

' Mrs. Brummegan ? '

' Sure,' condescendingly. ' You've heard of Mrs.
Brummegan ? '

' Oh . . . er. Yes. Sure I've heard. So she does
Mrs. Brummegan ? '

' Raised the roof in the provinces, I understand.'

' Oh. The provinces ! ' more coldly.

' London next,' blandly.

' London ? '

' Sure. Phil Goldberg's behind her. Comedy star
of his new revue. Sharing honours with Delysia
LaFosse.'

' Why, now you mention it, I believe I heard,' agreed
Miss Somers.

' You never can tell. Nobody one day. Queen of
London the next.'

' Ah, yes. Think I'll have a word with her.'

Miss Pettigrew received them all : eyes shining, face
radiant, hair loosening—but very artistically, still in
Miss Dubarry's waves. Ear-rings twinkling with worldly
sophistication : cheeks now developing a natural flush :
bosom heaving with so much excitement.

Miss LaFosse touched her arm. Miss Pettigrew
turned from her latest admirer.

' That's Tony,' whispered Miss LaFosse.

Miss Pettigrew looked ; an average-sized young man,
with brown, untidy hair, hot, smouldering eyes, and
something rugged and stubborn about his face.

' Oh ! ' thought Miss Pettigrew in relief. ' A nice
face. I expected . . . I expected . . . a lounge lizard.
Just shows how you can misjudge a girl's appearance.'

Miss Dubarry and Tony had had a meeting.

' Howdy, Tony ? ' said Miss Dubarry airily.

' Grand party,' said Tony equably.

Miss Dubarry passed on. They were very cool and

poised about it, very modern and nonchalant. After
that they avoided each other. Miss Dubarry was full
of life in one corner. Tony full of life in another.

'Ah!' thought Miss Pettigrew. 'Very conscious of
each other. Showing off. Oh dear, what a pity!
Shows they care for each other.'

Later Miss Dubarry came up.

'That's Tony,' she whispered.

'I know,' agreed Miss Pettigrew.

She looked at Miss Dubarry. Tony wasn't looking
their way and Miss Dubarry let her gaze rest on him.
For a brief flash Miss Pettigrew thought she glimpsed a
sick look in her eyes, then Tony turned and Miss Dubarry
was laughing with some one else.

Suddenly Miss Pettigrew was not so interested in the
people round her. After all, they were strangers, but
Miss Dubarry was her friend. She couldn't feel so
happy again, knowing how Miss Dubarry felt.

She edged away and found a corner by herself at the
end of the bar. She discovered a high stool and sat
down.

'Oh dear!' thought Miss Pettigrew sadly. 'I do
hope that young man comes to his senses. I can't bear
Miss Dubarry to be unhappy like that. One is young
for so little a time.'

Miss LaFosse came up.

'Guinevere,' said Miss LaFosse, 'meet Tony, a pal
of mine.'

'How-do-you-do?' said Miss Pettigrew.

'How-do-you-do?' said Tony.

'Have a confab,' said Miss LaFosse cheerfully. She
disappeared.

'Fetch you a drink,' offered Tony amiably.

'Thanks,' said Miss Pettigrew thoughtfully, 'I think
I will.'

'I have had two already,' thought Miss Pettigrew judiciously, 'and feel no ill effects. One more can do no harm and an affirmative answer seems to impress them a great deal more.'

Tony eyed her critically. He liked to think he was a nice judge of a woman. He noted the sly twinkle of the ear-rings, the sleek cut of the gown. He judged accordingly.

'Snake's Venom ?'

'Oh . . . er. Is it ? Yes of course,' said Miss Pettigrew, somewhat taken aback.

Tony brought a drink. Miss Pettigrew drank nearly half in a gulp. Tony eyed her admiringly. For a wild moment Miss Pettigrew wondered whether it really had been poison. She sat perfectly still in her chair. She didn't dare move. Fire ran down her throat. The room heaved. Her chair swayed. Her eyes played tricks. Then everything settled. The room was not moving. Her chair was quite stationary. She was still seated safely upon it. She made a tentative movement. She could still retain her balance. Miss Pettigrew beamed.

She felt grand. She felt brimming with authority and assurance. It was a marvellous sensation. She thought scornfully of her former timid self. A futile creature ! Fear ! Had she once known fear ? Impossible. She felt surging with pugnacious intentions. She wanted to do battle with some one for the sheer sake of downing them gloriously and proving her powers. She eyed the room with the light of battle in her gaze. Who would offer her combat ?

Tony was standing very submissively by her side. He did not seem to want to return to the crowd. He struck a chord of memory in Miss Pettigrew's mind. She saw that his eyes followed Miss Dubarry when

Miss Dubarry wasn't looking at him. She remembered.
Very slowly and very carefully Miss Pettigrew stood up.

'Ha!' barked Miss Pettigrew. 'So you're Tony?'

He started.

'Sure. I'm Tony.'

'I wanted to meet you.'

'Very kind of you, I'm sure.'

'Not at all. Stupid young men,' said Miss Pettigrew,
'always interest me.'

'What?' Tony gasped in surprise.

'Stupid,' said Miss Pettigrew.

'*Me?*'

'You.'

'Oh!' said Tony engagingly. 'I didn't know you
knew me.'

'Too well.'

He looked interested.

'But why stupid?'

'Oh, you wouldn't be interested,' said Miss Pettigrew haughtily. 'I merely take an academic interest
in hearing of the follies of young people. I'm past the
age, you see, when I can be a young fool myself, so
the interest has no repercussions.'

'What's that got to do with me?' Tony glared.

'You happened to be one I heard of.' Miss Pettigrew
glared back.

'Who's been calling me a fool?' demanded Tony
belligerently.

His face began to glower and his eyes to smoulder.

'No one . . . precisely,' said Miss Pettigrew with
cutting meaning. 'It was merely my own interpretation
when I heard.'

'Heard what?'

'I'm not at all interested in giving you details,' said
Miss Pettigrew loftily. 'I merely happened to think

what a fool that young man was and thought I'd like to see him. Now I have I'm satisfied.'

'Satisfied with what ?'

'My interpretation.'

'My God !' cried Tony. He glared. 'Who've you been talking to ? I won't have anybody going round calling me a fool.'

'You shouldn't act like one then.'

'Me ?'

'Of course,' said Miss Pettigrew with a surge of pity, 'it's not all your fault. Young people never have any discernment. By the time you reach my age, you'll have learned to know when people are telling the truth and when not.'

'I don't need to reach your age before I know when people are telling me the truth.'

Miss Pettigrew smiled condescendingly. Tony went red in the face.

'Now what are you grinning at ?'

'Smiling,' said Miss Pettigrew with dignity, 'and quite kindly. But don't mind me. I like to hear young people talk. It amuses me. How clever they think they are ! It makes me glad I've reached the age when it's hard to be fooled.'

'No one's fooling me.'

'Only yourself.'

'What . . .'

'But there !' said Miss Pettigrew, now becoming cynical, 'you're quite right. There's nothing to this love business. When you're my age you'll realize it and be thankful that you did act in the right way for stupid reasons.'

'Woman,' cried Tony furiously, 'if you say your age and my age again I'll do something desperate.'

'But mind you,' continued Miss Pettigrew, 'I think

the woman's just as lucky. As I said to Miss LaFosse, it's a good thing she's got rid of him. I don't know your friend very well, but I do know when women are telling the truth. You've got to, in my profession. Children lie so. One gets a sixth sense for knowing when they're lying or not.'

'My God!' cried Tony desperately. 'What the devil are you talking about now?'

'My profession,' said Miss Pettigrew with dignity.

'What's that?'

'I teach.'

'Teach what?'

'Children.'

'Oh Lord!' said Tony weakly. 'Be calm,' he implored. 'Be cool. Be collected. Now . . . think. What are we talking about?'

Miss Pettigrew thought. She pondered deeply. Concentration, she discovered, was rather difficult. Question and answer. She had an inspiration.

'Your late fiancée of course.'

'Edythe,' exploded Tony.

'Well,' said Miss Pettigrew indignantly, confusing what she had thought at the time with what she had said, 'as I said to her, why bother with a young man who is perpetually making scenes merely for his own enjoyment. It gets boring.'

'I don't create scenes merely for my own enjoyment,' said Tony furiously.

'Well,' said Miss Pettigrew. 'You certainly don't think much of yourself.'

'Holy suffering mackerel! Where are we now?' cried Tony in despair. 'What's that got to do with it?'

'Oh tut!' said Miss Pettigrew forcefully. 'Be yourself. Do women usually forget you once you're out of sight?'

'They do not.'

'Nonsense.'

'Nonsense. Nonsense what? What do you know about it?'

Miss Pettigrew looked irritatingly bland. Her mind felt beautifully light and clear. Nothing troubled her. Brilliant repartee simply leaped to the tongue. This young man was no match for her.

'Well, if you had such a conceit of yourself as you make out, it would never occur to you that any woman would prefer another man in your absence.'

'Neither they do.'

'Then why,' demanded Miss Pettigrew, becoming indignant again, 'pretend? It's just a cowardly way of getting out of an entanglement. A *very* cowardly way, I should say. Oozing out of the back door. Distinctly sordid,' concluded Miss Pettigrew triumphantly.

'What entanglement? Whose back door?' cried Tony, beginning to feel like tearing his hair.

'A paltry tale. Why didn't you say before you were tired and be a man.'

'Tired of what?'

'Of Miss Dubarry.'

'I'm not tired of Miss Dubarry.'

'Well, good gracious me!' said Miss Pettigrew warmly. 'It seems very odd to me. You say you are not tired of Miss Dubarry and she says she's not tired of you . . . well, really, what is an outsider to think?'

'Who's asking outsiders to think?'

'Murder will out,' said Miss Pettigrew with a glower. 'I started by thinking it. I still do.'

'Do what?'

'Think you're a very stupid young man.'

'Oh, you do, do you?'

'Yes. I do.'

They glared at each other. Miss Pettigrew had never been so rude to any one in her life before. Suddenly she realized this. What had she been saying ? She began to feel a little flustered. She discovered the other half of her drink still in her glass. She swallowed another gulp. It ran hot down her throat. She felt better at once. He deserved all he got. He had hurt very deeply her dear friend Miss Dubarry. She renewed her indignant glare.

' After the way she cared for you.'

' Oh ! She cares for me, does she ? ' asked Tony sarcastically.

' Didn't she say so ? '

' Oh. She *said* so.'

' Don't you know ? '

' Well, she . . .'

' Ah ! ' said Miss Pettigrew with brilliant sarcasm. ' Youth's discernment. . . .'

' Yes, she *did*,' Tony shouted.

' Didn't you ? '

Tony glared. He gulped. Went red in the face.

' Yes,' said Tony, ' I did.'

' Well,' said Miss Pettigrew, ' I've never heard anything sillier in my life. I hope she keeps her promise and has nothing further to do with you.'

' Oh, she said that, did she ? '

' Yes, she did,' said Miss Pettigrew heatedly. ' And I fully agree with her. I don't like to be so frank, but my age allows me a little licence. After meeting you, young man, I think Miss Dubarry will be much wiser to find some one of a more stable temperament, and more sustained power of thought. Marriage is a serious business.'

' So you'd marry her off to some one else, would you ? ' demanded Tony furiously.

'That's what I'd recommend,' said Miss Pettigrew with equal anger. 'I'm very glad she's finished with you.'

'So she's finished with me, has she?'

'Hasn't she?'

'Oh, has she? We'll see about that.'

Tony turned and glared around. Miss Dubarry was sitting near them, quite within glaring distance. She had edged up very carefully. Miss Pettigrew and Tony, talking in a corner, seemed far too important to her for her to remain out of reach. She must be on hand should circumstances demand her presence. They did.

'Edythe,' called Tony in a low, carrying, concentrated voice.

Miss Dubarry came up nonchalantly.

'So you've finished with me, have you?' said Tony in a low, explosive voice.

Miss Dubarry did some rapid mental gymnastics. She glanced sideways at Miss Pettigrew. Some subtle work had been going on here. Carelessness might ruin something. When in doubt, repeat the question.

'Have I?' repeated Miss Dubarry carelessly.

'So you don't think I'm stable enough?'

'Well,' asked Miss Dubarry cautiously, 'are you?'

'Ha!' exploded Tony again. 'So you think you'll marry some one else.'

'Well,' said Miss Dubarry, still wildly feeling her way, 'I mean, I'm not in my teens. It's time I was thinking of settling down . . . and if you don't want to marry me . . .'

'So you hope never to see me again, do you?'

'Oh!' said Miss Dubarry warily, 'I wouldn't be so hard as all that, Tony. That was said in the heat of the moment when you'd hurt me. I don't see why we shouldn't be friends.'

'Friends!' said Tony with another explosion.
'Friends! So you did say it?'

'Well, yes, I said it,' agreed Miss Dubarry a little
nervously. This conversation was getting dangerous.
She had no clue. A pity she hadn't been able to get

A pity she hadn't been able to get behind the curtains, but
then, how could she have emerged with dignity?

behind the curtains, but then, how could she have
emerged with dignity?

'So you think I'm the kind of man you can get
rid of as easily as all that, do you?' demanded Tony.

'Well, no,' said Miss Dubarry wildly. 'I mean . . .
you always were a sticker.'

'You bet I am.'

'Well, there you are.' Miss Dubarry collapsed.

'I'm glad you agree,' said Tony belligerently. 'Women don't pick me up and drop me as they think fit.'

'Of course not.'

'I'm glad you realize it.'

'Of course I do.'

'Well, what about it ?'

'Oh !' Miss Dubarry's heart took such a wild leap she almost expected to see it jump out of her body. Her instincts were to open her arms wide and gather Tony to her bosom, but her native guile saved her.

'Oh, I don't know,' said Miss Dubarry haughtily. 'No girl likes to be told she's a liar, even if she is one, but when she's actually telling the truth . . .'

'Oh well.' Tony's eyes smouldered. 'I've apologized . . . but if that's the way you feel about it . . .'

He made signs of departure.

'*Tony*,' wailed Miss Dubarry.

'Edythe,' said Tony in a husky voice.

Miss Pettigrew stood beaming on them benignly. She had very little idea now what she and Tony had been talking about and their present remarks sounded very cryptic to her, but the result seemed to please both of them and that was all that mattered. Miss Dubarry looked so happy Miss Pettigrew forgave Tony everything.

She glanced round the room a little anxiously. Such a public display of emotion was a trifle embarrassing and on a lady's part hardly quite . . . well, just hardly quite.

But no one was taking the slightest notice. Every one was talking. No one listening. Tony could have been murdering Miss Dubarry instead of gazing at her with such worship for all any one in the room would have noticed. Miss Pettigrew gave a modest sigh of relief.

Miss Dubarry swung round. She gazed at Miss Pettigrew with what is technically known as a starry look.

'Oh!' gasped Miss Dubarry. 'You wonderful darling.'

Miss Pettigrew looked surprised. Miss Dubarry gave her a hug and whispered in her ear.

'How can I ever thank you?'

Miss Pettigrew was extremely pleased. She quite understood a reconciliation had taken place, but did not understand why.

'Oh, my dear!' whispered Miss Pettigrew. 'I wish you every happiness.'

Regardless of make-up, regardless of the importance of her appearance, regardless of the fact that Tony might inadvertently see what she really looked like, tears came into Miss Dubarry's eyes and one or two actually rolled over, leaving in their tracks faint, black smudges of mascara.

'Oh!' gulped Miss Dubarry. 'I look a sight.'

'You look perfect,' said Tony adoringly.

'I'll have to go to the cloakroom,' said Miss Dubarry in a fluster.

'I'll come with you,' said Tony.

They went away. Miss Pettigrew watched their progress with a benign, maternal, indulgent gaze.

'The dear things,' she thought sentimentally. 'Just a little lover's tiff. Forgotten as soon as they saw each other again.'

She gave a very mild hiccup.

'Tut, tut,' thought Miss Pettigrew; 'indigestion. I must take some magnesia to-night.'

CHAPTER NINE

6.21 p.m.—7.25 p.m.

MISS PETTIGREW was extremely happy. She felt so delightfully light and airy she was almost sure she could make the passage to the door by simply floating through the air. She discerned a small portion of liquor still in the bottom of her glass. She drank it down.

She only hoped she wasn't too late

Miss LaFosse was gazing at Miss Pettigrew from the other side of the room. For the past quarter of an hour all her interest had been centred in Miss Pettigrew's corner of the room. She had noted the length of Tony's stay. She had noted Miss Dubarry join them. Her curiosity had reached fever heat. Then an acquaintance had blocked her vision, held her in conversation, and when next she had been free to gaze, Tony was gone; Miss Dubarry was gone.

Miss Pettigrew was standing alone with a rakish air, face radiant, eyes beaming, hair a little awry, an empty wineglass in her hand.

Miss Pettigrew was looking blissfully happy. Miss Pettigrew was looking too happy. Miss LaFosse knew that look. Her heart missed a beat. Her conscience smote her. Guinevere had been on the loose alone too long. She had completely forgotten to warn Tony not to judge her friend by the fur coat and the black dress; a most reprehensible lack of thought. She only hoped she wasn't too late.

She gave a distracted answer to a friend, rudely left him and ploughed her way across the room towards her charge, a dubious eye on the empty wineglass. Miss Pettigrew gave her a beaming welcome.

'Guinevere,' said Miss LaFosse anxiously, 'you haven't been imbibing?'

'Imbibing?'

'The pins aren't wobbling.'

'The pins?' repeated

M.T.

Standing with a rakish air

Miss Pettigrew. She raised her chin haughtily.

' The *legs*,' said Miss Pettigrew with much dignity,
' are perfectly steady.'

' Demonstrate,' said Miss LaFosse sternly.

Miss Pettigrew walked two steps back and two steps
forward again. She managed it with commendable
steadiness.

' Thank God ! ' said Miss LaFosse thankfully.

' Your suspicions,' said Miss Pettigrew reproachfully,
' hurt me deeply.'

' No offence,' apologized Miss LaFosse. ' My suspicions were not of you but of Tony.'

' A charming youth,' said Miss Pettigrew sentimentally, ' if a little erratic. But your suspicions are again
quite unfounded. One small drink only was all he
offered or I accepted.'

' I know Tony's drinks,' said Miss LaFosse, still
grimly doubtful.

But her curiosity overcame her worry. She could
contain her anxiety no longer.

' Where is he ? ' demanded Miss LaFosse expectantly.

' Where's who ? '

' Tony.'

' In the cloakroom,' said Miss Pettigrew dreamily.

' Oh ! ' exclaimed Miss LaFosse with a shock of
disappointment.

' Where's Edythe ? ' she asked hopelessly.

' In the cloakroom,' said Miss Pettigrew sentimentally.

' Oh ! ' cried Miss LaFosse again, excitement charging
her voice. ' Oh, Guinevere, don't say it . . . don't say
it . . .'

' Say what ? '

' They're not . . . together ? '

' Why not ? ' asked Miss Pettigrew. ' To the pure,
all things are pure.'

' Oh, you *darling* ! ' cried Miss LaFosse. ' You're

marvellous . . . you're wonderful . . . you're a miracle. How did you do it? Didn't I say you would! Oh, I'm so happy! I think you're the most wonderful woman I've ever met. Nobody but you could have done it. Tony and Edythe together again.'

Miss Pettigrew looked worldly-wise.

'My dear! All young people quarrel. It means nothing. Once they got together again, it was all quite simple. All they . . .'

'Of course it was simple . . . to you. No one else could have brought them together again. You don't know Tony when he gets a bee in his bonnet . . . I do. You're the world's miracle worker.'

Miss Pettigrew gave it up. If her charming friend liked to talk in riddles, let her talk. She, Miss Pettigrew, didn't care. She didn't care about anything. She only knew she had never felt so delightfully gay and irresponsible in all her life before. Let them all talk in riddles if they liked. A habit they obviously liked. What did she care? Nothing.

'As you say,' said Miss Pettigrew benignly.

'Let's go,' said Miss LaFosse.

Miss Pettigrew felt a stab of apprehension. She turned a wild look towards the door. It seemed remote. She was abruptly invaded with a strong disinclination to attempt the passage.

'My dear,' said Miss Pettigrew with dignity, 'if you do not mind I will take your arm. My head is a little dizzy. It is the heat, I think. I am not accustomed to such a crowded room with no windows open.'

'There now!' said Miss LaFosse heatedly. 'I knew. What the hell's Tony been giving you? You were all right when I left you. I'll take his head off when I see him. He should have known.'

'Oh!' gasped Miss Pettigrew. 'Please. It isn't

true . . . it isn't possible. . . . I'd never get over the shame. I assure you, the heat. I'm positive the heat.'

' There now, there now,' soothed Miss LaFosse. ' Of course it's the heat. Don't get upset. You're quite all right. You'll be fine when we get outside. The air in this room is lousy.'

Miss LaFosse took firm hold of Miss Pettigrew and piloted her across the room. Voices assailed them on all sides.

' Not going yet ? '

' Drunk your fill already ? '

' The tap's still running.'

Miss Pettigrew beamed on them all indiscriminately. Miss LaFosse fended them off with easy rejoinders. They reached the door and escaped.

In the passage Miss Pettigrew stopped and gasped.

' Oh dear ! I have failed to thank my hostess for a perfectly charming time. What will she think ? I must return.'

' Not on your life,' said Miss LaFosse hastily. ' It'll keep. And in any case it wouldn't be fair to shock Moira. She's not accustomed to it.'

Miss Pettigrew felt a great deal better in the cool air of the passage.

' Just as I said, my dear. It was the hot air in the room.'

' You've said it,' agreed Miss LaFosse with a twinkle. ' They'd talk the hind leg off a donkey in there.'

' I beg your pardon,' said Miss Pettigrew.

' Hot air,' explained Miss LaFosse.

' Oh ! ' said Miss Pettigrew. It dawned. ' Hot air . . . Oh how funny ! How extremely funny ! '

Miss Pettigrew began to laugh. She laughed and laughed until the tears ran down her face.

'Well,' said Miss LaFosse cheerfully, 'you have had one over the eight.'

But she felt very pleased her mild joke had such an appreciative audience. Together they mounted the stairs in hilarious accord. Miss Pettigrew refused further aid. She took firm hold of the banisters and drew herself up.

Outside the bedroom which was being used as the ladies' cloakroom Miss LaFosse beat a tattoo on the door. Then she opened it.

'Well, well,' said Miss LaFosse. 'Do mine eyes deceive me, or is there a *man* present ? Oh, shades of virtue, where hast thou flown ?'

'Cheese it,' said Tony.

'Delysia,' cried Miss Dubarry. She was no tidier, in fact, a great deal less tidy than when Miss Pettigrew had seen her depart ostensibly to repair her make-up.

'Edythe,' responded Miss LaFosse. She suddenly smiled tenderly. Miss Dubarry flew to her arms and gave her a hug.

'Delysia. We're going to be married.'

'No !' cried Miss LaFosse. She embraced Miss Dubarry with equal joy, then firmly removed her friend's arms and insisted on embracing Tony likewise. Tony did not take it amiss.

'Congratulations, you old sinner. Why the devil did you wait so long ?'

Tony grinned.

'I hadn't the price of a licence.'

'You could always have borrowed it from Edythe.'

'Well,' said Tony seriously, 'I thought I'd better wait a bit before showing quite so obviously why I was really marrying her. I mean, it was no use throwing away the ship for a ha'porth of patience.'

'None at all,' agreed Miss LaFosse. 'The restraint does you credit.'

'I'm glad you appreciate my manly capabilities,' said Tony modestly.

'Oh, all of them,' said Miss LaFosse earnestly. 'I'll be godmother for the first two, but after that I refuse further responsibility.'

'The thirteenth as well,' begged Tony. 'It must have some luck to counteract its fatal number.'

'You darling,' said Miss LaFosse. 'You certainly deserve another kiss for that.'

She kissed him again. Tony appeared to enjoy it. Miss Pettigrew, by this time, was beginning to get hardened to so much indiscriminate affection. No one else seemed to mind it, why should she ? She was slightly puzzled. The atmosphere did not appear to be quite in keeping with the occasion. Shy smiles and blushes were completely absent from Miss Dubarry's countenance, and an air of grave awareness of his future responsibility did not mantle Tony. It was very difficult to give voice to all the beautiful and tender sentiments which surely the moment demanded. But she could contain herself no longer.

'Oh,' broke in Miss Pettigrew shyly, in a flutter of romantic enjoyment, 'may I . . . may I offer my congratulations as well.'

'Thanks,' said Tony.

'Young love . . .' began Miss Pettigrew.

Miss LaFosse and Miss Dubarry swung towards her. By a certain look in Miss Dubarry's eye, Miss Pettigrew knew she was about to descend upon her again. She was right. She did. Miss Pettigrew found this whole-sale display of affection very bewildering, but extremely gratifying. It was not at all in keeping with the rules for a gentlewoman's behaviour. It lacked that becoming touch of the 'English reserve' so esteemed on the continent, but for once Miss Pettigrew didn't care a damn for a gentlewoman's reticence.

Miss Dubarry swooped and gathered Miss Pettigrew in a mighty hug.

'Oh, you dear, dear thing. How can I ever thank you!' Tears actually trembled in her eyes again.

'Oh, Guinevere,' cried Miss LaFosse, equally moved, 'what would we have done without you?'

'I can never repay you,' said Miss Dubarry in a quiver of happy emotion. 'If there's anything you ever want, come to me. A wrinkle removed. A change of hair. A fresh face.'

'What the devil *are* you talking about?' demanded Tony.

'Nothing,' chorused Miss LaFosse and Miss Dubarry.

'Nothing for male ears,' said Miss LaFosse kindly. 'A purely feminine matter.'

Miss Dubarry gathered her wraps.

'See you to-night,' said Miss LaFosse.

'We'll be there,' said Miss Dubarry.

The door closed behind them.

'A very delightful girl,' said Miss Pettigrew, 'but a little beyond my comprehension.'

'We'll scram,' said Miss LaFosse, 'before the rest pile up.'

They left the house. Miss LaFosse hailed a passing taxi and bundled Miss Pettigrew inside. She stopped at a florist's and got out.

'There,' she said cheerfully on return, 'I've ordered your buttonhole. Who said I had no memory?'

'Oh, how kind you are!' whispered Miss Pettigrew, tears in her eyes.

'After what you've done for Edythe!' said Miss LaFosse. 'What's a buttonhole?'

'But,' began poor Miss Pettigrew, 'I assure you I don't . . .'

'No depreciation,' said Miss LaFosse. 'I won't hear it.'

They arrived at Onslow Mansions. They went into the building, rode up in the lift, walked along to Miss LaFosse's door and Miss LaFosse inserted her key in the lock.

Miss Pettigrew had a strange sensation of coming home. The afternoon's visit had been an exciting, thrilling experience, food for thought for many a day, but it was nothing like the feeling as of content after a good meal which invaded her the minute she crossed Miss LaFosse's threshold again. The sense of simple joy was so poignant it was almost pain. She would not let herself think of to-morrow when all this would only be a dream. This was to-day.

Miss Pettigrew bustled in. She turned on the electric light: switched on the electric fire: punched cushions to plump invitation. All the lights had deep crimson shades so that the room was filled with a comfortable, red, glowing look of warmth.

Miss LaFosse flung off her fur coat.

'Thank God for a moment's peace.'

She sank into a comfortable chair in front of the fire.

Miss Pettigrew took off her fur coat and laid it aside with a great deal more care. The borrowed gown gave her a luxurious feeling of importance. She could not help walking with a new show of dignity. The rich, black velvet compelled a sense of majesty.

'Sit down, Guinevere,' said Miss LaFosse. 'You'll tire yourself out.'

'I'm not a bit tired,' said Miss Pettigrew blissfully. 'I'm much too excited to be tired.'

'Legs O.K. ?'

'My legs,' said Miss Pettigrew with renewed dignity, 'were always all right. My head was only a little fuddled with the heat, that is all.'

'Have it your own way,' said Miss LaFosse with a grin.

Miss Pettigrew came and sat beside her happily. The electric fire sent out a glow of warmth after the chill, dark November streets. She and Miss LaFosse were alone in the room with a comfortable, cosy sense of intimacy. Curtains drawn, doors shut, chairs drawn up to the fire. She felt it was about the happiest moment in the whole of a marvellous day. But she only wanted it to be a breathing space. There was a great many years stretching ahead of her which would be simply packed with quiet, uneventful periods. At the present time peace was decidedly not her desire. Quite the reverse. Something must happen again soon. If it didn't she would feel cheated, but surely the fates had been far too kind to her so far to turn round and desert her now. Something would happen. She would be sensible and enjoy this relaxation while it lasted to allow her to recuperate before events started happening again.

'I don't know about you,' said Miss Pettigrew daringly, 'but I could just do with a nice cup of tea.'

'Oh!' said Miss LaFosse.

'The other drinks were very nice for a change,' said Miss Pettigrew earnestly, 'and certainly give one delightfully odd feelings, but I always say you can't beat a really nice . . . cup . . . of . . . tea.'

'You're quite right,' said Miss LaFosse kindly. 'I shall go and make one.'

'Sit still,' said Miss Pettigrew firmly. 'If you only knew how I . . . how I *enjoy* doing it . . . particularly for some one who *appreciates* it.'

Miss LaFosse allowed her to have her own way.

Miss Pettigrew hurried into the kitchen. She moved around in a happy swirl of busy domesticity. It was so different working for Miss LaFosse. A pang shot through her heart. How blissful to own a place like this for oneself! Never to work for any one else again: never to sit on the outskirts while others basked in the centre: never to be ignored, looked down on, disregarded. She pushed the feeling away. Her day was not yet over. Obviously it was not over. Miss LaFosse had planned for the night as well, or why the flowers from the florists ?'

The electric kettle boiled. Miss Pettigrew made the tea. She put it on a tray with some biscuits and carried it to the waiting Miss LaFosse.

'You're quite right,' said Miss LaFosse; 'this tea is definitely refreshing.'

Above her own fragrant cup Miss Pettigrew beamed contentedly.

'I always say, a nice, refreshing cup of tea and you're set up for hours.'

'What time is it ?' asked Miss LaFosse.

'Nearly seven,' said Miss Pettigrew.

'Ah !' said Miss LaFosse luxuriously. 'Hours before I need change.'

'I understand,' said Miss Pettigrew with careless sophistication, 'that you sing at a night club.'

'That's right. The Scarlet Peacock. Nick's place, you know.'

'Oh !' said Miss Pettigrew with foreboding.

'Didn't Tony and Edythe look happy ?' sighed Miss LaFosse. Her face took on a dreamy, ruminating look of the female ripe for a little male attention. Miss Pettigrew's heart sank still lower.

'The culmination of all true romance,' said Miss Pettigrew sternly, 'is marriage. Unless the thought of marriage enters both partners' heads, you may be sure there will be no permanent happiness.'

'You're quite right,' said Miss LaFosse meekly.

'And I hope,' said Miss Pettigrew, 'you are not contemplating marriage with Nick. I really couldn't advise it.'

'Lord love you, no,' said Miss LaFosse, shocked. 'Nick . . . married ! He wouldn't be faithful five minutes.'

'I congratulate your acumen,' said Miss Pettigrew. 'He would not.'

'But he's a grand lover,' said Miss LaFosse wistfully.

'No doubt,' said Miss Pettigrew. 'All practice makes perfect.'

'He reaches marvellous heights,' pursued Miss LaFosse pleadingly.

'What interests me,' said Miss Pettigrew, 'is the staying power.'

'Oh !' said Miss LaFosse.

'You see,' said Miss Pettigrew.

'I see,' agreed Miss LaFosse sadly.

'Time you did,' said Miss Pettigrew sternly.

'You do damp a girl's enthusiasm,' sighed Miss LaFosse.

'Only when necessary,' retorted Miss Pettigrew.

'You're getting so stern,' said Miss LaFosse with a twinkle, 'I'll be afraid of you soon.'

'And very good if you were,' said Miss Pettigrew. Miss LaFosse chuckled.

'What's in a drink !'

'Oh !' Miss Pettigrew subsided in a fluster. 'Oh, my dear Miss LaFosse . . . I assure you . . . you are quite wrong. I was . . .'

'There . . . there,' soothed Miss LaFosse. 'Just a

joke. What about a spot of dinner ? What shall I order ? '

' Dinner ? ' said Miss Pettigrew. ' For me ? Oh no, thank you. I'm much too excited to eat. I should get indigestion and possibly hiccups again and my night would be ruined.'

' I'm not very hungry myself,' agreed Miss LaFosse lazily. ' Shall we leave it over then, and have a bite of supper later on ? '

' Much the best plan,' concurred Miss Pettigrew.

She poured herself out another cup of tea. This interlude was very pleasant, but it was getting a little protracted. Something should happen soon. She had only known Miss LaFosse for part of a day, but something had happened the whole time. She sat waiting for something to happen now. She would have been gravely disappointed if events had not kept up to standard. She was not a bit surprised when the bell rang. She leaped to her feet at once, expectancy in her eyes, nerves attuned for battle, murder or sudden death. Miss LaFosse made preparations for uprising.

' I'll go,' said Miss Pettigrew.

But it was only the flowers. Miss Pettigrew slowly returned with the package.

' There,' said Miss LaFosse when she opened the box, ' the very thing.'

A single scarlet rose, in a nest of feathery green, glowed with a brilliant colour. Miss LaFosse tried it on Miss Pettigrew's shoulder.

' Just as Edythe said,' exulted Miss LaFosse. ' That one touch of colour against the black gown and the green ear-rings and necklace gives just the right air of . . . of . . . ! Perfect,' she ended, words failing.

She laid it carefully on the table and sat down again. Suddenly a sense of guilt descended on Miss Pettigrew.

All day she had accepted benefits, chattered in equality with Miss LaFosse, visited Miss LaFosse's friends. What would Miss LaFosse think when she discovered her real mission ? No excuse to say she had tried to tell her. They had been very half-hearted attempts. Obviously, had she really wanted, she could have made the opportunity. There had been numerous periods during the day when it had never even come into her head to try and tell Miss LaFosse. Conscience smote Miss Pettigrew.

She began to tremble, trying to push away the small, clear voice. She wanted to go where they were going to-night, with a pathetic, passionate eagerness. She wanted to visit a night club, to partake of its activities, to be at one with the gay world. Simply and honestly she faced and confessed her abandonment of all the principles that had guided her through life. In one short day, at the first wink of temptation, she had not just fallen, but positively tumbled, from grace. Her long years of virtue counted for nothing. She had never been tempted before. The fleshpots called: the music bewitched: dens of iniquity charmed. She actually wanted to taste again the wonderful drink Tony had given her, which left one with such a sense of security and power. There was no excuse. She could not deny that this way of sin, condemned by parents and principles, was a great deal more pleasant than the lonely path of virtue, and her morals had not withstood the test.

She glanced despairingly round the room. The thought of losing this last, perfect finish to a perfect day rendered her sick with disappointment. But she could accept no further kindness from Miss LaFosse under false pretences. Her conscience had been trained too rigorously.

She came and sat in front of Miss LaFosse.

' There's a little matter,' began Miss Pettigrew in a

135

husky, quivering voice, ' I really think we should get settled before . . .'

' I had no mother,' said Miss LaFosse.

Miss Pettigrew gaped.

' At least,' amended Miss LaFosse, ' there was a woman who brought me into the world. But I didn't choose her. I don't miss her.'

' Your mother ! ' gasped Miss Pettigrew, shocked.

' She wasn't a very nice woman,' said Miss LaFosse simply. ' In fact, she was a very unpleasant woman. You know, the kind that sends shivers down your back when you think of them. Not good for children at all. A very bad influence. Seeing you sitting there, you're just the kind I'd choose if I had my choice. Not, mind you,' said Miss LaFosse earnestly, ' that you're old enough to be my mother. I know that. But that's what I feel. You inspire confidence and affection. I'm glad I've met you.'

' Oh, my dear ! ' quavered Miss Pettigrew. ' I can't bear any more kindness. No. I can't. I'm not used to it.'

Miss Pettigrew's eyes flooded with moisture.

' If you only knew . . .' she faltered.

Rat-tat-tat. Bang-bang-bang. Thump–thump–thump, thundered some one's fist on the door.

' There,' said Miss LaFosse in an annoyed voice. ' Who can that be ? As if they couldn't use the bell respectably. Suppose I'll have to answer it.'

But Miss Pettigrew was on her feet. Her tears had dried like magic. She was electrified, galvanized, quivering like a hound at the scent. That knock heralded no ordinary visitor. Gone was her confession.

She was across the room in a flash. Eyes beaming, face radiant, body tensed, Miss Pettigrew flung open the door.

136

CHAPTER TEN

7.25 p.m.—8.28 p.m.

'HA!' thundered a loud, masculine voice. 'Don't tell *me* she's not in, because I won't believe it.'

'Come in,' said Miss Pettigrew ecstatically.

The visitor strode into the room: a tall man, in evening dress. Black coat, not properly fastened: silk hat aslant: white muffler, floating loose. A magnificent body, a rugged face, a fighter's chin, a piercing eye, a stormy expression. A Hercules of a man: a Clark Gable of a man.

He flung off his hat, tore off his muffler, cast gloves on the floor and glared round the room with the quenching, thrilling, piercing, paralysing eye of the traditional strong hero, but not, like him, silent. His gaze fastened on Miss LaFosse.

'So, you little devil,' he said furiously, 'I've caught up with you at last, have I?'

'Oh dear!' said Miss LaFosse.

She did not even rise to greet her guest. She seemed fastened to her chair by pure fright or shock, or dismay, or at least some strong emotion, Miss Pettigrew diagnosed. Strong emotions, however, at the moment, were Miss Pettigrew's meat. She revelled in them. She got ready to interpose her body between Miss LaFosse and a possible assailant, but the latest visitor whipped past her as if she were not there and towered above Miss LaFosse.

'Well! What have you got to say for yourself?'

'No excuse,' quavered Miss LaFosse; 'no excuse at all.'

'I'm glad you're frank,' he said curtly; 'I wouldn't take even a bilious attack.'

The irate young man grasped her shoulders

'I never have bilious attacks,' said Miss LaFosse indignantly; 'I never overeat. I've got my figure to think of.'

'Stand up.'

Miss LaFosse stood up obediently with a glimmer of smiling relief in her eyes, but to her own, and Miss Pettigrew's complete shock, the irate young man grasped her shoulders and began to shake her soundly.

Miss Pettigrew started forward with a cry of indignation; then she stopped. She didn't know why. Here was a strange young man maltreating her friend and she simply stood like a stuffed dummy and did nothing about it. Nor did she want to. Miss Pettigrew gasped at herself. But quite suddenly she felt that this magnificent young man was quite dependable, would never really hurt Miss LaFosse and that Miss LaFosse probably deserved all she was getting. Yes. Miss Pettigrew admitted that to herself. Quite frankly she confessed in her innermost mind that much as she adored Miss LaFosse she must in truthfulness acknowledge that her friend would be quite capable of doing some deed worthy of righteous anger and obviously this was a case in point. Her wits, sharpened by the day's adventures, were rising to amazing heights of discernment. They leaped at understanding. From the small scrap of conversation heard Miss Pettigrew deduced immediately that Miss LaFosse had done something to the young man meriting anger, for which she had no excuse. She had admitted that herself. The punishment then was only just. Having dealt with children all her adult life, and what, after all, was Miss LaFosse but a grown-up child, Miss Pettigrew had a wholesome respect for a little requisite punishment. She decided to await events. Plenty of time to interfere if it became really necessary. First she must endeavour to grasp what it was all about.

The young man ceased shaking Miss LaFosse.

' I've been waiting to do that for thirty days. Now what have you got to say ? '

' I d . . . deserved it,' said Miss LaFosse breathlessly, but with surprising meekness.

He gave her a grim glance.

' So that's the stunt, is it ? You needn't try and get round me.'

' No . . . no ! ' said Miss LaFosse hastily.

He loosened his hold.

' Because you can't do it . . . not this time.'

' I'm not trying to,' said Miss LaFosse humbly.

He stood back.

' Oh yes, you are, but it won't work any longer. You've made a sap out of me for the last time.'

' Oh, please,' said Miss LaFosse in distress, ' don't say that. Do anything you like. Shake me again.'

' I don't want to shake you again.'

A smile of relief broke through Miss LaFosse's agitation.

' I'm so glad. I didn't really like it.' Her smile became coaxing. ' Well, now that's over, aren't you going to kiss me now ? '

' Oh no, my girl. I don't share any more.'

Miss LaFosse raised a sudden, startled gaze to his. He answered her unspoken question grimly.

' Yes, I'm through.'

' But . . .' began Miss LaFosse.

' There's no more buts, no more evasions, no more excuses. I've finished. You can fool me once, but not twice. I don't stand that from any man . . . or woman.'

' Oh ! ' whispered Miss LaFosse.

' I'm only letting you know. I'm a damn fool over you, and you know it, but I've got limits. You've reached them. You've played fast and loose with me for the last time. You either toe the line . . . or I quit.'

His last words were grim. Miss Pettigrew knew they were true. Felt that Miss LaFosse knew they were true. Miss LaFosse went a little white. Miss Pettigrew came and sat down. Her heart was hammering with excitement. She settled down to the enjoyment of a new situation, but keeping her senses alert to step in and do any rescue work should it be necessary and her powers capable.

'Well,' said the visitor grimly, 'I'm still waiting for the explanation.'

Miss LaFosse crumpled into a chair.

'Oh!' wailed Miss LaFosse, 'I funked it.'

'Thank you,' said the young man. 'I'm glad to learn your opinion of me.'

He ran his hand with an angry gesture through his hair. It was very nice, thick hair, smoothed back in the most correct modern fashion. Not fair, not dark. A comfortable inbetween shade, which left a man a man, without casting him for a blond hero or a dusky villain. He was not exactly young. Not in the twenties. Perhaps the early thirties, but all men, under forty, were young to Miss Pettigrew.

'Oh, please,' implored Miss LaFosse. 'It wasn't that. It was just at the last minute I felt I couldn't go through. Oh! I can't explain. I'm terribly, terribly sorry. I dreaded when you should come back.'

'I can quite understand that,' he said calmly. 'Deliberately to raise a man's hopes, 'til he's sitting on top of the world, then smash 'em in smithereens for a new whim, I suppose! It wasn't a particularly commendable action. If you hadn't agreed . . . but you did. That made all the difference.'

Miss LaFosse gave him another pleading look. Suddenly she began to cry a little. The new-comer frowned, then pounced again. He gathered Miss LaFosse in his arms and kissed her. It acted miraculously. Miss LaFosse gave a watery smile through her tears.

'I never meant to hurt you,' she gulped. 'I never thought you'd feel . . . quite like that.'

'Stop making your eyes red or you'll blame me for that later,' said her kisser peremptorily. 'I know you're just doing it for effect. Unfortunately the effect is telling on a susceptible male. I'll stop yelling, though I'm not sorry I bawled you out. I'd do it again, under similar circumstances, only there won't be any similar circumstances. That, I hope, is firmly in your head.'

His voice went a little grim again on the last words. Miss LaFosse looked at him. He looked at Miss LaFosse. He bent and gave her another kiss, then put her on her feet. He frowned at her a moment, then turned and grinned at Miss Pettigrew.

'How-d'you-do? Don't mind our little skirmish.'

'Not at all,' said Miss Pettigrew.

'Delysia likes an audience. She's accustomed to it. The tears were for your benefit to make you think I was a brute.'

'Oh, please,' said Miss Pettigrew in a fluster, caught between loyalty to Miss LaFosse and sympathy for this odd young man.

'Do I look like a brute?'

'No,' said Miss Pettigrew.

'Do I look like a cannibal?'

'No,' gasped Miss Pettigrew.

'Do I look like a wife-beater?'

'Certainly not,' denied Miss Pettigrew indignantly.

'There,' triumphed the new-comer. 'What more could you expect in a man? Not a brute, not a cannibal, not a wife-beater. A testimonial from your own sex. Damnation, I think I'm too good for you.'

Miss LaFosse began to giggle. She couldn't help it. Miss Pettigrew sat up with delighted interest. The big man's smile was extraordinarily engaging.

'Oh, please,' giggled Miss LaFosse. 'Do behave.'

'That's rudeness,' said the visitor indignantly, 'that's

ingratitude. That calls for a pick-me-up. I want a drink. Good Lord, woman, where's your sense of hospitality ? Where's that admirable gift of a true hostess, anticipation of a guest's wants ? '

' There's plenty in the back,' said Miss LaFosse.

' I'll get it,' offered Miss Pettigrew.

' You'll do no such thing. I can carry a bottle, can't I ? ' He banged into a table. ' My God, Delysia, who the devil furnished this room, it's like the seduction scene in *From Chorus Girl to Duchess.*'

' It's very nice,' said Miss LaFosse heatedly. ' I chose it myself.'

' Your taste is deplorable.'

He charged into the kitchen. They heard him thumping round the kitchen, clattering chairs and table, banging cupboard doors, rattling glasses on a tray.

' A very noisy young man,' said Miss Pettigrew happily.

' You've hit the nail on the head,' agreed Miss LaFosse.

Suddenly howls of rage were heard in the kitchen.

' Oh ! ' said Miss Pettigrew.

' Oh ! ' said Miss LaFosse.

His irate face appeared in the doorway.

' Good God, woman ! ' he roared. ' How many times have I to tell you that Whiskey, W-h-i-s-k-e-y, is a man's drink ? There's rum there, there's port there, there's sherry there, there's even that damn-awful gin there, but not one drop of whiskey. Where's your sense ? Where's your consideration for your visitors ? '

' Oh dear ! ' said Miss LaFosse weakly. ' Won't *any* of it do ? '

' It will not. At the moment I want a *drink*. At the moment I feel I *need* a drink. At the moment I must have a drink. That porter seemed to have an intelligent face. I won't be a minute.'

He stamped across the room and banged the door behind him.

'Oh dear,' quavered Miss Pettigrew.

'That,' said Miss LaFosse gently, 'was Michael.'

'*Michael?*' gasped Miss Pettigrew.

'Michael,' said Miss LaFosse.

'Good . . . good gracious!' said Miss Pettigrew feebly.

She groped for a chair and sat down. It took her quite a minute to gather her faculties together again: banish her preconceived notions of Michael: readjust her mental attitude towards the man in the flesh. Then her eyes began to shine, her face became pink, her body quivered with delight. She sat straight. She fixed shining eyes on Miss LaFosse.

'Oh, my dear!' said Miss Pettigrew joyfully. 'I congratulate you.'

'Eh!' said Miss LaFosse. 'What about?'

Miss Pettigrew was not to be damped. She was now a partisan, and there is no stronger partisan anywhere than a middle-aged spinster with romantic ideals.

'If I were twenty years younger,' said Miss Pettigrew with a radiant face, 'and could, I'd steal him from you.'

'Would you really?' asked Miss LaFosse with interest.

'I've been worried,' stated Miss Pettigrew happily, 'secretly worried, my dear, though I didn't show it, but it has gone. I'm quite serene now.'

'I didn't think you liked Michael,' said Miss LaFosse. 'Your previous tone certainly gave me that impression.'

'I hadn't seen him then,' apologized Miss Pettigrew.

'It just goes to prove how wicked it is to indulge in preconceived ideas.'

'And you recommend . . . Michael ?' said Miss LaFosse in surprise.

'For you . . . absolutely right,' said Miss Pettigrew firmly.

All her troubles had fled. Miss LaFosse's future was assured. No life with Michael could possibly be dull, obscure, frustrated. A fig for her ridiculous fears. He was the perfect mate. Miss LaFosse, married to Michael, would continue to live the gorgeous, colourful life that was her due. Who could imagine a mediocre existence with that young man ? All was well. A load had been lifted from her heart.

'White velvet and a veil and orange blossom,' said Miss Pettigrew blissfully. 'Oh, my dear. I know it's presumptuous in so short an acquaintance, but if you will only let me know the date, if it's the last thing I do, I'd like to get to the church.'

'Oh, Guinevere !' chuckled Miss LaFosse. 'You're going much too fast.'

Her face sobered. She fiddled with the fastening of her sleeve.

'It isn't as simple as all that.'

'Why not ?' demanded Miss Pettigrew boldly. 'He wants to marry you, doesn't he ?'

'He did,' said Miss LaFosse dubiously.

'Did !' Miss Pettigrew's heart sank. 'You *told* me he did,' she implored.

'I hadn't seen him then.'

'What's that got to do with it ?'

'Well. You saw how he was.'

'Yes,' said Miss Pettigrew, 'he seemed a little annoyed over something.'

'I think he was very annoyed,' said Miss LaFosse.

145

'If . . . if I could be of any assistance,' said Miss Pettigrew hopelessly.

'It's very complicated,' said Miss LaFosse.

'Not again,' said Miss Pettigrew.

'It's not a very appetizing story.'

'I can bear it.'

'Well,' sighed Miss LaFosse, 'I'd better try and explain before Michael gets back. Michael wanted to marry me. He kept pestering me. Then in a rash moment I thought if I married Michael, I'd be safe from Nick. So I said yes. He got a special licence and we arranged to get married at once at a registry office. Then Nick came that morning . . . and . . . well . . . I just didn't turn up. Michael went on a blind and when a bobby was trying to run him in for being drunk and disorderly he socked him one and got thirty days, no option. I thought he might have cooled off before he came out, but he doesn't seem to have cooled off.'

'A blind !' said Miss Pettigrew faintly. 'Socked him one.'

Her mind was in a whirl of excitement. By giving the closest attention to Miss LaFosse's story, she had managed to construe it correctly. Through heart-breaking disappointment Michael had gone out and got drunk and struck a policeman. He was a gaol-bird : a drunkard : a man who had committed the most heinous of sins under the British Constitution. He had assaulted a policeman in the performance of his duty. He was branded for life with a prison record. He should at once be consigned to the lowest depths of her contempt. But was he ? He was not. He went rocketing still higher in Miss Pettigrew's esteem. She thrilled at the very thought of him. He was a man among men. All her sympathies poured

146

out to him. Who would not excuse folly when committed for love ? Even Miss LaFosse must be moved
by this powerful proof of the depth of his heart-break.
She turned with quivering expectancy towards Miss
LaFosse.

'He was quite right,' Miss LaFosse was saying. 'I

. . . socked him one

was only pretending I funked it. It wasn't really that.
If it weren't for Nick I think I *might* marry Michael
. . . though I don't know,' said Miss LaFosse darkly.
'It takes a lot of thinking about. When you think
how . . .'

'Oh, but now !' broke in Miss Pettigrew breathlessly, 'I mean now . . . when you've seen them both
on the same day . . . when you see there's no com-
parison . . . surely . . .'

147

Miss LaFosse stood up. She leaned her head against the mantelpiece.

'You don't understand,' she said in a muffled voice, 'I still feel the same about Nick.'

Miss Pettigrew had no words. How could any woman prefer Nick before Michael, however fascinating Nick might be ? The one was gold, the other just gilt. But who was she to advise a young lady with three lovers all at once, when she had never had even one in all her life ! She made a valiant effort.

'Oh, but my dear Miss LaFosse,' said Miss Pettigrew agitatedly, 'please, please consider. Michael is a man. Nick is only a . . . a disease.'

'It's no use,' said Miss LaFosse hopelessly. 'Haven't I told myself all that before ? '

'Does Michael know about Nick ? ' asked Miss Pettigrew sadly.

'He knows we're friendly,' said Miss LaFosse cautiously, 'but, well, not quite so friendly as we are.'

'I should hope not,' said Miss Pettigrew severely.

'What the eye doesn't see . . .' said Miss LaFosse sententiously.

'Quite,' agreed Miss Pettigrew with abandon, without a thought for her old moral standards.

'And now,' said Miss LaFosse gloomily, 'I suppose I'll have to say good-bye to Michael.'

'Oh no !' said Miss Pettigrew, almost in tears.

'Well, you see,' explained Miss LaFosse simply, 'I've never fooled myself about Michael, even if he thinks I have. I knew all along a time would come when he said "the end". I would have to say yes or no. It's come. You heard him. He means it. I know Michael. Oh dear. I know it's dog in the mangerish. But I didn't want him to go.'

'Oh please!' begged Miss Pettigrew. 'Couldn't you say yes. Once it's over you'll never regret it, I'm sure.'

'I don't know,' said Miss LaFosse again darkly; 'there's reasons why . . .'

Michael banged on the door again. Miss LaFosse's reasons remained unexplained. She hastily powdered her nose. Miss Pettigrew opened the door.

'What did I tell you?' asked Michael. 'That man has intelligence. A little tact. A little persuasion. A small inducement, and immediately the necessary is produced.'

He plonked a whiskey bottle on the table. Miss LaFosse produced a corkscrew. Miss Pettigrew brought glasses.

'Say when,' said Michael.

'When,' said Miss LaFosse.

'Soda?'

'No, thanks.'

'Stout girl.'

Miss Pettigrew stood braced for adventure.

'When?' asked Michael.

'*When*,' gasped Miss Pettigrew.

'Oh, come!' expostulated Michael.

'Quit pressing,' said Miss LaFosse. 'Guinevere's refined. She's not like you. She doesn't go round getting drunk and bashing coppers. Put some soda in.'

'I always wanted to taste whiskey,' said Miss Pettigrew happily. 'I've never had it, ever, even when I've had a cold, as medicine.'

'Where were you brought up?' commiserated Michael.

'Sip it slowly,' begged Miss LaFosse.

'Bottoms up,' said Michael.

Miss Pettigrew sipped. She pulled a face. She slipped her glass surreptitiously on the table.

'Ugh!' thought Miss Pettigrew, disappointed. 'Not what it's cracked up to be. Why men waste money getting drunk on that, when they can get a really cheap palatable drink like lemon squash . . . !'

'I feel better,' said Michael.

He put his empty glass on the table, tactfully ignoring Miss Pettigrew's full one.

'Have another,' offered Miss LaFosse. 'Have two more.'

Michael gave her a calculating look.

'Getting me drunk, my good woman, will not alter my sentiments towards you. I always sober up eventually.'

'I didn't think it would,' sighed Miss LaFosse, 'but one can always try.'

'Well. Quit trying. It's no good,' said Michael calmly. 'Now I feel a man again we'll get back to business. What's the answer, yes or no?'

Miss LaFosse went a little white. She stood looking back at him. He continued to gaze at her composedly and her eyes dropped nervously. He dug his hand in his pocket, found a cigarette-case, lit a cigarette and stood waiting, blowing long spirals of smoke into the air.

'Tears in the eyes,' said Michael, 'curls delightfully disarranged, frock just a little too low, mouth pathetically quivering, expression childishly appealing, will have no effect.'

Miss Pettigrew felt her heart tighten. Miss LaFosse caught hold of the back of a chair.

'This,' said Michael gently, 'is for the last time of asking.'

Miss LaFosse flung a hopeless glance of appeal at

Miss Pettigrew. Miss Pettigrew drew a deep, quivering breath.

'Don't you think,' said Miss Pettigrew, not placatingly, not pleadingly, not persuasively, but craftily, in an impartial, conversational voice: the voice of a detached onlooker merely taking an academic interest, 'don't you think, on such a momentous question, a little time should be allowed ? All ultimatums have a time limit. The female mind, unlike the male, is not given to quick decisions. A quick decision is often rescinded. They possess none of that male pride which makes them stick to their word. Time must be allowed them to settle on a point.'

Michael drew in a lungful of smoke and expelled it with a sharp breath.

'Ha ! Perhaps you are right. As you say, due warning is always supposed to be given of an ultimatum. I have perhaps led her falsely to expect I would always dance to her tune. In fairness, notice must be given of a change. A week. A week will always give me time to display all my best points and perhaps sway her in the right direction.'

Miss Pettigrew let out a deep, soundless breath. Miss LaFosse lost her expression of strain and at once looked more cheerful.

Michael swung round abruptly and fixed a stern eye on Miss Pettigrew.

'You appear to be a sensible woman. Look at me.'

Miss Pettigrew looked, with no difficulty.

'Do I look sober ?' demanded Michael. 'Do I look steady ? Do I look honest ?'

'Oh dear !' said Miss Pettigrew in a fluster. 'Must I answer ?'

'You must.'

151

'Oh dear . . . well. Not sober,' said Miss Pettigrew earnestly. 'Not steady, but . . . but *honest.*'

'What?' said Michael, taken aback. He grinned.
'Woman, there's something to you.'

He came and sat beside Miss Pettigrew on the chesterfield. Miss Pettigrew thrilled.

'Do you think it would harm her to marry me?'

'Would it harm her to marry me?' demanded
Michael.

'It would be the very best thing for her,' said Miss
Pettigrew with decision.

Michael beamed cheerfully.

'Discerning female,' he exulted. 'You and I are
friends. Didn't I say you had sense?'

'You mentioned it,' said Miss Pettigrew.

' Have you any influence over that ridiculous mistake she calls a mind ? '

' I don't think so,' said Miss Pettigrew unhappily.

' I thought not. She hasn't got the sense to know when an influence is good.'

' Oh, but she's so nice,' begged Miss Pettigrew.

' She's a damned, irritating wench.'

' But very lovely,' pleaded Miss Pettigrew.

' Yes, confound her, but not the sense of a mouse.'

' But does she need it ? ' asked Miss Pettigrew earnestly.

' A bit of grey matter would do her no harm.'

' But I thought men didn't like brains in women.'

' I do. That's why I'm different, so God knows why I picked on her.'

' She has sense,' said Miss Pettigrew spiritedly.

' Then why doesn't she use it ? '

' I don't know,' sighed Miss Pettigrew.

' Because she hasn't got any.'

' I'm in the room, you know,' said Miss LaFosse in her lovely, chuckling voice.

' Be quiet,' said Michael. ' This talk is serious. We don't want folly intervening.'

' I beg your pardon,' said Miss LaFosse meekly.

' Granted.'

Michael turned back to Miss Pettigrew.

' You and I understand things.'

' I hope so,' said Miss Pettigrew weakly.

' I've had a lot of women in my life.'

' Oh ! ' gasped Miss Pettigrew.

' I've enjoyed them.'

' Oh ! ' a little weaker.

' They've enjoyed me.'

' I can imagine it,' fainter still.

' But I've never wanted to marry them.'

' No.'

' But Delysia. She's different.'

' Obviously.'

' Marriage is a serious business.'

' Assuredly.'

' Now Delysia's a little devil and there's times I could flay her alive, and obviously she needs a little physical correction, but I'm the only right man to do it. But I feel, which I never did with the others, that if Delysia really said yes and married a man, she'd play straight with him. I never felt it with the others.'

' It's the morality of my middle-class upbringing,' put in Miss LaFosse again, very eager to join this interesting conversation about herself. ' When it comes to marriage, a girl can somehow *never* get away from her earlier influences.'

' You're not in on this,' said Michael crushingly.

' Oh !' said Miss LaFosse meekly again. ' I'm sorry.'

' Then act as though you were.'

He turned back to the confused, shocked, thrilled Miss Pettigrew.

' You're a close friend of Delysia's ?'

' Yes,' lied Miss Pettigrew wickedly.

' Well, tell her not to be a damned fool and that I'm the man for her and not that black-haired, oily, knife-throwing dago. Don't think I'm blind.'

' He's not a dago,' said Miss LaFosse furiously.

' If the cap doesn't fit,' said Michael blandly, ' how do you know who I'm talking about ?'

' You . . . you . . .' cried Miss LaFosse hotly and inadequately.

' His great-great-grandfather was an Italian and blood will out. You can't fool me.'

Michael jumped to his feet and glared ferociously round.

'Has that blankety-blank **Caldarelli** been here to-day ?
I can smell him a mile away.'

'Only when I was here,' said Miss Pettigrew hastily,
connecting Caldarelli and Nick at once.

'Ha ! Then you've seen him ?'

'Yes.'

'A bounder.'

'I agree.'

'Not God's gift to women.'

'Decidedly not,' traitor-
ously agreed Miss Pettigrew,
stilling her flutters at the
remembrance of Nick's dark,
passionate glances.

'Not fit to be in the
presence of a lady.'

'I'm not a lady,' broke in
Miss LaFosse hotly.

'No,' agreed Michael,
'you're not. Save me from
ladies. I used the wrong
word. I apologize.'

'I accept it,' said Miss
LaFosse with dignity.

'Not fit to be in the
presence of a white woman,'
amended Michael insult-
ingly.

'. . . singing mushy songs
to mushy *señoritas*'

'Safer away,' agreed Miss Pettigrew.

'What does he remind you of ?'

'Ice-cream,' said Miss Pettigrew.

'What ?' said Michael. His face lit with joy.

'Woman,' he cried in delight, 'your acumen is
marvellous. I could only think of him singing mushy
songs to mushy *señoritas* in mushy films.'

'But how *lovely* he would do it!' thought Miss Pettigrew wistfully.

'Ice-cream,' crowed Michael. 'Marvellous. Caldarelli's ice-cream. A perfect association.'

He swung round towards Miss LaFosse.

'Ha!' said Michael triumphantly. 'Caldarelli's ice-cream. She prefers the son of an ice-cream vendor to *me*.'

'How dare you?' cried Miss LaFosse indignantly. 'You know Nick's father never sold ice-cream in his life. And *your* father sold fish.'

'Fish!'

Michael jumped to his feet. He exploded into oratory. He strode up and down the room. Miss Pettigrew cast nervous eyes on chairs and ornaments.

'You compare *fish* . . . with ice-cream,' cried Michael. 'Fish has phosphorus. Fish feeds the brain. Fish is nutritious. Fish is body-building. Fish has vitamins. Fish has cod-liver oil. Fish makes bonny babies bigger and better. Men give their lives for fish. Women weep. The harbour bar moans. You compare fish . . . with ice-cream. And look me in the face.'

'Oh dear!' choked Miss LaFosse. 'Michael. Do behave.'

He stopped and grinned.

'Be calm. I can't think of anything else. I don't think castor oil comes from fish or the allusions might become more lurid.'

Miss Pettigrew blushed and looked away hastily. Miss LaFosse's gaze fell on the clock.

Michael took the glance as a hint.

'Fixed for to-night, I suppose?'

'I'm singing at the Scarlet Peacock.'

'I'll come.'

'I didn't ask you.'

156

'I'll meet you there. I have a date with another female—pure bravado—but I'll go and cancel it. Not very scrupulous conduct and not usual behaviour, but critical emergencies need drastic measures. If I've only a week to make an impression I'd better start at once.'

He gathered hat, gloves, scarf in a storm of activity. He came across and kissed Miss LaFosse. Miss Pettigrew watched with vicarious pleasure. His face went serious.

'No fooling,' he said quietly.

Miss LaFosse caught her breath.

'I know.'

He came over and gave Miss Pettigrew a resounding kiss. Miss Pettigrew didn't see him go out. She sat back dazed and breathless with bliss. The door banged behind him.

CHAPTER ELEVEN

8.28 p.m.—12.16 a.m.

THE room was quiet for a minute. Miss LaFosse stood soberly by the fire. Then she gave herself a little shake. Miss Pettigrew came out of deep waters.

' Well,' said Miss LaFosse, whose volatile nature never remained depressed for long, ' I don't know about you, but any kind of excitement always stimulates my appetite. What about a spot of dinner after all ? It's past my usual hour, but we've still got heaps of time. I'll order something to be sent up. We needn't have every course.'

She reached for the telephone. She would listen to no refusal from Miss Pettigrew, who protested genteelly she could not touch a bite. Miss Pettigrew's conscience was worrying at the cost. She had accepted so much already from her new friend.

' Nonsense,' declared Miss LaFosse. ' You'll soon find your appetite when the food's in front of you.'

She was quite right. When dinner arrived Miss Pettigrew found her appetite had miraculously returned. No one, brought up on the deadly monotony of insipid stews, tasteless mince, tough roast beef, which had been Miss Pettigrew's lifelong diet, could remain indifferent to the kind of food in which Miss LaFosse indulged.

But though the dinner was delicious enough to excuse

any one forgetting anything but eating, Miss Pettigrew was not to be diverted from her main purpose. Somehow or other Miss LaFosse must be persuaded to give up Nick and marry Michael. Through soup, fish, roast and sweet the battle went on, Miss Pettigrew on the offensive, Miss LaFosse on the retreat. Miss LaFosse would resort to stratagem. When she found herself too hard-pressed by Miss Pettigrew's stern logic she would deftly switch the conversation. With great cunning she would begin telling Miss Pettigrew some highly coloured anecdote of her varied career, and Miss Pettigrew would grow so enthralled at hearing this inside dope on 'How the other half lives' she would be momentarily sidetracked from her main attack. But not for long. The minute the story was over Miss Pettigrew's guns were at once trained on their original objective again.

Time fled unnoticed and just when Miss Pettigrew was thinking triumphantly that at last Miss LaFosse's resistance was wearing thin, Miss LaFosse noticed the time and jumped to her feet with a cry.

' Oh dear ! Look at the time. I'll have to fly. I'm all to change. It's after eleven and I promised to be there at twelve.'

She made for the bedroom in an access of energy, but Miss Pettigrew was not going to let her escape while they were still alone together to carry on the argument.

' May I watch ? ' asked Miss Pettigrew with stern determination.

Miss LaFosse gave up trying to escape.

' Sure,' she agreed resignedly. ' I'm a public figure.'

Miss Pettigrew ensconced herself happily in a chair beside Miss LaFosse's dressing-table. Miss LaFosse's rush died down. The rites of dressing demanded a slow tempo and she was not one to be unduly worried about punctuality.

She took off her frock. She went into the bathroom and came out again. She chose an evening frock. She smiled cheerfully at Miss Pettigrew. She had quite recovered her former good spirits. She sat down in front of her mirror.

' I do often think,' she said cheerfully, ' that the nicest part is the getting ready.'

Miss Pettigrew for once was not to be put off by enticing digressions.

' Can nothing I say persuade you ? ' implored Miss Pettigrew.

' Oh, Guinevere,' said Miss LaFosse, ' you make me feel like an ungrateful pig.'

' I don't care,' said Miss Pettigrew sternly and courageously ' I must speak my mind. You know in your heart of hearts Nick will not remain faithful to you. Some day you are bound to get older. He will not look at you then. When he is fifty, he will still ogle the young girls.'

Miss LaFosse sighed.

' Oh dear ! You do make it so depressing.'

' Why not take the plunge,' begged Miss Pettigrew, ' and risk marrying Michael ? You know,' added Miss Pettigrew craftily, madly flinging to the winds last traces of honour and virtue, ' if it didn't work you could always go back to Nick. It's not as though you wanted to marry Nick.'

' Oh, Guinevere ! ' said Miss LaFosse with a grin.

' I know.' Miss Pettigrew flushed guiltily.

' You artful sinner,' accused Miss LaFosse. ' You know perfectly well I wouldn't dare. He'd beat hell out of me.'

' My dear ! ' expostulated Miss Pettigrew. ' Aren't you . . . aren't you a little extravagant ? '

'I wouldn't like to bet on it,' said Miss LaFosse.

'But there's so much in its favour,' pleaded Miss Pettigrew. 'Try and put Nick entirely out of your mind. Then would you marry Michael?'

'Ah!' said Miss LaFosse darkly. 'I'm not so sure about that.'

'But why?' asked Miss Pettigrew. 'He's good-looking. He's got plenty of money—at least he seems to have. He loves you. What's wrong?'

'He's not respectable,' said Miss LaFosse earnestly. 'Nothing could make Michael respectable. A woman's got to sow her wild oats, but when it comes to *marrying*! It's a serious business. She's got to be careful. There's . . . there's the future generation to think of.'

'Oh!' gasped Miss Pettigrew, utterly flabbergasted, wind knocked out of her sails.

'There you are,' said Miss LaFosse.

Miss Pettigrew refused to be downed. She rose. She clasped her hands. Her face became earnest, imploring.

'I am impertinent,' said Miss Pettigrew. 'I am forward. I am rude. You will turn me out. But I must speak. I like you too much. I can't see you unhappy in the future. This life you lead. Where will it end? Please, please marry Michael.'

'Dear, dear,' smiled Miss LaFosse. 'You mean to put me on the path of virtue.'

'If I only could.'

'Is it so much the best?'

'Indeed, indeed it is,' began Miss Pettigrew. Then stopped. She was not fifty yet, but some day she would be, with no home, no friends, no husband, no children. She had lived a life of spartan chastity and honour. She would still have no home or memories. Miss LaFosse would reach fifty some day. Suppose

161

she reached it equally without home and friends. What then ? How full would *her* memories be ?

' No,' said Miss Pettigrew. ' I don't know whether it is the best.'

' Oh, my dear,' said Miss LaFosse gently.

Miss Pettigrew raised her head. She spoke breathlessly in a rush.

' I have never,' said Miss Pettigrew, ' been loved in my life. I want to know. I've always wanted to know. There are hundreds like me want to know. *Is It Worth It ?* '

' Yes,' said Miss LaFosse, ' to me.'

Miss Pettigrew sat down.

' I am older than you,' said Miss Pettigrew ; ' I am a stupid woman. I haven't your brains, nor your beauty, nor your cleverness. I don't advise marriage from virtue or custom, but from experience. I have no friends, no money, no family. I only wish to save you from that.'

' Oh, my dear,' said Miss LaFosse again.

' As long as he is kind, that is all that matters. I have known,' said Miss Pettigrew, ' in my life a lot of good people, but few were *ever* kind.'

' Oh, Guinevere,' said Miss LaFosse.

' Now the first one, he was kind too,' said Miss Pettigrew earnestly, ' but, well, my dear. I wouldn't advise marrying him. I don't like to jump to conclusions but I *think* there was a little Jew in him. He wasn't *quite* English. And, well, I do think when it comes to marriage it's safer to stick to your own nationality.'

' Certainly,' agreed Miss LaFosse demurely.

' And Nick—well, Nick will *not* make you happy in the long run. I think you know that yourself. But Michael, well, Michael ! ' said Miss Pettigrew, her face shining, ' I won't say much more, because I've been very forward as it is, but I've never met a young man I liked better. And he's *all* English.'

'In fact,' said Miss LaFosse, 'what you mean is Michael's made a conquest.'

'Yes,' said Miss Pettigrew.

'You darling!' said Miss LaFosse. She could restrain herself no longer. She leaned forward and hugged Miss Pettigrew and gave her a kiss.

'I'll think about it, I promise.'

Miss Pettigrew felt quite weak after so much expenditure of force.

'Oh dear! I do hope you don't mind me being so frank. I just had to speak.'

'Mind!' said Miss LaFosse. 'Me? Didn't I tell you I had no mother. No one's ever cared to lecture me before. It's been lovely. I wouldn't have missed it for worlds.'

She turned back to the dressing-table. Miss Pettigrew watched operations with intense interest. She shook her head.

'My dear,' said Miss Pettigrew, 'do you think that so much make-up is, well, lady-like?'

'I acted a lady once,' said Miss LaFosse. 'When it comes to marrying, having a lord as a hubby can help no end in the profession. You've no idea. He was a lord. Or about to be one when the old man died. I always get a bit muddled with titles. So I put on the refined act. I *heard* he didn't like lipstick —he liked kissing. You see the connexion. He was a bit careless about traces and the old lord had very good eyesight and a moral nature.'

Miss Pettigrew, stepping on the accelerator of her worldly wisdom, thought she saw the connexion.

'Well, I acted the lady,' said Miss LaFosse. 'No lipstick, no legs showing. You know. Aloof and keep your distance. None of the come-hither about me. I saw him next week with a bitch of a woman, all lipstick, legs and lust.'

'My dear,' broke in Miss Pettigrew. 'I mean, well, you know, there are other words.'

'Than lust? Well, teach me a worse. I'm willing to use it.'

All lipstick, legs and lust

'No, no,' said Miss Pettigrew, blushing; 'the—er—female dog.'

'But she wasn't a female dog. She was a mongrel bitch.'

Miss Pettigrew thought discretion the better part of valour. She was still bewildered. She thought Miss LaFosse's explanation very un-explanatory and a bit involved and not at all clear, but at the rate she was progressing along the road of dissipation she was much more interested in the lord who didn't like lipstick.

'What happened to the lord?'

'He married the lipstick and legs,' said Miss LaFosse simply, 'when the old man died. I learned my lesson.'

She applied her lipstick thoughtfully. Miss Pettigrew nodded profoundly.

'I see,' said Miss Pettigrew, 'there are very many points to learn in collecting a husband. My ignorance is abysmal.'

'You'll learn,' said Miss LaFosse.

'I am willing to be coached,' said Miss Pettigrew with complete abandonment, 'but my days of conquest are past.'

'Never say die,' said Miss LaFosse.

She applied a last dab of powder.

'There. That's that. Now come along, Guinevere. Your turn now. Remove the old traces.'

Miss Pettigrew hurried into the bathroom. She came back, skin shining like a schoolgirl. Miss LaFosse gathered together the materials for removing the shine. Miss Pettigrew took her place in front of the mirror.

Already there was a mild look of disarray about her person. Miss Dubarry's neat waves were all out of place. Her gown was a little crumpled. Miss Pettigrew had scrubbed her face like a miner from the pit. That subtle air of 'chic' had vanished. The black velvet gown had lost its sophisticated air. It seemed to have set in definite crumples.

'Tut, tut, Guinevere,' remonstrated Miss LaFosse. 'You are falling to pieces.'

She set to work rapidly to reconstruct Miss Pettigrew No. 1 back again into Miss Pettigrew No. 2.

'It's no use,' said Miss Pettigrew resignedly. 'I'll

come apart again. Dowdy I always have been and dowdy I always will be.'

'Nonsense,' disagreed Miss LaFosse sternly. 'That's merely an inferiority complex. If you can look good once, you can look good always. Merely a little practice.'

'I'll never have enough.'

'Don't be pessimistic.'

'You can't turn a sow's ear into a silk purse.'

'You can turn rags into paper.'

'One girl's smart, one girl isn't,' said Miss Pettigrew, warming to the argument. 'Both have the same figure. You don't know why. I'm just the isn't one.'

'Pure nonsense,' said Miss LaFosse. 'Tummy in, shoulders back. That's the secret. If you will walk with a slouch your clothing gets a slouch.'

She completed operations on Miss Pettigrew's face. She firmly and securely fastened Miss Dubarry's waves back into place. She pinned the red rose on Miss Pettigrew's shoulder. Miss Pettigrew smiled radiantly at her reflection.

'For the first time in my life I am enjoying being with myself.'

She donned her borrowed fur coat. Miss LaFosse appeared in a magnificent black evening wrap with a white fox collar. She hastily collected gloves, handkerchief, evening bag.

'My goodness, I daren't think how late we are!'

She suddenly developed another craze for speed. She fled for the door. Miss Pettigrew trotted after. If the small voice of conscience did pipe up, Miss Pettigrew turned a wickedly deaf ear. Not the king and all his horses and men should deprive her of her enjoyment now. She had an excuse. Events had happened so rapidly all day she could claim she was not quite herself. She was in a state of mental exaltation and that covers a multitude of aberrations.

She gambolled after Miss LaFosse, natural colour deepening the artificial, eyes shining, breath excited. She was bound for adventure, the Spanish Main a night club. The very name filled her with a glorious sense of exhilaration. What would her dear dead mother say if life came back to her body ? To what depths of depravity was her daughter sinking ? What did Miss Pettigrew care ? Nothing. Freely, frankly, joyously, she acknowledged the fact. She was out for a wild night. She was out to paint the town red. She was out to taste another of Tony's cocktails. She was a gentlewoman ranker out on the spree, and, oh shades of a monotonous past, would she spree ! She was out to enjoy herself as she had never enjoyed herself before, and all the sermons in the world wouldn't change her course. She was set for deep waters, the multitudinous seas to incarnadine.

She trotted beaming down the passage after Miss LaFosse. Too impatient for the lift Miss LaFosse skimmed downstairs, Miss Pettigrew not a foot behind. A taxi squealed to a halt at the porter's whistle. Miss LaFosse turned towards the driver, but Miss Pettigrew moved her aside. Radiantly, haughtily,

' The Scarlet Peacock,' said Miss Pettigrew, ' and make it snappy.'

They got in.

They went roaring through the lighted streets. Miss Pettigrew sat up straight and stared with glittering eyes out of the windows. No longer were the damp November streets dreary. Fairy signs glittered on buildings. Magic horns hooted insistently. Palace lights shed a brilliant glow on the pavements. Avalon hummed, throbbed, pulsed, quivered with life. Bowler-hatted

knights and luscious ladies hastened with happy faces
for delightful destinations. Miss Pettigrew hastened
with them, though much more aristocratically than on
her own two legs. Now she, herself, had a destination.
What a difference that made! All the difference in
the world. Now she lived. She was inside of things.
Now she took part. She breathed Ambrosial vapour.

Miss LaFosse, seated beside her, slim, graceful, poised,
groomed down to the last wicked little curl, was her
friend. She, Miss Pettigrew, spinster, maiden lady,
dull nonentity, jobless, incompetent, was bound for a
night club, clad in splendour: painted like the best of
them, shameless as the worst of them, uplifted with
ecstasy.

'Oh!' thought Miss Pettigrew blissfully, 'I think
I'd like to die to-night before I waken up.'

They arrived.

CHAPTER TWELVE

12.16 a.m.—1.15 a.m.

A TALL building, discreet, dignified, met Miss Pettigrew's gaze. She stared. Her heart fell. She turned reproachful eyes on Miss LaFosse. Was Miss LaFosse letting her down? Was this a Night Club? A modest light glowed above a double door. A Commissionaire bowed politely.

' A wretched evening, Miss LaFosse.'

' It is indeed, Henry.'

Miss LaFosse mounted the steps. Miss Pettigrew followed much more slowly. The doors opened and closed behind her. Miss Pettigrew gasped. A vision of splendour burst upon her gaze. They were in a large foyer. She had a sense of light and colour, music and scent. At the far end a broad staircase mounted to regions above. Women walked by in gorgeous evening gowns. Men attended them in their suave black-and-white uniforms. All was gilt and glitter, voices and laughter. Miss Pettigrew revived again. Her eyes began to shine. This was like a night club. This was as things should be. This was as the screen portrayed them. A door opened on their left and a surge of music throbbed from the hidden room. Her nose began to twitch like a hound after a scent.

' This way,' said Miss LaFosse.

'Lead on,' said Miss Pettigrew.

Miss LaFosse mounted the stairway. Miss Pettigrew followed. The passages upstairs were equally splendid. No mere show downstairs hiding inferiority above. Miss Pettigrew nodded with approval. This was the thing.

They passed various discreetly closed doors. They

'A wretched evening, it is indeed, Henry'

went into the ladies' cloakroom. Rich carpets, shaded lights, glittering mirrors, attendants hovering to assist them. They took off their wraps, powdered their noses, shook their frocks into place, and went downstairs again.

An attendant hastened to open the door of doors. They passed through. Miss Pettigrew faltered and stopped. An open space, with a shining floor, surrounded by tables, met her gaze. At the distant end the band was silent. All occupants of the tables were free to stare. As Miss Pettigrew gazed panic-stricken, the room grew bigger and bigger. She must walk across that immense floor the cynosure of all eyes. Her courage oozed out of her toes.

'Now remember,' whispered Miss LaFosse urgently, 'tummy in, shoulders back. You will notice there are mirrors. I will seat you strategically and an occasional peep will give you pep. You look swell.'

She moved. Miss Pettigrew took a deep breath and dived after. Miss LaFosse smiled at some one at nearly every table. At nearly every table some one greeted her. They crossed the entire room, and at the far end, near the band, Miss LaFosse stopped.

Miss Pettigrew's knees were trembling: her heart pounding. A further ordeal awaited her. The table was surrounded by people. Dozens and dozens of vague blobs of faces. She managed to produce the sickly smile of a stranger butting into a group of friends. What mad impulse had brought her here where she didn't belong?

Her terrors were groundless, her fears without cause. She focused her eyes at last. There was Miss Dubarry beaming. There was Tony grinning. There was Michael leaping to his feet. Certainly there were other people present. But what did they matter? She was among friends. Miss LaFosse. Miss Dubarry. Tony. Michael. There could be a thousand other people present. Miss Pettigrew's smile spread into a real one of breathless joy.

'Where the devil have you been?' demanded Michael.

'You're late,' accused Miss Dubarry.

'We'd given you up,' said Tony.

'Waiter,' called Michael. 'More chairs.'

'Where the devil have you been?'

They were seated at last. Miss LaFosse did a little unobtrusive manœuvring. Miss Pettigrew found herself in clear proximity to a mirror. She had a quick peep for reassurance, but she was beginning to lose the need for it. She was engulfed in friendliness. She had Tony on one side of her and Michael on the other. Miss Dubarry had flung a hasty whisper in her ear.

'I'm so happy. It's all due to you. Don't forget your promise to visit my beauty parlour.'

Miss Pettigrew didn't yet know what all these passionate thanks were for, but their spirit moved her to joy. Her face began to shine again.

Finding herself so close to Tony, however, she began to feel overcome with embarrassment. She made desperate attempts to remember what she had said to him during the afternoon, but she couldn't. She only had a definite impression that she had been very rude: not at all like herself. She began to grow hot at the thought. Under cover of the general barrage of remarks, she turned to him in shy desperation and touched his sleeve. Tony gave her a comradely smile.

'Oh, please!' stammered Miss Pettigrew in a low voice. 'This afternoon. I'm afraid I was very rude. I can't remember. But I'm sure I was rude. I have a feeling. I don't know what to say. I . . . I'm very much afraid Miss LaFosse was right after all. It must have been the drink you gave me. I'm not accustomed to it. It must have gone to my head. I'm deeply ashamed. What can I say? Please, please forgive me. I didn't mean to be rude.'

'Rude?' said Tony. 'To me?'

'Yes.'

'When?'

'This afternoon.'

'I don't remember.'

'When I was talking to you.'

'We had a most remarkable talk.'

'But I wasn't polite.'

'I don't meet any polite women, I wouldn't know if you were, so I wouldn't know if you weren't.'

'Oh, please,' said Miss Pettigrew in agitation, 'I'm serious.'

'So am I.'

'But you're not.'

'Not what?'

'Not serious.'

'Of course I'm not.'

'But you said you were.'

'I'm sure I said no such thing. Do I look the kind of a bloke who never laughs?'

'I never said you never laughed.'

'You implied it. Never,' said Tony bitterly, 'did I think I looked like Henry.'

'Henry!' cried Miss Pettigrew helplessly. 'Who's Henry? What's Henry got to do with it.'

'You said I never laughed.'

'I said you weren't serious.'

'Why should I be? I have no White Ship.'

'Oh, please,' cried poor Miss Pettigrew. 'I don't know what you're talking about.'

'And you,' said Tony in a voice of bitter disillusionment, 'are an educated woman.'

'What's that got to do with it?'

'Did you never hear of King Henry the First?'

'Of course I've heard about Henry I,' said Miss Pettigrew hotly.

'Then why pretend you didn't and lead the conversation astray?'

'I pretended no such thing. It's you who won't talk sense.'

'Sense about what?'

'About this afternoon.'

'But we weren't talking about this afternoon.'

'Yes we were.'

'Now wait,' said Tony. 'Let's be very cool again. Let's be collected. Let's gather our thoughts with care. What *were* we talking about?'

'About my being rude.'

'Then why,' said Tony simply, 'bring in History?'

'Oh!' gasped Miss Pettigrew.

She stared at him helplessly. Tony gazed straight in front of him. Miss Pettigrew struggled between bewilderment and indignation. Suddenly light dawned. She giggled.

'Young man,' said Miss Pettigrew, 'I think you're teasing me.'

Tony's eyes slid round. They held a twinkle.

'Tit for tat,' said Tony slyly.

'I don't know what you mean,' said Miss Pettigrew, 'but I expect it has something to do with this afternoon. I suppose I'll have to apologize for it as well.'

'Ah!' said Tony. 'Now you're at it again. What's all this apologizing about?'

'My rudeness this afternoon.'

'What rudeness?'

'Not again,' begged Miss Pettigrew, 'please, not again.'

'All right,' agreed Tony, 'but you'd better phrase it differently.'

'My conversation this afternoon.'

'I enjoyed it,' said Tony. 'I was out of my depth, but I enjoyed it. I like originality in women. One meets it so seldom. No apologies are necessary.'

'Are you sure?' pleaded Miss Pettigrew. 'You're not just being polite?'

'Would I,' asked Tony, 'be conversing with you now with such amiability and joy if you, as a complete stranger, had grossly insulted me in the afternoon? Do I look the type to forget insults? I warn you now, an answer in the affirmative will definitely be counted as the first insult.'

'That's right,' agreed Miss Pettigrew more happily. 'It's such a load off my mind.'

'Friends?' said Tony.

'Friends,' said Miss Pettigrew, completely happy.

'There is now no need,' pleaded Tony, 'to keep the conversation on such a high intellectual plane.'

'None at all,' chuckled Miss Pettigrew.

'Thank God!' sighed Tony. 'My historical anecdotes are strictly limited to Henry I never smiling, William the First landing in 1066 and the Crown being lost in the Wash. Connected in some manner by joke once heard.'

'Well,' came Miss LaFosse's cheerful voice, 'if you two can stop flirting for a minute, Guinevere might like to meet the rest. Apologies for putting the dangerous woman beside your man, Edythe.'

'Oh dear!'

Miss Pettigrew turned in a fluster and blushed for her rudeness, soon to forget her momentary upset in a lively interest in the other occupants of the table. There was a stocky young man, with a bullet head, fair, short hair, brilliant, light blue, wary eyes and an expressionless face. He looked like an explorer. Beside him, very close beside him, was a gorgeous woman. She had masses of deep auburn hair and great violet eyes. She was not plump, yet she gave the impression of soft, rounded curves and comfortable hollows. She had an air of Mona Lisa, the Lady of Shalott. All her movements were slow with a lazy, languid indolence. She was dressed in brilliant purple. A great, glowing emerald shone on her finger. Beside the other women, so slim, modern and English, she seemed like some luxurious blossom from another clime. Miss Pettigrew thought romantically the young man must have brought her back from some rich, tropical land.

'Guinevere,' said Miss LaFosse, 'meet Julian. If you want to make your rival tear her hair with envy, go to Julian. He'll dress you. But he makes you pay. He has to stay friendly with me because I owe him a lot of money and he knows if he doesn't stay friendly I won't pay.'

Julian's mouth parted and Miss Pettigrew had a quick flash of white teeth.

'How-d'ye-do?' said Julian briefly.

'He never says much,' explained Miss LaFosse. 'He simply sits and undresses every new-comer in his mind and then re-dresses her as she should be, and when she comes to him eventually, which she always does, he just gives one glance and says at once what she must wear, so she thinks he's marvellous and always goes back.'

'Oh dear!' thought Miss Pettigrew. 'How embarrassing if he looks at me. I shall blush all over.'

'Well, you can't complain of my methods,' said Julian mildly, 'if the results are so satisfactory.'

'Rosie,' said Miss LaFosse, 'meet Guinevere. A friend of mine.'

'Welcome,' said Rosie.

'You mustn't order steak and onions,' said Miss LaFosse earnestly to Miss Pettigrew. 'Rosie's on a diet. She daren't eat them and she adores them. The tantalizing smell would ruin her night. Or worse: she might succumb and fall to temptation.'

'I won't,' promised Miss Pettigrew hastily.

'I went to a doctor,' said Rosie gloomily. 'Damn his eyes. White meat. Chicken! I ask you? I loathe chicken. No body to it. Nothing to fill a girl's stomach. No rich foods. No fatty foods. No fried foods. No potatoes. Hardly any butter. No cakes. What's left? I ask you? Is it worth it?'

'Oh yes,' chorused the other girls, shocked.

'Figures might change,' said Miss Dubarry consolingly, 'then you'll reach the correct standard quite naturally, while we'll all have to sit around all day and cut out dancing and drink pints of cream, 'til we're sick of the sight of it.'

'When I'm fifty,' said Rosie pessimistically, 'when I won't care whether I'm fat or thin.'

The music started.

'Shall we dance?' asked Julian.

He and Rosie took the floor. Rosie melted into his arms with a clinging surrender that imbued the formal hold with a close, personal intimacy. They danced off, cheek to cheek.

Miss Pettigrew watched them with fascinated eyes.

'What a lovely woman!' admired Miss Pettigrew. 'I've never seen any one like her before. Is she a foreigner?'

'She'll grow fat,' said Miss LaFosse darkly. 'You mark my words. You can't say "no" always.'

'She's a harem woman,' said Miss Dubarry. 'I don't like harem women. They let down their sisters.'

'I do,' said Tony. 'They know where they belong and don't get ideas into their heads. One man, he's master. The others don't exist. Their place is the Seraglio. They seek no other. Their duty is to provide the full quiver and attend to their lord's needs. What more can they ask? What more can he ask? Very satisfactory I call it.'

'Bah!' said Miss Dubarry scornfully. 'I like independence in a woman. So do men that are men. He'll tire six weeks after they're married. Dash it all! Strawberry's and cream are all very well for a change. But for a permanency . . .! Fancy living with a woman who never said no.'

'I agree with Tony,' began Michael. 'The women of to-day . . .'

'Be quiet,' ordered Miss LaFosse. 'No arguments. We all know *your* ideas. Out of date. Guinevere, meet the Lindsays, Peggy and Martin. Married a year and not separated yet.'

Miss Pettigrew turned to the remaining couple. Both had smooth, young, lively faces. Both had straight brown hair, blue eyes and cheerful grins. They might have been twins. Martin's hair was brushed smoothly back: Peggy's was cut in a fringe across her forehead and brushed smoothly down over her ears.

'Professionally,' explained Miss LaFosse, 'the Lindsay Twins. Better publicity than husband and wife. Comedy turn. Revue, Variety or anything offered.'

Miss Pettigrew met all these people with delighted interest. Her wide, shining eyes surveyed the room. The drums boomed: the cymbals clashed: the saxophones wailed: the violins wept: the piano cascaded. The music dragged one to one's feet. Made one want to dance. Miss Dubarry and Tony moved away. The Lindsays joined them. Miss LaFosse shook her head unseen by Miss Pettigrew. A young man sang through a microphone. The lights dimmed. Shuffling feet made a rhythm of their own.

'So this,' said Miss Pettigrew blissfully, 'is a *Night Club*! And I was told they were wicked places.'

Miss LaFosse thought of discreetly shut doors upstairs.

'Well,' said Miss LaFosse cautiously, 'there are

179

night clubs and night clubs. You're not likely to meet Royalty here.'

'I have no desire,' said Miss Pettigrew, 'to meet Royalty. It would fill me with too much awe. I am quite happy as I am.'

The music stopped. The lights went up. Their table filled again. The conductor made signs to Miss LaFosse. Miss LaFosse nodded. Miss Pettigrew heard her friend's name announced. A storm of clapping greeted the news. The lights went down and there was Miss LaFosse, flooded by a spotlight, crossing the floor alone, completely at ease, with a careless swing of her shoulders, a masterly sway of her hips. She reached the grand piano and stood leaning against it, one hand on hip, the other laid idly across the polished piano-top. She wore daringly a gown of sheer white. Over a sheath-like slip of white satin, which outlined with cunning design every curve of her fascinating figure, flares of transparent tulle, billowing to the ground, yet managed to convey an impression of artless innocence. There was no contrasting colour except her bright gold hair. The spotlight turned it into a nimbus.

There was a crash of chords and Miss LaFosse began to sing. Miss Pettigrew sat up slowly with breathless attention. Her experience of professional entertainers was small. Her experience of night-club entertainers confined solely to her view of them at the talkies, her lone secret vice. Seeing and hearing one in the flesh was altogether another matter. The white figure, posing against the piano, caught her attention, with that of every one else in the place, and held it breathless.

The professional Miss LaFosse was quite a different woman. Without any definable change of pose or expression she was suddenly surrounded with that compelling aura of the Star. Lounging against the

Delysia

piano with indolent grace, Miss LaFosse gazed round the room with a slow, indifferent glance. Lazy lids drooped over drowsy eyes, which would suddenly open wide with a wicked, mocking humour. She had a deep, husky voice. It was hardly singing. Miss Pettigrew was not quite sure what to call it. Sometimes it was more like talking, but it sent delightful shivers of enjoyment down her spine. Miss LaFosse sang a naughty, delicious song, called ' When Father left for the Week-end, what did Mother do ? ' Miss Pettigrew enjoyed every tantalizing minute of it, even though she went quite pink at what she thought some of it might mean. When it came to an end the room rang with applause. Miss LaFosse sang a popular song hit, then another. After that she refused the encore. She returned to their table.

' O.K., honey,' said Miss Dubarry. ' You were great. No wonder Nick doesn't want to lose you. Glad I'm not a rival, or I'd hate to say whether the friendship would stand it.'

' When do you sing again ? ' asked Michael.

' About half-past two,' said Miss LaFosse.

' Oh Lord ! ' Michael groaned. ' Must I wait until then ? '

' No one's asking you to,' said Miss LaFosse mildly.

' Let's have a drink,' said Tony.

Miss LaFosse leaned discreetly over to Miss Pettigrew and whispered urgently,

' Now remember, don't mix them. Nothing more fatal when you're not used to 'em.'

' What's yours ? ' asked Tony.

' I will have,' said Miss Pettigrew, ' a small glass of sherry, thank you.'

Tony's eyes popped.

' I heard aright ? ' he said anxiously. ' The old ears aren't going back on me ? '

' When you reach my age . . .' began Miss Pettigrew. Tony looked round wildly.

' Not again,' he implored. ' You're not starting again. Wasn't this afternoon enough ? Sherry it shall be.'

Miss Pettigrew looked bewildered.

' Trifle,' said Rosie suddenly. ' Spongecake and

Slowly sinking lower and lower

raspberry jam and being giddy with a tablespoonful of sherry in . . . I'll have a whiskey.'

' You and me,' said Michael. ' Waiter . . .'

They all drank. Various people stopped at their table. Miss Pettigrew ceased troubling with these birds of passage. One's capacity for remembering names and faces was limited.

' Here's Joe and Angela,' exclaimed Miss Dubarry.

Miss Pettigrew's fascinated eyes were on a man at the next table who was slowly sinking lower and lower in his chair. Soon he would disappear out of sight altogether underneath the table. Would, or would

183

not, his companions rescue him in time ? She took
no notice until Miss LaFosse said,

'Guinevere, meet Mr. Blomfield. Joe, meet my
friend, Miss Pettigrew.'

She was so surprised at the formality of the introduction she turned her head.

Joe was looking down at her: a big man, not a
young man, possibly the early fifties. No sign of
middle-aged spread. What might be called a well-
preserved figure. A man looked better with a well-
covered body in the fifties. He was immaculate in
evening clothes: shirt-front gleaming, flower in buttonhole. Massive head, powerful jaw, humorous eyes,
no-fooling-me mouth, hair greying a little, bluff manner,
genial, red face.

His gaze lighted on Miss Pettigrew's face with surprise. Then his lips parted, his eyes lit, his face expanded, with a surprised, warm, friendly smile. One
contemporary acknowledged another. Miss Pettigrew
stared in equal surprise at him, then suddenly her own
lips parted in a shy, diffident, hesitantly intimate smile.
They gave each other greeting. He and she belonged
to a different generation. They reached common ground
for a moment.

'Guinevere, meet Angela. Angela, my friend Guinevere.'

Miss Pettigrew looked at the young woman.

'How-do-you-do ?' said Miss Pettigrew shyly.

'How-d'do ?' said Angela in an indifferent, drawling,
faintly complaining voice.

She was the first friend of Miss LaFosse to intimidate
Miss Pettigrew and bring back all her old nervousness.
She was so very young, so very hard, so very brittle,
so very assured. She seemed to see straight through
Miss Pettigrew's borrowed finery down to what Miss

184

Pettigrew really was and despise her. Miss Pettigrew flushed a little for no reason and sat farther back in her chair.

Angela was dressed in a vivid scarlet gown that fitted her like a sheath, outlining high, tiny breasts, slim diaphragm, narrow hips, tapering thighs. She had pale silver hair. Miss Pettigrew stared at it with fascinated eyes; a platinum blonde in the flesh.

' Dye,' thought Miss Pettigrew with stern satisfaction. ' Dear Miss LaFosse's is natural.'

Angela's face was a lovely expressionless mask, perfect as to detail, but with no life in it to give it appeal. She had great blue eyes, surrounded by long, curling lashes, a straight nose, a lovely pink and white complexion, a perfect, scarlet, rosebud mouth, a coiffure without a curl out of place. She was a finished production of feminine art, but Miss Pettigrew, not having seen her come from her bath, reserved judgment.

Miss Pettigrew sighed inwardly and drew away her eyes. What a pity that such a nice man should be caught by a young chit ! Every sensible woman knew that young creatures never really went with older men except for what they could get, but men were notoriously stupid and susceptible in their middle age.

Mr. Blomfield and Angela were obviously intimate friends.

' Join us,' said Michael.

' If we're not intruding,' said Joe.

' A pleasure,' said Rosie.

' Thank you,' said Joe.

Angela said nothing. She had once heard that too much talking, too much laughing, too much animation, aged one. Apart from the primary consideration that she never had anything to say, she meant to keep her looks.

'Waiter,' called Tony, 'more chairs.'

Their circle was enlarged by the addition of another minute table and two chairs. The band started a tune. Every one got up and danced except Miss Pettigrew, Miss LaFosse and Michael. Miss Pettigrew began to feel a little uncomfortable because of Miss LaFosse. She would assure her she did not mind sitting out a dance alone. She would tell her next time. Even Joe, with rather a martyred expression, was walking ponderously around the floor with the slim Angela in his arms. The music stopped. There was another interval of delightful general conversation. The music started again.

'Shall we ?' said Tony to Miss Dubarry.

'Ours,' said Julian to Rosie.

'Shall we show 'em ?' said Martin to Peggy.

One by one they disappeared. Miss Pettigrew looked after them a little wistfully, thinking of forgotten youth and lost opportunities.

Joe stood up. He loomed above Miss Pettigrew, large, expansive, genial.

'May I have the pleasure ?' said Joe.

CHAPTER THIRTEEN

1.15 a.m.—2.3 a.m.

MISS PETTIGREW started. She gasped.

'Are you asking *me* ?' asked Miss Pettigrew incredulously.

'If I may have the honour,' said Joe with a beautiful bow.

'Alas !' said Miss Pettigrew tragically. 'I can't dance.'

Joe beamed.

'Neither can I,' said Joe. 'I only pretend.'

Serenely he pulled out Tony's vacant chair and lowered himself comfortably beside Miss Pettigrew. He sighed with pleasure.

'Too old,' said Joe. 'Too much stomach.'

'You are *not* fat,' said Miss Pettigrew indignantly.

'Good tailor,' said Joe, 'good belt. Signs though.' He patted his stomach comfortably.

'Indeed there are not,' said Miss Pettigrew still indignant. 'Just a nice filling-out. A splendid figure, if I may be so bold as to say so. Middle-aged men are meant to be solid.'

'Am I middle-aged ?' asked Joe.

Miss Pettigrew looked aghast.

'Oh dear !' she thought in distress. 'Have I offended ? Some men are as touchy as women about

their age. Does he pretend he is still young ? I must
say something.'

Then she thought, why should she ? Hoity-toity !
She wouldn't wickedly flatter a silly old man whom she
would never see again. She looked at him severely.

' Middle-aged you are,' said Miss Pettigrew with spirit,
' and middle-aged you can't escape being.'

' Bless you, lady,' said Joe in his booming, comfortable
voice. ' I'm glad you realize it. Now I won't have to
pretend to hop around like a two-year-old.'

He settled himself lower in his chair with a comfortable
air of permanence.

' Joe.' Angela's high, complaining voice came across
the table. ' Shall we dance ? '

' No,' said Joe, ' we will not. Not this one. My feet
aren't up to it.'

If glances could be daggers, those which Angela
threw at Miss Pettigrew would have transfixed her.
Miss Pettigrew became all hot and flustered, but behind
her trepidation was a wicked sense of rapture. For the
first time in life some one was jealous of her. She became
so exhilarated with the thought she shelved all ideas
of fair play and deliberately hoped Joe would stay.
Joe looked round equably. At the next table the occupants made haste to beam at him.

' Oh, George ! ' called Joe cheerfully, ' Angela wants
to dance and I don't. What about it ? '

A young man rose with alacrity.

' That's good of you, Joe. Come and oblige,
Angela.'

Angela rose with equal alacrity. They danced off.

' I've a lot of money,' said Joe. ' I find people very
willing to oblige.'

' How sordid,' said Miss Pettigrew sternly.

' George likes Angela,' said Joe peacefully, ' and

Angela likes George, but she likes my money better. They'll be quite happy.'

Miss Pettigrew didn't know what to say to this, so said nothing.

'Well, well,' said Miss LaFosse's cheerful voice,

Someone was jealous of her

'sitting out already. I'm surprised at you, Guinevere. Come on, Michael. Two's company's, four's a crowd.'

They danced away.

Miss Pettigrew sat and thrilled. A man had deliberately elected to sit out with her. And such a presentable man! No forced circumstances either. He chose the situation himself. Even if it were only politeness it was a very nice gesture. Her face shone with gratitude.

'Thank you very much,' said Miss Pettigrew. 'It is

very kind of you to sit with me. I was beginning to fear I was spoiling Miss LaFosse's evening. She wouldn't dance and leave me sitting alone. Now at least she can have one dance.'

'Kind,' chuckled Joe. 'My dear Miss Pettigrew, the pleasure is all mine. You're saving me aching bunions and stabbing corns. When I was born my feet were only made to carry eight pounds. The rest of me has grown out of proportion.'

Miss Pettigrew smiled at the mild joke. She was a little nervous about conversation. She was quite unused to entertaining strange men tête-à-tête and didn't know what to say, but she soon discovered her worries were groundless. Talk just happened. No difficulty. It simply arrived.

There were drinks to be offered and refused. There were present friends. There was Joe's career.

'Corsets!' said Joe. 'There's a lot of money to be made in corsets. *If* you can get in touch with the right people. I did. If you can take an inch off a woman's . . . well, I won't mention the place, but you can guess . . . you can make a fortune. Talk about the age of corsets being gone! My eye! You've no idea how these society women fly to me to give them the perfect figure they lack naturally. Do you think Julian's gowns would look the way they do without my groundwork underneath? No, sir, they wouldn't. A protruding, well, dash it all, you can guess . . . back *or* front, could ruin the look of any creation.'

Miss Pettigrew sat fascinated. This was an amazing topic of conversation between a man and woman meeting for the first time, but she found it a thousand times more interesting than discussing the weather. It was not indelicate. It was Big Business. Who would have dreamed yesterday that to-day she would be sitting talking on equal terms with Big Business! Her gentle mouth was tremulous with interest and sympathy. Joe expanded. Angela loathed discussing corsets. Miss Pettigrew loved it. No mistaking real interest. He eyed her professionally.

'Now you've got a splendid figure for your age,' said Joe earnestly. 'I don't think even "Blomfield's Correct Corsets" could do anything more for you. How do you do it?'

'Short food and continual nervous worry,' thought Miss Pettigrew. But to-night she was Cinderella and refused to contemplate her shabby background.

'Oh!' said Miss Pettigrew negligently. 'Nothing at all. I assure you. It's just natural.'

'No children,' said Joe brilliantly.

'I am not married,' said Miss Pettigrew with dignity.

'Men are blind,' said Joe gallantly.

Miss Pettigrew was weak with joy. All these compliments were going to her head. She could have done with more, but the dance came to an end. Tony looked sternly at Joe. Joe said blandly,

'Youth must needs take second place, my boy.'

'Ha!' said Tony, 'monopolize the belle, would you?'

Miss Pettigrew squirmed with pleasure. Joe stayed planted in the chair beside her. Miss Pettigrew was radiant. George had joined the party and sat with unobtrusively adoring eyes on Angela.

'I'm hungry,' said Miss LaFosse. 'I can't sing any more on an empty inside.'

'I thought one was supposed to,' said Julian.

'I'm different,' said Miss LaFosse.

'I'm hungry too,' said Michael. 'The effect of my dinner has also worn off.'

Supper was ordered. The music began again, a

dreamy, melting melody. The couples left the table again until supper should arrive. Joe looked at Miss Pettigrew.

'Our dance, I think,' said Joe.

'But I told you I couldn't dance,' said Miss Pettigrew with deep regret.

'I am quite confident,' said Joe, 'that you do the Old-fashioned Waltz perfectly.'

Miss Pettigrew's face lit.

'Is it the Old-fashioned Waltz?'

'It is so,' said Joe.

Miss Pettigrew stood up.

Joe bowed. He put his arm around her waist. They hesitated a few beats then swung into the crowd. Miss Pettigrew shut her eyes tight. This was the crowning moment. See Naples and die. She simply surrendered herself to Joe's arms and the dreamy, lilting rhythm.

Joe danced it well. Despite his dark hints, Miss Pettigrew felt his bulk only as a comfortable pressure against her own body. In her youth, at the very few social assemblies she had attended which permitted a little mild waltzing, her lot for partners had always fallen among the elderly generation, and Miss Pettigrew well knew the rather embarrassing awkwardness of a partner's over-generous waistline.

'Perfect,' said Joe. 'The modern generation don't know how to waltz. I wouldn't have missed that for worlds.'

Treading on air Miss Pettigrew returned to her seat with flushed cheeks and shining eyes.

'Well, you giddy old fraud,' accused Miss LaFosse. 'Telling me you couldn't dance. You only wanted to sit out with Joe.'

'Oh, please,' said Miss Pettigrew, pink now with

embarrassment. 'I assure you the Waltz is the only dance I know.'

She was haughty with Joe for several minutes in case he should think things. Supper arrived. Miss Pettigrew found surprisingly she was quite hungry again. She set to with a will.

'Have an ice,' offered Michael.

'I will,' said Miss Pettigrew.

She slowly turned each ambrosial spoonful round her tongue

He winked.

'Should be good here. Owner's speciality, I understand.'

Miss Pettigrew relapsed into giggles, despite Miss LaFosse's indignant glare at Michael. But the ice was a marvellous concoction. Miss Pettigrew had never thought she was greedy before, but this was no chilled custard. There was cream and fruit and nuts and ice-cream and a wonderful syrup, all skilfully blended. She slowly turned each ambrosial spoonful round her tongue.

The band started a slow, drowsy foxtrot. The lights were lowered. Only a dull glow pervaded the room. Miss Pettigrew looked up with dreamy enjoyment and saw Nick approaching their table. The ice suddenly lost its flavour.

Nick came threading his way slowly between the tables, his gaze on Miss LaFosse. His face was quite expressionless, his eyes blank, yet suddenly Miss Pettigrew shivered. She had a feeling that only a thin shutter of restraint was drawn over his eyes. Any second it might open to reveal them in full flame.

Miss Pettigrew glanced wildly round the table. No one else had seen Nick. The lowered lights, the treacly music, the rich food, were all conducive to repose and romance. Each couple had edged a little closer together. Michael was the closest of all. His arm was obviously round Miss LaFosse and his brown head bent above her fair one. He was talking earnestly. Miss LaFosse's face wore a serious, almost shy expression.

Nick reached the table.

' Delysia,' said Nick. ' Our dance, I think.'

Every one at the table was suddenly still. The band played on. Dancing couples crossed the floor. The lights remained discreetly lowered. No one noticed the tables in the corner.

Miss LaFosse's body gave a jerk and her eyes came round to meet Nick's. Her face shone white in the dimness.

' Oh ! Nick ! ' said Miss LaFosse in a dazed whisper.

Michael went rigid. Two muscles on each side of his jaw stood out. He shifted his hold very slightly on Miss LaFosse's shoulder.

' Sorry, old man,' said Michael, ' Delysia's sitting this one out with me.'

'Delysia has forgotten,' said Nick in a quiet voice. 'I have a prior claim.'

Turbulent thought surged through Miss Pettigrew's mind. She gazed hopelessly round. All the other couples, with discreet, non-committal faces, were gazing somewhere else. This was between Nick, Delysia and Michael. None of their business and Nick wasn't a pleasant enemy. No help there. But something must be done. Miss LaFosse was slipping. The snake had fixed its eyes and the rabbit was helpless. Slowly, inch by inch, Miss LaFosse was drawing away from Michael's restraining hold. Miss Pettigrew almost sobbed.

There Nick stood, as handsome as sin, brilliant eyes beginning to show smouldering lights, dark face bitter and compelling, body charged with a tense, violent, jealous male anger, willing, forcing Miss LaFosse into the brief paradise of his passionate desire.

Miss LaFosse was already sitting upright on her chair, her wide eyes full on Nick's.

'Are you coming, Delysia?' said Nick.

'I . . .' began Miss LaFosse. She stood up.

With a convulsive jerk Michael stood beside her.

'Delysia.'

Miss LaFosse caught in her breath with a little, hopeless sound. She flung a look of wild appeal at Nick.

'I'm afraid this dance is booked,' said Michael in a choking fury.

'Sorry if there's been a mistake,' said Nick smoothly, 'but I have something to say to Delysia. It's important.'

He turned the full strength of his compelling gaze on Miss LaFosse again. Miss LaFosse took a step forward.

'Lost . . . lost' wept Miss Pettigrew's thoughts. 'If she goes now she will never escape him.'

Gone was all Miss Pettigrew's thought of herself. Every faculty, every nerve, was bent on the hopeless task of saving Miss LaFosse. Her eyes ranged wildly between the protagonists. Michael's desperate face, Miss LaFosse's helpless air of submission, Nick's hard, dark, compelling glance.

Miss LaFosse moved a hesitating step forward. Helplessly Michael exhorted,

'Delysia.'

'I'm . . . I'm sorry,' said Miss LaFosse helplessly. She gave him a tragic glance.

'Oh !' thought Miss Pettigrew, her eyes smarting. 'What will Michael do ? He'll go on a blind again. He'll sock another policeman. They'll give him sixty days next time. What can I do ? What can I do ?'

A light broke on her mind.

'We might be a while,' said Nick.

'*Sock him one*,' hissed Miss Pettigrew.

Michael socked. Nick went down, taking a chair and a table with him. He leaped to his feet, face pallid, eyes blind with fury. Michael danced on his two feet, a look of unholy joy on his face : body poised for action, eyes shining, a glorious grin on his mouth.

Nick's furious leap carried him almost to striking distance ; then he stopped. The faintest, tiniest quiver of hesitation came over his face. The fastidiousness of the Latin. Michael cared nothing for dignity. Nick did. Three waiters rushed to intervene. He didn't stop them. Lights went up. Dancers came to a standstill and looked round in surprise. The band blared out. More waiters appeared. Voices rose in a babel of sound. Miss Pettigrew grabbed Michael's arm.

'Out,' hissed Miss Pettigrew, mistress of fate, kingmaker.

Michael obeyed. Reluctantly : but Delysia was worth more than the satisfaction of a glorious blood lust.

Michael grabbed Miss LaFosse's arm and towed her

towards the door. She went. Tony grabbed Miss Dubarry, Julian grabbed Rosie, Martin grabbed Peggie, George made hay while the sun shone and grabbed Angela. General Pettigrew urged on the troops. Joe rumbled behind her,

'Never did like the fellow.'

They reached the door and tumbled into the vestibule, leaving behind the braying band, the excited voices, the soothing waiters, the raging Nick. The girls hastened to the cloakroom. Miss Pettigrew grabbed her fur coat; then they were downstairs again, the men were waiting, and they all spilled into the street.

The cold, damp November air struck their faces. It was raining in a miserable, half-hearted fashion. Miss Pettigrew's eyes blinked in the gloom after the brilliant lights inside. In the darkness they seemed a far bigger crowd than inside. Every one was talking excitedly, laughing hysterically. There seemed to be about ten voices calling 'Taxi, taxi'. Every female was linked possessively by some male. All but herself. Suddenly, in the crowd, Miss Pettigrew had a lost, frightened, lonely feeling. Her bubble of exaltation was pricked. Suddenly she remembered she was a stranger. Then, loud above the others, a voice was heard shouting,

'Miss Pettigrew. Where's Miss Pettigrew? I'm taking Miss Pettigrew home. Where's Miss Pettigrew?'

CHAPTER FOURTEEN

2.3 a.m.—3.6 a.m.

'HERE,' said Miss Pettigrew in a tiny voice.

Joe loomed above her. He said no word, but his arm went through hers with that glorious, proprietary, warding male attentiveness never hitherto experienced by Miss Pettigrew. She simply leaned on him weakly.

Taxis appeared. Couples bundled in. Miss Pettigrew made to follow, but Joe's grasp was firm. The taxis disappeared. Another cruised by hopefully.

'Ours, I think,' said Joe.

'Where to, sir?' asked the man.

'Just drive on,' said Joe; 'I'll let you know later.'

Miss Pettigrew found herself in the cold, dark interior, out of the rain, alone with a man. The taxi quivered. Miss Pettigrew quivered. But not with fear. With excitement, with bliss. Her thoughts raced with such wild elation she was almost dizzy. She couldn't believe it.

'But I never asked him,' thought Miss Pettigrew happily; 'he chose me all himself. I wasn't even near. He deliberately said he was taking me home. I wasn't even thinking about it. He never need have said a word. It's unbelievable, but he simply must have wanted to. What other explanation is there?'

She was weak with sheer gratification, but she thought

that such unruly jubilation was not quite modest and felt guilty.

'Oh dear!' said Miss Pettigrew. 'What about Angela?'

'Angela,' said Joe comfortably, 'is with George. Didn't you see? They were the first to get in a taxi. He will see her, if less safely, quite as competently home.'

'Won't she be offended?' asked Miss Pettigrew timidly.

'I'll buy her a present,' said Joe. 'She's never offended if I buy her a present.'

'Oh!' said Miss Pettigrew, nonplussed.

'I wouldn't worry about Angela,' said Joe consolingly. 'She wouldn't worry about you.'

'To take another woman's escort . . . !' began Miss Pettigrew, half in real concern, half in a wicked meekness, because she was thoroughly enjoying all this reassurance.

'You didn't take me,' said Joe. 'I took you.'

Miss Pettigrew abruptly cast scruples to the winds. Angela had everything: youth, beauty, assurance, another man. She could spare Joe for one night.

'The address,' said Miss Pettigrew, 'is Five, Onslow Mansions.'

'Isn't that Delysia's address?'

'I am staying with Miss LaFosse,' lied Miss Pettigrew.

'You can't go there yet,' said Joe earnestly.

'Oh dear, why not?' asked Miss Pettigrew nervously.

'Well, live and let live,' said Joe. 'They've only just got together, haven't they? They'll want a little time to themselves. Didn't you notice they grabbed a taxi on their own?'

'Oh dear, what shall I do?' said Miss Pettigrew with a sinking heart.

'That's easy,' said Joe cheerfully. 'We'll drive around a bit first.'

'In a *taxi* ? ' said Miss Pettigrew, scandalized.

' Sure. Why not ? ' said Joe.

Miss Pettigrew sat up.

' Certainly not,' said Miss Pettigrew severely. ' And the meter simply *ticking* round. It would cost you a *fortune*. I couldn't dream of letting you. I am a very good walker, I assure you. Perhaps, if we got out, we could walk back. I'm sure it's fair now. I . . . I wouldn't trouble you to come with me, only I am very nervous in the dark, and I know I wouldn't be able to find my own way.'

She looked at him with nervous apology. Joe went into a low rumble of laughter.

' If they'd all been like you I'd be a wealthier man than I am,' chuckled Joe.

He found the speaking-tube.

' Drive round 'til I give you an address.'

' Oh, please,' said Miss Pettigrew in distress.

' Listen,' said Joe. ' There's a lot of money in corsets. My bank manager eats out of my hand.'

He sank back comfortably. He was finding it a most original experience to be with some one who worried that he should spend rather than that he should not.

' If you're quite sure ? ' said Miss Pettigrew from her rigid posture.

' I'll buy you the taxi,' said Joe.

Miss Pettigrew slowly settled back herself. It was his business. He knew best. She had now quite obviously betrayed her lack of wealthy background. She hoped he wasn't laughing at her, but it was too late now to make amends. Suddenly she just couldn't be bothered to pretend any longer.

' I know there are people with a lot of money,' said Miss Pettigrew humbly, ' but I find it quite impossible to think in terms of pounds. I count in pence.'

'Once,' said Joe, ' my greatest dissipation was a gallery seat at a music hall.'

' Oh, said Miss Pettigrew happily, ' then I'm quite sure you understand.'

She settled more happily. The cold November wind found chinks in the cab and came sweeping in. She drew her fur coat with luxurious bliss more closely round her.

' My bank manager eats out of my hand'

' It is cold,' said Joe, and calmly put his arm round Miss Pettigrew and held her close.

Miss Pettigrew sat in a taxi with a strange man and he had the effrontery to put his arm round her, and Miss Pettigrew . . . Miss Pettigrew relaxed. She sank in her seat. She laid her head on his shoulder. She had never been so wicked in her life and she had never been so happy. She wasn't going to pretend any more. She heard her own voice saying very loudly and very firmly,

'I am forty,' said Miss Pettigrew, 'and no one, in all my life before, has flirted with me. You mayn't be enjoying it, but I am. I'm very happy.'

She found his free hand and very firmly took hold of it. Joe's returning clasp was warmly reassuring.

'I am very comfortable myself,' said Joe.

'Mr. Blomfield . . .' began Miss Pettigrew.

'Why not Joe?' said Joe persuasively. 'Let's thaw.'

'Joe,' said Miss Pettigrew shyly.

'Thank you.'

'My own is Guinevere,' offered Miss Pettigrew timidly.

'So I had heard,' said Joe. 'If I may . . .'

'I'd like you to.'

'I'm very happy to know you, Guinevere,' said Joe.

'I've had a wonderful day,' said Miss Pettigrew confidentially. 'You wouldn't believe it. At first it was watching things happen to other people, but now I am right in it myself. I'll never forget this day in all my life. You are giving it the perfect finish.'

Miss Pettigrew was the oddest lady Joe had ever put his arm around, but he found her oddity giving him a peculiar sense of contentment. She was different, and even a man in the middle fifties can like a change. Certainly her odd conduct, her bewildering remarks, her shy delight, were something he had never struck before. They gave him a most comfortable sense of satisfaction. What, after all, was a baby face . . . only something to look at . . . against the sense of complacency Miss Pettigrew inspired in a man.

'Comfortable?' said Joe, giving Miss Pettigrew a comforting squeeze.

'Very,' said Miss Pettigrew shamelessly.

This was obviously a perfect excuse to draw her closer, and Joe was no slowcoach. He drew her closer. Miss Pettigrew came.

'I don't care,' said Miss Pettigrew suddenly, 'whether you are wishing you were with Angela or not.'

'I am not,' said Joe solemnly, 'wishing I was with Angela.'

Miss Pettigrew turned her head a little and looked at him. Was it the sherry she had taken, or Joe's encircling arm that gave her a sense of audacity?

'I cannot understand,' said Miss Pettigrew severely, 'how sensible men like you can get taken in by the young creatures. You only suffer in the long run and I should not like to see you hurt.'

'I am never,' said Joe, 'taken in by young creatures.'

'Oh!' said Miss Pettigrew doubtfully.

'You see,' explained Joe, 'when I was a kid I had no fun at all. No parties, no dances, no girls. So that now, when I have a bit of money and leisure, I like a bit of life and movement. I buy them a few presents and in return they are very . . . charming. Their youth brings back mine. We both get what we want, but they don't fool me. No, sir, not me.'

'I quite understand,' said Miss Pettigrew surprisingly. 'I have *never* had any fun or amusement. To-day has taught me a lesson. I have discovered a lot of frivolous tendencies in myself hitherto quite unsuspected.'

'Excellent,' said Joe. 'We can enjoy life together.'

The words were only a phrase, Miss Pettigrew knew, but she had a sudden vision of a life rich, varied; a little vulgar perhaps. He would get drunk sometimes. He would undoubtedly shock her. He was not refined. He would bring odd people to the house. Her standards would be turned topsy-turvy, but what a sense of ease, of security, of fullness he would bring to existence!

She stole a look at him. Big, bluff, hearty, a hint he could be a little brutal maybe, but also kind and considerate. He was not a gentleman. Her mother would have been shocked by him. Mrs. Brummegan might have cut him, if she had not first heard of his money. Her father would definitely not have admitted him within the circle of his intimates. She was lowering her dignity as a well-bred gentlewoman in accepting his attentions, but she had sunk so low in one short day she simply didn't care whether he was vulgar or not.

Joe's conventionally encircling arm was now definitely a warm, comfortable embrace. Miss Pettigrew, there was no other word for it, simply snuggled in. She was quite shamelessly happy.

The rain outside had not stopped, but turned to a horrid, wet sleet, neither snow nor rain, that plastered one window of the taxi where the wind blew against it. Miss Pettigrew watched it from the serene comfort of the warm interior of the taxi.

'You were quite right,' said Miss Pettigrew. 'It's not a night to be out in.'

'Catch your death of cold,' agreed Joe.

'Especially in this modern evening wear,' said Miss Pettigrew.

'Very attractive,' said Joe gallantly, 'but not sensible.'

'No real warmth in a single garment,' admitted Miss Pettigrew.

'We have to wear silk too,' said Joe gloomily.

'Wool,' said Miss Pettigrew. 'I don't care what people say. Wool is still the best wear for winter.'

'I quite agree,' said Joe fervently. This was a vital subject.

'But the young girls!' Miss Pettigrew shook her head. 'Silk it is and silk it has to be. No warmth at all. I don't know how they don't all die of pneumonia. You cannot make them understand that they look *better* for wool. A warm body means a glowing face. A cold body means a pinched look and a red nose.'

'What about the men?' said Joe with earnest gloom. 'I'm used to wool. I was brought up on wool. My mother insisted on wool. I like my woollen vest and pants. But dare I wear them! No. I don't. They'd think I was an old fogey. They think I should wear silk as well as themselves. I'd blush if they discovered me in wool.'

'I presume,' said Miss Pettigrew scornfully, 'you are speaking of the young girls you are so fond of. You are a very stupid man. You should remember your age. No. I will not flatter you. You are *not* a young man. You will undoubtedly get rheumatism. You go straight home to-night and to-morrow insist on pure woollen underwear. Whether I am rude or not, let me tell you this. They won't get romantic over you whether you wear silk or wool. So you may just as well wear wool and be comfortable.'

'Could you?' asked Joe.

'Could I what?'

'Get romantic over me?'

Miss Pettigrew blushed. She positively wriggled with pleasure. She looked almost arch. This, thought Miss Pettigrew delightedly, is flirting Why had she waited so long to savour its enjoyment?

'I,' said Miss Pettigrew subtly, 'am not a young girl.'

'Ah!' triumphed Joe, who was all there. 'Then you could?'

'I might,' said Miss Pettigrew coyly.

'I insist.'

'I am not in the habit,' said Miss Pettigrew with tremendous boldness, 'of getting romantic over every handsome man I meet.'

'Me?' said Joe, pleased. 'Handsome?'

'No mock modesty,' said Miss Pettigrew. 'You know there is no need for you to worry over looks.'

'I return the compliment,' said Joe.

They were both pleased. Joe beamed. Miss Pettigrew felt immensely at ease. She ventured another sly allusion.

'Woollen underwear,' said Miss Pettigrew.

Joe's delighted, booming laugh rang out. His wits were never slow.

'It leads one's thoughts astray,' chuckled Joe, 'but in the right direction.'

Miss Pettigrew looked demure.

'I will revert to sense and warm vests to-morrow,' promised Joe.

A common belief in woollen underwear was a bond to shatter the last barrier of constraint. They obviously had important tastes in common. Miss Pettigrew held very firmly to his warm, free hand. Joe's arm remained around her. They were both content. To Joe, the knowledge that at his age, fifty-five, his arm round a woman definitely thrilled her, gave him a thrill in return. It made him feel years younger. With those brazen young girls, you were never sure.

'Speaking of clothes,' said Joe, 'I know a bit about clothes. Got to in my job. Your black get-up lacked only the one touch.'

'What's that?' asked Miss Pettigrew, faintly dashed, but intensely interested.

'Pearls,' said Joe. 'A string of pearls and you were perfect.'

'Pearls!' gasped Miss Pettigrew. 'Me? I've never even owned an imitation string in all my life.'

'I'll buy you some,' said Joe simply.

Miss Pettigrew sat very still. It had come at last. A man was trying to buy her with presents. It was the first step: a crucial moment. Always, in films, when the man produced the first gift of jewellery, you *knew* that danger hovered. He was that sort of man! No good man offered a lady gifts. Not jewellery! There was something sinister, subtly immoral about the offer of jewellery. Chocolates, yes, flowers, handkerchiefs, extravagant dinners and theatres, but not jewellery, not fur coats. Fur coats and jewellery were the bad man's betrayal: the good girl's warning.

'All my life,' said Miss Pettigrew, 'I've longed for some jewellery. I'd love some.'

'I'll get you some to-morrow,' said Joe.

'I'll accept,' said Miss Pettigrew.

'Why not?' asked Joe in surprise.

'Ladies don't,' said Miss Pettigrew.

'Are you a lady?'

'Yes,' said Miss Pettigrew.

'I knew it,' said Joe gloomily. 'I suspected it. I felt you were different.'

'I'm sorry,' said Miss Pettigrew humbly.

'It does rather complicate matters, doesn't it?' said Joe sadly.

'Does it?' said Miss Pettigrew.

'Doesn't it?' said Joe hopefully.

'No,' said Miss Pettigrew. 'I find it much pleasanter not to be a lady. I have been one all my life. And what have I to show for it? Nothing. I have ceased to be one.'

'Ah!' said Joe, brightening. 'That simplifies matters.'

'What matters?' asked Miss Pettigrew.

'A kiss matters,' said Joe tentatively.

'Oh!' said Miss Pettigrew.

She became bold.

'I'm not so sure.'

'Then . . . suppose we try it.'

They tried it. Inexpertly, it is true, on Miss Pettigrew's part, but Joe's tuition was sound, his technique polished.

When Miss Pettigrew at last left Olympus and came back to earth, she was a changed woman. She never need hang her head again. She could now speak with authority. She was inexperienced no longer. She had been kissed soundly: with experience, with mastery,

' Then . . . suppose we try it '

with ardour. Her face had such a radiance Joe felt humble.

' I've never been kissed before,' said Miss Pettigrew.

' Then I'm a lucky man,' said Joe. ' I shall make up for lost time.'

Miss Pettigrew started.

' Oh dear ! I had forgotten all about the time. What will Miss LaFosse think ? I must return at once.'

Miss Pettigrew became agitated. Joe was a sensible man. He acted the gentleman at once. He sat up and picked up the speaking-tube.

'Five, Onslow Mansions,' said Joe.

The taxi slowed, wheeled, turned.

'If I may,' said Joe, 'I will call at Delysia's in the morning and take you to lunch.'

Reality, like a thousand tons of bricks, came tumbling about Miss Pettigrew.

'I won't be there,' said Miss Pettigrew in a flat voice.

'That doesn't matter. Where will you be ?'

'I don't know,' said Miss Pettigrew.

'Don't know,' said Joe in surprise.

Miss Pettigrew slowly sat up. She turned away her head. She fought to keep back weak, hopeless tears.

'I have been leading you astray,' said Miss Pettigrew in a muffled voice. 'I am not what you think I am. I never thought you would ever want to see me after to-night, so I didn't think you need know. I must tell you the truth now.'

'I often think,' said Joe cautiously, 'that truth is the better course, but if you don't want to tell me . . .'

'I have lied to you,' said Miss Pettigrew. 'I am not really a friend of Miss LaFosse.'

'But she said you were,' said Joe, bewildered.

'She was only being kind,' said Miss Pettigrew. 'These clothes I have on. They're not mine. They're hers. She only loaned them to me for the night.'

'What's that got to do with it ?' asked Joe.

'This face you see,' said Miss Pettigrew valiantly, 'which I . . . I think you like. It isn't really mine. Miss Dubarry and Miss LaFosse just made it up on top of my own. I'm really a very plain, dowdy, spinster. You wouldn't really like me.'

' I think I might,' said Joe, manfully keeping his face straight.

' I happened to do a little thing for Miss LaFosse this morning,' explained Miss Pettigrew in a tremulous voice, ' and she very kindly entertained me all day and brought me to-night, but she doesn't really know me.'

' Don't you think,' said Joe, ' if you, well, began at the beginning. I'm a little bewildered.'

' I met Miss LaFosse for the first time in my life this morning,' confessed Miss Pettigrew, ' when I went there to try and get a post.'

She thought she had better not tell Joe what kind of a post, as he might know nothing about the child, or children, Miss LaFosse probably had tucked away, so she skipped the employment tactfully and in a stammering voice told Joe the history of her day's adventures. Joe was delighted with them. He thumped his knee with appreciation.

' You're a world's wonder,' said Joe delightedly. ' What do I care whether you are in work or out of work ! What's your real address ? I'll call there.'

Miss Pettigrew flushed, then went white. She stammered painfully.

' I haven't any. I owe my landlady rent. She said if I did not get a post to-day, I had to leave. I have not got a post.'

' If I could be of any assistance,' offered Joe tactfully.

' Oh, perhaps you could.' Miss Pettigrew turned with eager hopefulness. ' You seem such an important man. You must know a lot of people. Perhaps among your numerous friends one of them might be wanting a governess and you could at least mention my name. That's what I am. A governess.'

' Oh ! ' said Joe, whose offer of assistance had meant a much more immediate pecuniary advantage.

'Of course I will,' he added hastily. 'I am quite sure I will be able to find you something. Have no fear.'

Miss Pettigrew's face lightened with pathetic relief, then clouded again.

'Oh dear!' she said in distress. 'I had better be honest. I mean, it wouldn't be fair to you, giving a personal recommendation, not knowing. I am not a very good governess,' said Miss Pettigrew hopelessly. 'It would have to be a very simple post. In my last place I'm afraid the term governess was only a polite fiction for a kind of nursemaid. You had better know the worst.'

'I quite understand,' said Joe. 'The difficulty is not insurmountable.'

'You are so kind,' stammered Miss Pettigrew.

'And now,' said Joe, 'I'm very lonely back here all by myself.'

He drew Miss Pettigrew back and his arm, very firmly, went round her again.

They arrived at Onslow Mansions. Joe dismissed the taxi and came into the building with Miss Pettigrew. The hall was empty. The night porter was not in sight. Joe prepared to ascend with Miss Pettigrew to have a private word with Miss LaFosse, but Miss Pettigrew stayed him.

'If you don't mind,' said Miss Pettigrew shyly, 'I had better go up alone. Miss LaFosse has been exceptionally good to me. I could not take it upon myself to bring up an uninvited guest. It would be trespassing on her kindness too much. I could not do such a thing. I am quite sure she would not like it.'

'Just as you wish,' said Joe, valiantly trying to reach Miss Pettigrew's standard of politeness, and to see Miss LaFosse as an outraged hostess. Delysia, he was well aware, wouldn't notice anything amiss if Miss Pettigrew arrived back with ten strange men.

'Here is my card,' said Joe firmly. 'You are to be there to-morrow at twelve prompt. If you do not come I shall put detectives on your track. Promise.'

'Oh!' whispered Miss Pettigrew. 'You really think you will be able to find something for me?'

'I am quite sure,' said Joe with such a meaning glance that Miss Pettigrew's heart missed two beats, 'I will be able to find some position for you.'

'Oh, thank you,' said Miss Pettigrew breathlessly. 'I . . . I wouldn't trouble you only . . . only I'm getting a little cowardly. It is so very worrying being out of a position.'

'No trouble,' said Joe. 'A pleasure. No more worrying.'

'Good night,' said Miss Pettigrew shyly. 'And thank you for the happiest night of my life.'

She held out her hand, but Joe was not accustomed to such formality. Miss Pettigrew was once more engulfed in a hearty masculine embrace and soundly kissed.

'Until to-morrow,' said Joe.

Miss Pettigrew walked up the first few stairs a little dazed with happiness.

Joe routed out the night porter and inquired Miss LaFosse's telephone number. He waited ten minutes and put through a call.

'Hallo!' said Miss LaFosse's voice.

'That you, Delysia?' inquired Joe.

'Yes,' said Miss LaFosse. 'Who's that?'

'It's me, Joe, but don't say anything. Miss Pettigrew there?'

'Yes.'

'Keep her to-night, will you?'

'Sure.'

'I'll explain in the morning. Don't tell her.'
'That's O.K.'
'I'll be around early.'
'Not too early. I'll keep the bird.'
'Right you are. Good-bye.'
'Good-bye.'
Joe hung up the telephone.

CHAPTER FIFTEEN

3.6 a.m.—3.47 a.m.

MISS PETTIGREW walked up the first few stairs like a sleep-walker. Her feet sank into the deep carpet. The building was silent. Dim lights lit the stairs and corridors. The quietness induced meditation. Slowly her sense of happiness departed. She faltered. Her steps lagged. Her fairy-tale world faded. She stared in front of her at a phantom fear which loomed ahead.

Her day was over. It had been a wonderful day, but it was over. She saw herself clearly again just as she really was: as she had been on her first trip up these stairs so short a time ago, penniless, out of work, nervous, unattractive. That was her real self. She had been something a little eccentric and highly entertaining to Miss LaFosse for a day, and Miss LaFosse was accustomed to indulge her whims, but she knew quite well what Miss LaFosse's final reaction would be.

She would arrive, give Miss LaFosse back her clothes, put on her old ones again, return to her old self, look a little seedy, a little down-at-heels, unprepossessing. Miss LaFosse would feel uncomfortable and a little irritated and would wonder how she could most conveniently rid herself of an encumbrance.

Miss Pettigrew couldn't bear her to think that. Anything rather than that. She made a terrified vow.

214

She would rush in, pretend she was in a hurry, hustle into her own clothes, give hasty thanks and make a quick departure. Miss LaFosse's memory of her shouldn't be tinged by a single minute's discomfort.

Having made this courageous vow, Miss Pettigrew's steps still refused to quicken. Instead they went even slower and slower, while she tried to fight off a paralysing terror. Mrs. Pocknall would never let her in now. She would never dare knock up Mrs. Pocknall at this scandalous hour. She would have to walk the streets for the remainder of the night. She leaned trembling against the wall.

After a few seconds' complete submission to panic she slowly resumed her upward climb. She reached Miss LaFosse's corridor: saw the now familiar door. Was it only this morning she had looked upon it as a strange door and approached it with timid apprehension, wondering what reception it had for her, dreading failure, praying for once her fear would be wrong, never in wildest imagination dreaming what did await her ?

'But it's over,' thought Miss Pettigrew. 'I've had my day. I have been very lucky. Some never even have that. I must be brave.'

She took another step towards the end. The silky fur of Miss LaFosse's coat still enveloped her, but it was only there in fact, not in spirit. In spirit Miss Pettigrew was again wearing her old tweed coat, her battered felt hat, her down-at-heels shoes. In spirit she was the ineffective governess again, with neither courage, initiative nor charm. No man would ever like her as she really was. Flirting was a charming game. Men knew you expected them to flatter you and gratified your wish, but they expected you also to greet their remarks in like spirit. It was only her stupid inexperience which had made her take everything seriously.

If she turned up to-morrow in her true guise, would not Mr. Blomfield wonder what in heaven's name to do with her and how to get rid of her politely? She would sit in an agony of hurt and shame and embarrassment. She could not face it. She would never go near him again.

'No . . . No. Never that,' whispered Miss Pettigrew to herself. 'At least he shall always think of me as he saw me to-night.'

She stood at Miss LaFosse's door while the seconds ticked a minute. She could not bring herself to ring, to end everything.

'You have been very kind, my dear,' thought Miss Pettigrew; 'I will not embarrass you.'

She lifted her hand slowly and pressed the bell. The bell trilled inside. There was a short wait. The door flew open.

'Guinevere,' cried Miss LaFosse. 'You naughty girl. You giddy old kipper. Where have you been? I thought I'd lost you. Come in at once. Has Joe seduced you? Tell me the worst.'

'I must hur . . .' began Miss Pettigrew feebly, still determined on her resolve, but Miss LaFosse, standing there, looking as lovely, but much happier than the first time she saw her, and greeting her with obvious pleasure and welcome, made a coward of her again.

'Come in to the fire at once,' ordered Miss LaFosse. 'You look half-frozen. Michael, move that sheer hulk from in front of the warmth.'

Miss Pettigrew was drawn towards the fire. Michael bounded to his feet. He descended on Miss Pettigrew. She found herself enveloped in a mighty hug. He swung her off her feet and kissed her soundly.

'I've never wanted to hug a woman so much before. No. Not even you, Delysia. I'd have stayed here all night till you came.'

216

Miss Pettigrew was bewildered. She had no idea what all this exuberance was about. She was too wrapped up in her own troubles. But that did not mean she did not enjoy it. She did. She had never thought kissing was so truly delightful before. She was getting greedy for kisses. What she would do, when she returned to her old life and no more came her way, she did not know. Pink with pleasure she was put on her feet again. Miss LaFosse hovered solicitously, beaming at them both.

'Let me help you off with your coat,' offered Miss LaFosse.

'Sit here,' said Michael.

The fire was glowing brightly. The chesterfield was drawn up to its heat. A pot of coffee and cups stood on a side table. Its comforting smell filled the room. Its aroma seduced her courage. Miss Pettigrew had to force herself to speak.

'I really must . . .' began Miss Pettigrew again bravely.

'Have a cup of coffee,' said Michael. 'You must have a cup of coffee. Chills are dangerous on a night like this. Give me clear frost any day.'

He picked up the coffee-pot. Miss Pettigrew found a steaming cup in her hand.

'I'll have another,' said Miss LaFosse.

'So will I,' said Michael.

'Sit down,' said Miss LaFosse again, to the still-standing Miss Pettigrew. 'Draw up to the fire. There's such a heap to talk about. Where have you been so long ?'

'Me first,' said Michael. 'I've simply got to know how . . .'

The telephone bell rang.

'Bother,' said Miss LaFosse, getting up. 'At this hour ! How do they know I'm not in bed ?'

217

'Knowing you, I expect,' said Michael.

Miss LaFosse picked up the receiver.

'Hallo ! . . . Yes. Who's that ? . . . Yes. . . . Sure. . . . That's O.K. . . . Not too early. I'll keep the bird. . . . Good-bye.'

Miss Pettigrew had stood up and laid down her coffee-cup. The telephone ringing was always momentous. It might presage anything. Michael had also risen and laid down his cup. His expression was slightly tense. If that bounder Caldarelli was trying a last-minute assault, he'd finish him. By God ! Even if he had to murder him.

'All serene,' said Miss LaFosse casually. 'Just a pal.'

Michael relaxed and turned beaming to Miss Pettigrew who was still standing a little uncertainly, trying to pluck up courage to begin her little act of exit.

'Sit down and tell me where you've been,' demanded Miss LaFosse again.

'I'm first,' said Michael. 'I've got to know. I can't rest until I do know. How did you do it ? How was the brainwave born ? How could a respectable maiden lady provoke such a shattering of all the canons of good behaviour ? I'm not conventional. I never have been, yet I must confess it never entered my head to flout all the rules and sock a man on the jaw. There I stood, like a stuck pig, and it took you at the critical moment to direct my brain to the sensible, masculine deed that should have been done months ago.'

'Oh !' exclaimed Miss Pettigrew, light dawning.

'Tell me,' pleaded Michael. 'Whence the inspiration ?'

Miss Pettigrew looked a little sheepish. It was all so simply explained, but if they liked to think she was marvellous, she could not resist the flattery.

Still standing a little uncertainly, trying to pluck up courage to
begin her little act of exit

'Expound,' begged Michael.
'Ethel M. Dell,' said Miss Pettigrew.
'Eh?' said Michael.
'Riddle-me-ree,' said Miss LaFosse.

'Simple,' said Miss Pettigrew modestly.

'To you,' said Miss LaFosse, 'not to me.'

'Speech,' said Michael.

The floor was Miss Pettigrew's. She took it.

'Oh !' said Miss Pettigrew tremulously, 'the explanation is simple. I have passed through life with very little experience, but I still have Feminine Instincts. Deep in the female breast burns a love of the conquering male. Ethel M. Dell knew her sex. All her men were he-men. I know my sex too, though I am stupid on other subjects. I remembered you were a he-man too. You had socked a policeman. If Nick had sprung up and given battle, all would have been lost. Even if you had beaten him, which was very likely, seeing you are a bigger man, his willingness would still have beaten you. But I banked on the fact that Nick would funk it. He seemed the kind who might. It was a gamble, but I risked it. It came off. That is all.'

Miss Pettigrew ended breathlessly.

'All,' breathed Michael.

'She knows everything,' said Miss LaFosse in awe.

'What a woman !' said Michael.

'What a witch !' said Miss LaFosse.

'I *must* do homage,' said Michael.

He kissed Miss Pettigrew again. All blushes, thoroughly enjoying it, Miss Pettigrew said happily.

'You will make Miss LaFosse jealous.'

'That you might,' agreed Miss LaFosse. 'But even if you did take him from me, I'd have to admit the best man won.'

'I was so terrified you would choose the wrong man,' gasped Miss Pettigrew in relief. 'You *have* chosen the right one, haven't you ?'

'Yes,' said Miss LaFosse.

' You bet,' said Michael.

' The relief . . . ! ' said Miss Pettigrew weakly.
' You've no idea.'

' Sit down,' triumphed Michael. ' Draw up and exult.'

' Your coffee,' worried Miss LaFosse; ' it must be quite cold. I shall get some fresh. Michael shall help.'

She winked at Michael. Michael followed her into the kitchen.

' That was Joe on the 'phone . . .' whispered Miss LaFosse out of hearing.

They brought back hot coffee. Miss Pettigrew found herself back in her chair in front of the warm fire, coffee-cup in hand, vow forgotten. She had to hear details.

' Tell me,' said Miss Pettigrew with excited, shining eyes.

' We're going to get married,' said Miss LaFosse.

' At once,' said Michael.

They sat looking like two happy children. It was impossible to have any one so intensely interested in their welfare as Miss Pettigrew without feeling gratification. It made their marriage not just one among a million, but one of some peculiar importance. Michael leaned forward and touched Miss Pettigrew's hand, his humour gone.

' Thanks to you,' said Michael in a low voice.

' I'm so happy,' said Miss Pettigrew shyly. ' All my fears at rest.'

' So am I,' said Miss LaFosse.

' Then you approve of me ? ' asked Michael.

' Yes.'

' Despite my . . . flamboyant temperament,' challenged Michael with a twinkle.

'Because of it,' said Miss Pettigrew.

'Expound the oracle,' said Michael.

'There are people and people in the world,' explained Miss Pettigrew. 'Some are meant for quiet domesticity. Some are not. Miss LaFosse is not. Neither are you. It is right you should mate. It's only when the wrong halves insist on trying to join that you get all the trouble.'

'Then you don't believe the wedding-bells should sound like closing-time?' asked Michael with rising spirits.

'I am no authority on inebriate psychology,' said Miss Pettigrew severely; 'though an outside observer, I've been on the inside of many marriages. This old-fashioned idea of settling down on marriage,' lectured Miss Pettigrew carefully, 'is quite right in its way, as long as the right couple settles down together. But if the right couple don't wish to settle down, they do not cease to be right. There is weight of evidence to support this view.'

'The weight of evidence has taken a load off my mind,' said Michael solemnly.

'It's a great comfort,' said Miss LaFosse, 'to be a right couple.'

'I have no wish to settle down,' decided Michael.

'Domesticity is dead,' concurred Miss LaFosse.

'Two minds with but a single thought,' said Michael.

'And that one bright, but hardly proper,' said Miss LaFosse.

'Once,' said Miss Pettigrew contemplatively, 'I thought otherwise. I belonged to the settling-down brigade. It was my highest ideal of married bliss. But to-day I have learned a lot.'

'Ah!' said Miss LaFosse with acumen. '"I hear those gentle voices calling." You got on well with Joe.'

' Mr. Blomfield is a very charming man,' said Miss Pettigrew with reserve.

' You couldn't call him a settler-down.'

' I gathered not.'

' But you like him.'

' We seemed to have tastes in common,' said Miss Pettigrew cautiously.

' Hark at the woman ! ' said Michael. ' What siren strains are these ? Tastes in common ! Pigging in to the fleshpots of Egypt ? What has she done to Joe ? '

' I insist,' demanded Miss LaFosse with interest, ' on learning what dark deeds you have been up to with my old friend Joe.'

' Yes, young woman,' said Michael. ' Explain. You arrive with complete effrontery, no explanation, three-quarters of an hour after us, although we all left together.'

Miss Pettigrew flushed and looked a little guilty.

' I know,' joyously claimed Miss LaFosse. ' He kissed her.'

' He'd be a fool if he didn't,' commented Michael.

Miss Pettigrew's face was a complete give-away.

' I knew it,' triumphed Miss LaFosse. ' You sly minx. After all your lectures to me. Taking poor Joe for a joy-ride. What chance had he against your charms ? '

' These abandoned women.' Michael shook his head.

Miss Pettigrew hastily gathered together the shreds of her tattered dignity.

' I assure you,' said Miss Pettigrew earnestly, ' I did it for the best. Mr. Blomfield said you had just got together and would definitely not want to be disturbed for a little while. He suggested a short run until you had time to . . . to get yourselves adjusted.'

Michael grinned.

'Sound man, Joe. I'll stand him a drink next time I see him.'

'I don't believe it,' said Miss LaFosse. 'You turned the glad eye on him and he couldn't resist you.'

Suddenly Miss Pettigrew giggled, looked naughtily wicked, a little arch. To be teased about a man ! It was definitely fascinating.

'I knew it,' repeated Miss LaFosse. 'Tell me the worst.'

'I admit,' said Miss Pettigrew with guilty pleasure, 'Mr. Blomfield placed his arm round me in the taxi. It was very cold and he did not wish me to get a chill.'

'Oh ! Oh !' cried Miss LaFosse. 'Excuses ! Such excuses !'

Miss Pettigrew found that she could not tell even Miss LaFosse and Michael about Joe's kisses. They were private between themselves : too precious to be detailed even to the best of friends.

'Oh, you tiresome Sphinx !' cried Miss LaFosse. 'He kissed you. Come. Confess.'

'Well,' said Miss Pettigrew grudgingly, 'he did kiss me good night. I understand it is the custom among people of your . . . your Bohemian tendencies.'

Michael and Miss LaFosse burst out laughing.

'Bohemian girls !' cried Miss LaFosse joyously. 'And old Spanish customs !'

'Stay me with flagons !' gasped Michael. 'Oysters are in. Her lips are sealed.'

'Never say die,' choked Miss LaFosse. 'Fetch me a tin-opener.'

Miss LaFosse teased her. Michael teased her. Miss Pettigrew grew pinker and pinker, her smiles broader and broader. She forgot all about departure. The clock crept round.

'Good Lord!' said Michael at last. 'I must be off.'

It was like the knell of doom sounding to Miss Pettigrew. Suddenly she remembered. She scrambled to her feet.

'Good gracious! I forgot the time as well. I must go too. I must rush. How could I forget? I must change your clothes at once. I will fly.'

'Nonsense,' said Miss LaFosse. 'You're staying the night, of course.'

Miss Pettigrew fought with temptation. She caught hold of a chair to steady herself. She could not speak for two or three seconds. She drew a deep, quivering breath.

'Thank you,' said Miss Pettigrew at last. 'You have been very kind, my dear, but I must go. You and I have had a very pleasant day to-day, but to-morrow will be different. I cannot trespass on your kindness further. I couldn't bear this day to be spoiled by a . . . an anticlimax.'

'Well,' said Miss LaFosse. 'After the way I'd counted on you! I didn't think you would be so unkind, leaving me in the lurch like this.'

'In the lurch?' said Miss Pettigrew, bewildered.

'If you won't stay, I'll have to,' said Michael. 'That's all there is to it. It's drastic, I know, and I hope no one will learn for Delysia's sake, but I'll have to do it.'

'That's right,' said Miss LaFosse firmly. 'I will not be left alone. Nick might turn up any time. I'd be afraid to be left alone.'

Miss Pettigrew looked from one to the other. They looked very serious, a little reproachful. Suddenly she remembered Nick had a key. Did Michael know? He could not. No wonder Miss LaFosse was nervous.

'If you really need me!' stammered Miss Pettigrew. 'I wouldn't intrude . . . but if you really *need* me?'

'You'll stay, cried Miss LaFosse. 'I knew you wouldn't let me down.'

'My eternal gratitude,' said Michael. 'I'd hate to compromise Delysia, but I'd have to do it. I can't have her upset.'

'Certainly not,' said Miss Pettigrew sternly. 'I wouldn't countenance such a thing. I'll stay if you are sure you want me.'

She thought there had been quite enough compromising of Miss LaFosse already, even if Michael knew nothing about it. It was high time a sensible woman like herself took charge. And it was almost a miracle that Miss LaFosse should really need her for the night. Things always looked so much brighter in the morning. She could set off in search of a job with renewed courage. She had not known quite how terrified she had been of spending the night outside until the need had gone. The flood of relief that poured through her left her quite weak.

'That's settled,' said Michael. 'I said we could count on you. Where's my hat? Where's my coat? Where's my woman? Good night, darling! Now's the time for your Bohemian tendencies.'

'Your coat,' gasped Miss Pettigrew. 'The bedroom. I will put it away.'

She seized Miss LaFosse's fur coat and beat a hasty retreat into the bedroom. There was an interval of silence. The door banged.

'All clear,' called Miss LaFosse. 'You can come out of hiding. Nothing to shock your modesty now.

CHAPTER SIXTEEN

3.47 a.m.—?

MISS PETTIGREW came out looking embarrassed.

'I understand,' said Miss Pettigrew, 'that young people always prefer their farewells to be in private.'

'You make an ideal chaperone,' said Miss LaFosse. 'I'll do as much for you.'

'Now,' said Miss Pettigrew, 'it is very late. I think you had better get straight to bed and get a good night's sleep.'

'Oh no,' pleaded Miss LaFosse. 'I'm not a bit tired. Do let's sit and have a little chat. Men are all right in their place, but I do like a nice feminine gossip.'

'Strange to say,' said Miss Pettigrew happily, 'I'm not at all tired myself.'

They sat in front of the fire.

'So you're really going to marry Michael,' said Miss Pettigrew contentedly.

'Yes,' said Miss LaFosse.

'I can't tell you how glad I am,' said Miss Pettigrew earnestly. 'It sets my mind at rest.'

'Were you as worried as all that?' asked Miss LaFosse.

'I was,' said Miss Pettigrew. 'I knew that in the end Nick would leave you unhappy. I know that it is very easy for an outsider to advise and very different when it is yourself suffering the pangs of love, but there are times in this life when all is *not* worth losing for love.'

'You're quite right,' said Miss LaFosse soberly. 'But without you I would never have been free. It was no use. The minute Nick said "Come" I had to go.'

Both women were silent a moment. Each was seeing in her mind's eye Nick slowly disappearing from the room, with his dark head, his brilliant black eyes, his bitter tongue, his compelling glances, his wicked little black moustache, his lithe, feline body. Nick had lost this once, but he would still carry on his conquering ways, still bring joy and sorrow to other women. Miss LaFosse would always hate her successors. Miss Pettigrew gave him a last regretful tribute. Wicked he might be, but fascinating he undoubtedly was.

'Some men are like that,' agreed Miss Pettigrew.

'Yes,' said Miss LaFosse in a low voice. 'Nick was.'

Miss Pettigrew leaned forward and caught Miss LaFosse's hand.

'But not now,' pleaded Miss Pettigrew urgently. 'Promise me not now. It doesn't matter whether he comes and goes down on his knees, promise me you won't go back to him.'

The door closed firmly on the wraith of Nick.

'Never again,' promised Miss LaFosse earnestly. 'It was just as you said. When Michael stood towering over him, I felt a surge of pride in Michael. When Nick sprang to his feet in a fury, I felt a surge of pride in Nick. And then . . . when he hesitated . . . I don't know. Something just went "click" inside me, and I saw that he was all just . . . just ice-cream. And he melted away. Just like that. He couldn't get me back now if he tried.'

'The relief!' sighed Miss Pettigrew. 'I can't describe it.'

'Such a day!' said Miss LaFosse. 'Everything went wrong and everything went right. But I daren't think what would have happened if you hadn't come.'

'Oh dear!' said Miss Pettigrew. 'Oh dear!'

She remembered suddenly. She had not yet told Miss LaFosse why she had come. She had been wickedly remiss about it up to now, but she could not sleep in comfort unless her confession was made. The time had come. She could evade it no longer.

'There is something I must tell you,' said Miss Pettigrew in a strained voice.

'Yes,' said Miss LaFosse expectantly.

'It's why I did come here,' said Miss Pettigrew bravely. 'I have tried to tell you once or twice, but you always interrupted.'

'I didn't want to hear,' said Miss LaFosse. 'It takes away the fun, knowing about people. Suppose you had come selling vacuum cleaners, what an anticlimax! Who could be thrilled over a vacuum salesman? You aren't, are you?'

'No,' said Miss Pettigrew. 'But you must listen now.'

'I'm quite willing now,' said Miss LaFosse. 'I'm really very interested. There I was, in the most desperate of straits, and bang, out of the blue a miracle-worker appeared and pulled me out of the fire.'

'I am a governess,' said Miss Pettigrew. 'I came in answer to your inquiry at Miss Holt's Registry Office for a governess.'

It was out at last. She looked away. She sat in her true colours, a supplicant for Miss LaFosse's patronage.

'*My* inquiry?' asked Miss LaFosse.

Miss Pettigrew nodded.

' Miss Holt gave me your address.'

' Oh ! ' said Miss LaFosse with an expressionless
face. There was a pause.

' Would you like it to be a boy or a girl ? ' asked
Miss LaFosse.

' Oh dear ! ' said Miss Pettigrew nervously. ' I
might name the wrong sex. But there ! I suppose we
all have preferences. I must confess I find little girls
rather more easy to deal with.'

' Would you mind if there were two ? ' asked Miss
LaFosse. ' One of each.'

Miss Pettigrew's head sprang round. She stared at
Miss LaFosse in dismay, then looked away hastily.

' Not at all, not at all,' said Miss Pettigrew hurriedly.
' I have had two before quite frequently.'

Miss LaFosse exploded into a peal of laughter.

' You solemn darling ! Don't get alarmed. I was
only teasing. I haven't any.'

' No children ? '

' No children. Not even a very little one.'

' Oh dear, I'm so glad ! ' gasped Miss Pettigrew in
relief.

' But you thought I might have,' said Miss LaFosse
with a sly dig.

Miss Pettigrew looked here, looked there, blushed
scarlet.

' I humbly apologize,' said Miss Pettigrew in a
fluster. ' Please forgive me. How could I think of
such a thing ! '

' Oh, quite easily,' said Miss LaFosse with a grin.

Miss Pettigrew looked reproving.

' Whose are the children then ? ' asked Miss Pettigrew
with dignity.

' Which children ? '

'Your children . . . I mean . . . the children . . . the governess . . . the registry office,' said Miss Pettigrew, getting confused.

'There aren't any.'

'No . . . no children?'

'None at all.'

'But . . . but your inquiry?'

'For a maid. My maid has just left. Miss Holt must have muddled the addresses.'

'Oh dear!' said Miss Pettigrew in a flat voice. 'Of course. There was an inquiry for a maid at the same time. I remember her mentioning it. Then I will be too late now. My post will be taken.'

'Well,' said Miss LaFosse cautiously, 'I hope, for my sake, it is.'

'Your sake?'

'I have a proposition to make,' said Miss LaFosse. 'I hesitate to make it. I know you are a lady. You will not be offended?'

'With you, never,' said Miss Pettigrew, secretly in a flutter.

'You see,' explained Miss LaFosse, 'Michael and I are getting married. Quite soon. But Michael has a kink. He will live in a big house with big rooms. He says he spent all his youth with a family of nine all cooped in a little flat with the walls closing in on him and never a room to himself, and He Will Have Space. He has his eye on a beautiful house now, but it is immense. We are both to live there. I can't look after houses. I know nothing about looking after houses. I shall be away at rehearsals too. I am distracted. Do you . . . could you possibly give up your present career and come to live with us and look after my house for me?'

'Me?' whispered Miss Pettigrew ungrammatically. 'Me . . . come to live with you and Michael?'

'I wouldn't interfere,' promised Miss LaFosse. 'I assure you. You could run it just as you thought right. There will be maids, of course. I hesitate to ask you to take on such work, but it would be so marvellous for me. I admit I'm selfish. But I can see it perfectly. My house run smoothly. Michael's meals always on time. You a perfect hostess at my parties, so that for once I could enjoy myself as a guest at my own parties without a frenzy of agitation, and knowing that everything will be absolutely right. Do please consider it. You need not decide at once.'

Miss Pettigrew began to tremble. It was like a great light bursting with a radiance that spread and spread. It was fear gone for ever. It was peace at last. A house to run almost her own. How she had longed for that! Marketing, ordering, like any other housewife. No more frightening, horrible children and their terrifying mothers. Flowers to put in rooms exactly as she wanted them. She could try her hand at cooking again. To reach forty, and never, since she had left home as a girl, really to have cooked anything properly! Loneliness banished. Oh blessed, blessed thought! It was unbelievable. It was heaven come to earth. It was rest. It was rest at last.

Suddenly she began to cry. She bent her head and wept. Miss LaFosse hastily put her arm around her.

'Oh, Guinevere!' said Miss LaFosse.

After a while Miss Pettigrew dried her eyes. Her nose was a little pink and her lids a little red, but her eyes were shining, her face alight.

Miss Pettigrew looked at Miss LaFosse.

'You know perfectly well,' said Miss Pettigrew, 'that you are doing *me* a favour, not yourself. I am a very poor governess. I am a very bad governess. I hate it. I loathe it. It's been a deadly weight all my

232

life. I can't manage children. I grow more afraid of them every year. Each post was worse than the last. Every one was cheaper. I was really only a nursemaid in my last. I am getting older. Soon not even the cheap ones will employ me. There was nothing for me but the workhouse, and now you offer me a home. I can't thank you. I don't know how. I'm not very good with words. But I'll look after your house from basement to attics and you'll never regret it.'

'Now, Guinevere, you mustn't work too hard,' admonished Miss LaFosse.

'I insist,' said Miss Pettigrew radiantly.

'I can't have you knocking yourself up.'

'Work you like is a pleasure.'

'Then I won't have you pleasing yourself too much.'

'I must have things done properly or not at all.'

'You can tell the maids to do them.'

'And have them put blue flowers in a green room and break the best vases and put damp sheets on the beds! Certainly not.'

'You can tell them if they don't do things properly they must leave.'

'I shall be there to see that they *do* do things properly.'

'You can't make yourself ill trying to be everywhere at the same time. I won't have it.'

'Are you,' asked Miss Pettigrew indignantly, 'or am I running this house?'

'You,' said Miss LaFosse meekly.

'Thank you.'

'Not at all.'

The question was settled.

Miss Pettigrew's face suddenly clouded. She looked apprehensive.

'What about Michael?' asked Miss Pettigrew nervously.

233

'It was Michael's idea,' reassured Miss LaFosse earnestly. 'He says you are his mascot and he doesn't want to lose you now. He says even if he does marry me, he still wants a comfortable home and I'm a rotten housekeeper.'

'How good you both are!' said Miss Pettigrew with radiant happiness. 'He flatters me. I will be a novice at first, but I will put my heart and soul into it. I will learn. You need not fear. I have cast out fear. I am a new woman.'

Abruptly she leaned towards Miss LaFosse and said breathlessly, intensely,

'Do you like me?'

'Like you?' repeated Miss LaFosse in surprise. 'Of course I like you.'

'I mean really and truly. Not just politely because you think I helped you a little. Do you really and truly like me?'

'I think,' said Miss LaFosse gently, 'I like you more than I have ever liked a woman in my life before.'

'Do you think a *man* could like me?'

'If I were his age,' said Miss LaFosse demurely, 'and you were yours, I'd fall like a ton of bricks. It was Joe on the 'phone just now. He's coming round to-morrow.'

Miss Pettigrew stood up. Her figure expanded. Her eyes shone.

'I think,' said Miss Pettigrew, 'I have a beau at last.'

Persephone Books publishes forgotten fiction and non-fiction by unjustly neglected authors. The following titles are available:

If you have enjoyed this Persephone book why not telephone or write to us for a free copy of the Persephone Catalogue and the current Persephone Biannually? All Persephone books ordered from us cost £10 or three for £27 plus £2 postage per book.

PERSEPHONE BOOKS LTD
59 Lamb's Conduit Street
London WC1N 3NB

Telephone: 020 7242 9292
sales@persephonebooks.co.uk
www.persephonebooks.co.uk